THE
CHOICE

THE
CHOICE

PENNY HANCOCK

MANTLE

First published 2022 by Mantle
an imprint of Pan Macmillan
The Smithson, 6 Briset Street, London, EC1M 5NR
EU representative: Macmillan Publishers Ireland Ltd, 1st Floor,
The Liffey Trust Centre, 117–126 Sheriff Street Upper,
Dublin 1, D01 YC43
Associated companies throughout the world
www.panmacmillan.com

ISBN 978-1-5098-6790-5

1 3 5 7 9 8 6 4 2

A CIP catalogue record for this book is available from the British Library.

Typeset in Sabon LT Std by Jouve (UK), Milton Keynes
Printed and bound by CPI Group (UK) Ltd, Croydon, CR0 4YY

Visit www.panmacmillan.com to read more about all our books
and to buy them. You will also find features, author interviews and
news of any author events, and you can sign up for e-newsletters
so that you're always first to hear about our new releases.

For my beautiful new granddaughters
Noa Jessie and Florence Josie.
Wishing you many happy years of reading

THE
CHOICE

PART ONE

RENEE

1

That day

The boats are turning their bows inland as the creeks slowly fill. A wind has got up, as it often does when the tide comes in. The clank of mainsails against masts provides a steady rhythm as the water loosens hulls from their mud berths. Apart from the distant thump of a hammer banging in the boat shed at the far end of the harbour, there's no sign of anyone out on the boardwalks now, or walking along the coastal paths. I glance towards the horizon again. The tide appears to be dragging the sky with it, draping cloud patterns over the mudflats.

I give a quick wave back through the houseboat window, then hurry along the boardwalks, those not yet submerged, and take the footpath to the village. My car's hidden away in the visitor car park, which is, fortunately, deserted at this time on a Monday afternoon.

In the car I sit for a moment, catch my breath. When my heart rate has slowed, I start the ignition and pull out onto the main road. There's an old Simon and Garfunkel song playing on the radio. 'Homeward Bound'. It feels serendipitous. I sing along at full volume as I drive away from the harbour. Up through the village, then along lanes lined with tall hedges. The sun has slipped out and burnishes the tops of trees. Their leaves are turning ochre and oxblood, complimenting the old gold of the fields.

I don't take the causeway back to the island but drive on, because the chemist in town is better stocked than ours, and I need to make sure Tobias has his medication today. That's what I tell myself. If my husband asks, I can say I've been in town. And have his prescription as proof.

'It'll be ready in twenty.' I wonder if the pharmacist looks at me oddly.

I'm being paranoid. Why would she? She doesn't know me, or my family.

I try to behave normally as I potter about the shops while my husband's medication is prepared. In the charity shop window there's a Burberry trench coat I quite fancy, the kind of thing my mother would approve of. Funny that she still influences me when I buy clothes, after all these years. I can hear her exacting tone. *Check that it's natural fibres. You don't want man-made at your age. At any age but especially now you're older.*

She's right, though. Anything synthetic against my skin sets off the heat, causing it to rush through me, up my neck and into my face. This makes me self-conscious, afraid it shows, not just the beads of sweat breaking out on my brow, but the sense of turmoil; that I'm losing my grip.

I ponder for a while, then decide to try the coat on, to kill time. The shop assistant takes it off the manikin and holds it out for me to slip my arms into, as if I were royalty. It fits perfectly. The twenty-five pounds I pay is a bargain. Leaving the shop, I experience that little lift of pleasure buying new (or nearly new in this case) clothes gives me. I keep the coat on and spring back the way I've come to the chemist's. The prescription is ready. Thanking the pharmacist, I push the paper bag of medication into my pocket and hurry back to my car feeling stylish and foolishly happy. Along with my husband's pills, I clutch the secret about where I spent this afternoon to my chest.

By the time I do finally arrive back at the causeway to the island, the spring tide – they happen twice a month but this one is even fuller than usual – means the road's completely vanished. A queue of cars, mostly Audis and four-by-fours and the odd Tesla, has formed in front of me and in the rear-view mirror I see more traffic arriving. There have been times when a vehicle has got submerged, its driver discovering the hard way that the water is deeper in the middle of the causeway than they envisaged. They forget that although it's the twenty-first century, we are still fundamentally linked, even in our top-of-the-range cars, to the phases of the moon, to the rhythm of the tides, to the weather, to the elements. We are still dependent on nature and ignore this truth at our peril. It's something Jonah and I often discuss, how we recognize, particularly as we age, that we belong to something bigger. He often talks of his renewed sense of awe for the environment that's been further kindled by his living on the boat.

At last the road surface emerges as the waters slip away and the cars in front move tentatively over the causeway. We've had to wait over half an hour to move. But this afternoon no one gets stuck. We crawl across safely.

At home, Tobias is at the computer as usual, sorting through family photos. A project he embarked on after his stroke.

'I hand over the curating of our married life to you, my love,' I'd said when he came up with the idea. It's true I wondered at the time what would remain when he'd reduced our life together to his key scenes, sorted into albums that he intends to give as gifts to Mia and George on their birthdays. As Tobias works through the photographs, he adjusts our family history, removing the things that don't fit with the facade he likes to present to the world. What tale will the photos tell when he's edited out what, or who, he doesn't want to remember? I've resigned myself to accepting his narrative, aware part of our family history will be confined to the rubbish heap. But with the best will in the world, you can't retain a record of every moment of all your children's and grandchildren's growing years. I have my own memories anyway, my own things that matter to me. I have diaries, drawings, cards made by the children when they were little or sent to me when they were older.

I stand in the doorway and watch my husband before he notices me. Tobias's once fair hair is beginning to grey. He still has that pale Scandinavian look about him that I found so attractive when I first met him. Still do, on occasion. But Tobias is a faded version of the man he was before, since his illness. In addition to physio, he had to have speech therapy for months, joining an Afasic group where he learned to name things, the way Xavier, our baby grandson, was doing at the time. Tobias still often gets his words muddled. Some days he seems more diminished by the stroke, poor man, than on others. He's still tall, slender, good-looking, with his high cheekbones and prominent chin. But his hairline's receded at the front, and he needs a haircut at the back where the darker grey is curling into his collar. Cutting my husband's hair used to be something I took pride in. The fact it's got so long and unruly speaks of my recent preoccupation. I've been neglecting him.

Leaning over his shoulder, I see he's reached a time three summers ago, when Mia had just moved up here with Xavier. Xav's three years old in the picture, wearing a yellow raincoat and too-big wellies. He's holding a fishing net on a stick and grinning at the camera.

'Where've you been?' Tobias talks to the screen.

'Getting your medication. Then the tide was up.'

Tobias doesn't ask any more about my day. He has these periods when he's remote. This isn't his fault either; it's a result of his medical condition. But I do sometimes feel I've lost him. The person he was before, I mean. I sometimes feel I'm battling on with what's left of our family life alone.

Of course, today Tobias's lack of curiosity works to my advantage. I don't have to spin elaborate lies. If he's not interested, then why should I tell him where I spent the afternoon?

'I'll have my wine now,' he says without looking up. 'And pistachios if we have any.'

It's not anywhere near wine o'clock, as Mia calls it, and my tenderness turns to irritation, which is unkind. Tobias has got into the habit of asking me to do the slightest thing for him. He objects to his disabilities yet he willingly adopts the role of dependent. It seems to me like surrender. Or even indulgence. Knowing I won't refuse him anything has turned him into a kind of lord of the manor who, at times, treats me like one of his subjects. But as I go through to the kitchen to get his wine, something he could have done himself, I wonder whether my irritation is, after all, a kind of sublimated guilt? Am I angry with myself for withholding the truth about where I spent the afternoon? Guilty of lying by omission to the man I've shared everything with for the last thirty years?

As a therapist I've noticed, in families like the Ollards who've been coming to me for some time now, that when one of a couple seeks something outside of the marriage, it's not usually to hurt or betray their partner; it's more likely to be a desperate attempt to feel alive again. To retrieve something of their former selves that seems to have been trampled on by the day-to-dayness of married life. Or to discover a part of themselves they have yet to know. And perhaps, in a slightly different way (no two unhappy families are alike, as Tolstoy famously said), it's like this for me too. I wonder if not telling my husband about my visit to the boat this afternoon, a little inlet out of my usual time, has given me back a sense of self I've been lacking for quite some time.

In the kitchen I get the glass Tobias likes from the shelf. He's not strictly supposed to drink. Yet removing one of his few remaining pleasures in life seemed so cruel, we made this compromise between us, that Tobias can have his early-evening glass of well-chilled Entre-Deux-Mers with a small snack, and then a glass of red Malbec with dinner. I hand him his wine and go back to the kitchen.

With the same radio station I had on in the car for cheering background music, I chop an onion and crush garlic under the flat blade of a knife. Adding celery to the onion, it all sweats in a sofrito. The diced sweet potato and carrot remind me of little cubed sweets the kids used to love, and they sizzle pleasingly as I add them to the pan with tins of tomatoes and leave it all to simmer. Later, this will go into a food box to deliver tomorrow between clients.

George rings as I'm washing the pans that don't fit in the dishwasher.

'Hi, Mum, thought I'd check in. How're you doing?'

'I'm fine, George. I'm actually very good.'

'You sound it. You sound . . . I don't know . . . brighter than you have for some time.'

I pause for a beat and temper my voice when I next speak.

'Well. It's been a beautiful day here.'

'And how's Dad doing?'

'He's doing well. Just having a glass of wine, in fact. Sorting photos. D'you want to speak to him?'

'Not if he's busy. Next time.'

'How are you, my darling? How's it all going?'

My son tells me about the latest role he's playing in a costume drama they're shooting opposite the Tower of London. 'It's a great setting,' he says. 'Loads of street food nearby. You must come. You could watch for a bit then I'll take you to eat.'

'If ever I find a moment, I'd love that, George.'

'OK. Let me know when you've got time. Say hi to Dad. I'll speak to him tomorrow. Got to go.'

'OK. Love you.'

When my mobile sounds again Mia's name flashes up on the screen. I pick up and she speaks straight away.

'Can I talk to him?'

'Hello, Mia.' I think how different she is to her brother – my youngest – who always asks how I am first. 'I'm fine, thank you, how are you?'

'Sorry, Mum. How are you?'

'I'm OK. Was just cooking.'

'It's just I'm missing him so much.'

'Missing him?' For a second I think she means her dad.

'I've popped back to the hotel between drinks and dinner. Wanted to say night night before he goes to bed.'

Night night?

'Xavier, Mum. I want to speak to him.'

Xavier.

'Mum?'

A ringing starts up in my ears.

'Xavier isn't here.'

'What do you mean, he isn't there? Where is he? You were picking him up from school today.'

'But it's Monday.'

It *is* Monday, not one of my usual Xavier days. But Mia's away, Mia's in Amsterdam on a course. I took Xav to school this morning and was supposed to pick him up this afternoon. The kitchen turns vivid, as if, until this moment, I've been viewing it through soft focus. The pans on the stove. The mixture inside them. The boxes of cereal I keep here specially for Xav with their bold lettering.

Xav, Xav, Xav. Xav should be right here with me, eating his tea, chatting about sea life creatures. The way he does three days every week. But not usually this day, not usually Monday. I grab the work surface to steady myself.

'Oh my God. I forgot.'

'*You forgot?* What do you mean? Where is he? Where's my son?'

'OK, Mia, listen . . . I'm going now, I'm going up to the school.'

The numbers on the cooker clock blink. *It's gone five!*

I should have been at the school gates an hour and a half ago! And no one has called. Why has no one from school called?

Tobias's voice comes from the sitting room. 'Darling, a little more wine?'

But Mia's speaking too. 'I don't understand. The school haven't tried to ring me . . . the school always ring if I'm late picking up. Why haven't they rung? Didn't *you* get a call? They must've tried to reach you when they couldn't get through to me.'

'I'm going. I'll call you back.'

I drag the stupid trench coat on as I run out of the door, berating myself for lingering on the boat, for making that detour to cover my tracks, for ambling around charity shops when I should have been at the school gates, for my vanity, for singing along to Simon and Garfunkel as if all my cares were over. And what am I going to tell them? About where I was when I should have been picking up my grandson?

It's a ten-minute jog to the primary school.

As I run, the thoughts pile in: Mia calling a few weeks ago to let me know about the course in Amsterdam; me promising I would pick up Xavier for her today.

Yes, I'd said, because I love spending time with my only grandchild. *Yes, I can take and pick up Xavier on Monday and Tuesday.*

And then, as if I'd already stored this promise on a calendar with a reminder, and so didn't need to look at it again, I carried on with whatever I was doing. Only I hadn't stored it on my phone calendar, or on anything else. And I clearly hadn't stored it in my mind either; instead, when I should have been getting ready to pick up my grandson, I'd gone blithely to the boat the minute Jonah called, my heart singing. I'd spent the afternoon there, then, afraid I'd be seen, made that unnecessary detour to the town for Tobias's medicine and got stuck at the causeway because the tide had come in. A spring tide, deeper than usual.

I'm here now, at school, sliding back the bolt and opening the gates, running over the tarmac to the main entrance, leaning against the bell. Cursing the fact schools have all this security these days, that you can't just march in, demand to see the teacher who is in loco parentis until you get there.

I didn't get a call. Did I? As I wait for a member of staff to let me in, I scroll through my 'recents', my texts, my WhatsApps but there's nothing. I bang on the door. A child's painting of a sun with a smiley face grins down at me.

Surely the staff must still be here? Someone must still be here, a cleaner, a caretaker? Someone has Xavier.

When I ring the school it goes straight to voicemail, telling me the office is now closed until eight thirty tomorrow morning.

The wind tosses the leaves about on the horse chestnuts. The play equipment is motionless, the primary colours vulgar now they're devoid of children clambering over them.

There's the rattle of the door and I swing round. Paul Kicks is there, the school caretaker, a dad I know from days when we used to take George to football.

'You OK?' He sticks his head round the door.

'I came for Xavier. I was supposed to pick him up. I'm terribly late.'

'The staff have gone. Some course they're on up at the education centre.'

'I don't know where he is.' I try to control the panic in my voice.

'Hmm. There was no one left in the classrooms or the office when I came in.' Paul opens the door wider. 'You sure he didn't go back with a mate?'

'I don't know. I don't think so. Someone would have said.'

My phone rings. Mia.

'Mum, is he there?'

'I'm just talking to the caretaker. He says the children had all gone when he came in.'

A fretful pause. Then she says, 'I just thought, there's a mum at the school, Harriet, who called last week to ask if Xav could come and play and I said sometime this week would be good. It's possible she took him home with his new friend, Poppy. I'm going to ring her.'

She hangs up.

'It'll be OK, you know. We'll find him.' I look up. Paul Kicks is speaking to me kindly. 'Children do not go missing in a place like this. Now you come in and sit down for a bit and I'm going to make some phone calls.'

My mobile sounds again.

'Harriet hasn't got him. She didn't see him at home time. Where is he, Mum? What's happened to my son? And *where the fuck were you?*'

2

Ten days earlier

I scrunch the T-shirt into a ball and throw it across the room. It's far too hot and clings to all the wrong places, which is bizarre. Only a year ago it looked fine. And I haven't put on any weight. I know because I weighed myself this morning and was the same as I've been for the last ten years. It's as if my flesh is shifting about on my body, deliberately seeking out new places to settle so my clothes no longer fit. I rummage about for something cool, although right now I could stand under a cold shower and still feel as if I have a furnace blazing inside. I want to tear my skin off. It feels like a thick, thermal, too-tight bodysuit. Sometimes, at night, as I lie naked under the sheets, I fantasize that there's a zip running down the front of my body that I can undo, so I can step out of this insulating layer and allow cold air to rush over me.

Rummaging for a cooler top makes me hotter still, exhausted and irritable. And it isn't yet seven o'clock and I've only been up half an hour. I grab another T-shirt and wipe the sweat from my brow then pull a crisper, white cotton shirt off a hanger. I want clothes that don't actually touch my skin. Clothes that let the air waft through them. Clothes that, as I listen to my clients, don't suddenly feel as if they are closing in on me, crushing the breath from me. I think of the sea swim I have planned at the end of the week with my friends and wish I could be there now, the cold water easing the heat away, chilling my bones from within like those icicles you stick into wine bottles.

The white shirt seems to work, with some wide-leg trousers like funnels that I wouldn't have looked twice at a couple of years ago when I still actually enjoyed the feel of skinny jeans close around my legs.

There's the sound of a car outside and I move to the window. Mia's little blue Nissan has pulled up at the kerb and she's getting Xavier out. Beyond them the estuary glitters in the morning light. Small triangular sails dot the horizon. The tide's in and it's a beautiful day. I glance back at Mia and Xav. For the first time ever, my daughter looks to me like a middle-aged woman. Mia is only twenty-seven. But there's something in her expression this morning as she says something to Xavier, in her posture as she hurries with him to the door, that reminds me of a much older woman.

I go down to open the door and catch a glimpse of myself in the mirror at the bottom of the stairs. A while ago I had my hair chopped into a short bob (a mistake with unruly curls like mine) and dyed a shade of brown that looks too harsh for my skin tone. It's messed up from pulling the shirt on over my head, and my mascara's smeared because of the sweat. I look slightly deranged, as if I'm unable to properly care for myself. But I'll fix that later because here is Xavier. Charging towards me, letting me pick him up and kiss him and blow raspberries on his deliciously cool cheeks. I hug him to me as I always do; oh, how I love the feel of him, how I love *him* for allowing me to be the most doting grandmother. I swing my grandson up and down and give him another squeeze, pressing my cheek upon his before releasing him.

'I'm late.' Mia's already on her way back out of the door. I wonder if she'll mention the date. I shouldn't be surprised when she doesn't. She glances at me.

'Mum. You've got mascara round your—'

'I know, I know. Don't worry, off you go, I've got him.'

Xav has found the blue bike we keep for him here and is peddling round the garden. The bike was a present from Irena on his fifth birthday. Mia refuses to have it in her house. Watching my grandson cycle round the garden, my chest contracts with love. It's been the case since he was tiny, since he first fitted into the crook of my elbow, since his tiny arms were covered in soft black down. I never expected this torrent of feeling for her child when Mia first told me she was pregnant.

More dear than the child is the child's child – where had I heard that? But it felt – still feels – true. I don't remember the same acute physical response with any of mine when they were newborn. Perhaps you're just too busy with your own children to notice the way your heart clenches with protection and tenderness. Suddenly I wonder. Did I fail somewhere along the way? At loving them all equally? At communicating my love to them? Is that why things have turned out the way they have?

When I look at Xavier, however, my love is tinged with a kind of melancholy. But why should loving Xavier make me sad? Having someone as innocent as my grandson in my life should surely make me happy? Well, there's a question I should be able to answer, as a therapist. Jonah says the feeling I've tried to describe is a type of introjection. Xavier's father has left and he's coping perfectly well. But I feel the little boy's loss as if it were mine.

And yet Xavier's loss is my gain. I was afraid, once upon a time, that I wouldn't be involved at all in Xavier's upbringing, when Mia and Eddie were determined to move down to the West Country. At that time, a few years ago, my mother was showing the first signs of dementia. We realized we'd have to move her from her house in France into a care home on the island. It would have been difficult to move away. Not to mention complicated, since I didn't know if Mia and Eddie actually wanted us near. I used to imagine going to visit them, arriving at their house and how Xavier would be terrified of this older white woman – me – who he'd rarely met, with her ageing, disabled husband. This scenario for some reason obsessed me. It was another 'loss' fantasy, Jonah told me, a fear of separation, of abandonment that had perhaps been ignited by something in my childhood (my father leaving? My mother's string of lovers?) and confirmed for me by what had happened to Tobias (I'd lost part of him to his stroke) and Irena. But then all that ridiculous gambling stuff with Eddie happened and the house they had only just bought was repossessed. And, due to what to my mind seemed Mia's intractability, she and Eddie split up.

Thank goodness someone needs me, I'd thought, when Mia told me she was moving back to the island. Which is ridiculous, because sometimes it feels as if my clients, as well as Tobias and my mother, need me a little too much. But I was overjoyed that I'd be seeing Xavier more often, be witness to his growing up. To help him get over losing regular contact with his dad. So yes, Mia and Eddie's break-up has had a silver lining for me.

In the kitchen I spoon heaps of coffee into the cafetière, breathing in its rich aromas.

My friend Maureen tells me if I want to control the hot flushes, I should give up caffeine, but it's a pleasure I'm not prepared to forgo. Irena, my middle child, is the only one of my children who used to love coffee the way I do. As I pour the water into the cafetière I picture her in Paris, leaning across one of those small round cafe tables, discussing activism with one of her earnest friends, espressos in tiny cups, paper sugar envelopes scattered across the table, cigarettes half-smoked, tin ashtrays. Perhaps she's having a croissant, a celebratory birthday breakfast? This image is complete fantasy. I know nothing about her life in France. I don't even know if she's in Paris any more.

'Thought you'd gone.'

Tobias is in the kitchen doorway, stabilizing himself with his good hand on the door frame. He's dressed in baggy trackpants and a T-shirt. 'I've got the physio,' he explains. 'Thought you'd left.'

Tobias and I sleep apart since he had a stroke. He's taken Irena's old room, where he can spend as long as he wants getting comfortable without disturbing me. It takes him a while to get up and wash and clean his teeth and he likes to do it by himself. Getting up early is my tacit way of giving him space. He turns and walks lopsidedly away from me into the garden to join Xav. I want to call him back. I want to ask, *do you realize what day it is today?* But his stance tells me he doesn't want me to say anything. He wanted me and Xav to be gone by the time he got up so he could avoid the conversation he knew I'd want to have.

The postman arrives. A pile of envelopes slithers through the box onto the mat.

I shuffle through them. They're mostly official stuff and charity circulars but there's one stiff envelope addressed to Irena.

It's a birthday card from someone who doesn't know. I'm tempted to open it, to see who it's from, because anyone can be a clue, anyone who knows or knew Irena may be able to throw some light on what's happened to her. There's a moral dimension to this that Tobias and I have argued about in the past. Tobias's argument was always that post is private and personal and we do not have a right to open our grown-up children's mail. But the desire to know something is too strong. And Tobias in his present state is not going to notice. I hold the envelope over the steam from the kettle like an old-fashioned sleuth.

It is barely stuck down and opens easily. Inside is a birthday card to Irena from Sunanda, one of my own old friends who is particularly good at remembering the birthdays of her friends' children. My heart sinks. No clue then. Sunanda has no idea Irena doesn't come home any more. And I can't forward the card, because I don't know where Irena is myself. There's a stash of Irena's mail behind one of the Kilner jars in the kitchen and this one joins it. Some of it has been there for over six years now.

Once I've dropped Xav at school, I cycle over the causeway to the counselling centre where I lease a room. The centre is in an old Tudor house on the edge of our local town on the mainland. My room has double aspect windows and is filled with light. It has wonky floorboards that I've covered with a tapestry rug. House plants that love the sun-filled room scramble up one corner with their varying textures and shades of green. The white walls are punctuated with abstract art collected during the island's open studios. The room smells subtly of lavender and rosewood, issuing from a reed diffuser. It is all designed to relax my clients, but it relaxes me, too, the minute I settle down to read my notes.

At nine thirty Amy comes in and drops onto the chenille sofa that I keep for my clients. I sit opposite in a leather chair I found in an antique shop and had reupholstered.

Amy's partner Yannis lollops in behind her as usual and leaves a significant half metre between them, angling his face away from both of us, avoiding eye contact. They've been coming for a few weeks now. They share the childcare of Amy's little girl, Sasha, but Amy began to mistrust Yannis after he left the child at home to pop out to the shop one evening. Yannis, a stockily built Albanian lorry driver, rarely speaks. I wonder whether Amy should indeed trust him with her young child, whether he has it in him to parent a child who isn't his. And yet Amy, who is as chatty as Yannis is silent, insists she wants him involved. And he, too, says he wants to be a father to Sasha. So that's what we're working on. Enabling Amy to trust Yannis, and Yannis to show Amy he's worthy of her trust.

After Amy and Yannis, I have Dan and Joe. They married a couple of years ago. When they first came to me, Dan explained he'd found a surrogate who was prepared to have a baby for them, but Joe had done a U-turn, saying he had cold feet about raising a child. This caused an ongoing rift between them. Joe believes they can have a good life together without children. But Dan is desperate to have a child and believes this is something they'd agreed on before they married. This morning for the first time, Dan admits that if Joe doesn't want a child, he'll consider leaving him, and having the baby via the surrogate even if it means doing so alone.

The room fills with a charged silence. It feels almost voyeuristic to be present when one member of a couple reveals something so earth-shattering in front of you.

My heart rate speeds up as I anticipate some emotional outburst from Joe.

Instead, Joe stays quiet, looking into his hands. I ask gentle probing questions, hoping these will lead them to their own route through this impasse. But other than that, all I can do is sit with their misery.

I see so much pain, so much heartache in my room. At times I wonder if I'm doing my clients any good at all.

When my last couple of the day have gone, I step outside and am met with air heavy with the late-summer scent of bramble, reminiscent of childhood – my own and my children's – and blackberry picking. I close my eyes for a minute and breathe. It's a relief to have finished, but I need some time to unwind before I can face Tobias and his needs. I unlock my bike, pull on my helmet, breathing in the warm fragrant air as I cycle the couple of miles down to the harbour where the houseboats are moored.

Jonah's sitting on the step outside his cabin. He's got his pan of water on the gas hob and he gets up when I arrive, to spoon instant coffee into two plastic beakers. Tobias sneers at instant coffee, and I've already had my daily fix. But this is Jonah, and I don't want to reject the efforts he's going to.

The houseboats occupy an area close to the harbour in a village a couple of miles from the town where I work. They're moored in what are known as 'mud berths', reached by little boardwalks that criss-cross the creeks on the nature reserve. Jonah lives on one of the boats but he also looks after a few of the others for a friend who keeps them for holiday lets. He likes to joke that he's become a kind of landlord, overseer of many homes, but in fact this is a defence. Jonah's marriage fell apart a while ago and he found himself on his uppers, so moved into this houseboat. Jonah keeps the truth from his clients. I am honoured that he's confided in me. But Jonah was my supervisor when I first started work as a therapist, and I still take my more complicated client cases to him to talk over. We've known each other for a long time now so perhaps keeping secrets from one another seems a little redundant. The only thing I don't know is what happened in his marriage, and I won't ask. Jonah will tell me, if and when he wants to.

I join Jonah on the cabin step. The wood feels warm, imbued with the heat of a long summer just coming to an end. I turn my face to the sun. The sky is high and blue, and the water reflects this as it seeps around the grassy tussocks. There's the smell on the breeze of salt, seaweed, brine.

Jonah's older than me, approaching his seventieth birthday. He has white hair and wrinkled skin bronzed by the sun, and shiny brown eyes. He's wearing blue sailing shorts and boat shoes and a faded orange hooded sweatshirt. His legs are sinewy and burnished by the elements.

'Looks like you've been out in your boat today, Jonah?'

'Well, as a matter of fact I have. It was beautiful early this morning on the creek.'

As well as his houseboat, Jonah keeps an old sailing dinghy. He isn't one of the yacht-club people (like Tobias used to be) who like the competition, the lifestyle. He just loves being out on the water. His dinghy's in need of some TLC, the varnish on the hull flaking, the seats rickety, but he says it's all he needs. To get out, to feel the wind, to hear the splash of waves against the boat. To hear the cry of the seabirds and perhaps spot some sea life before coming in feeling cold, and then wrapping up in the houseboat to warm his hands on the flame from the tiny gas ring or the wood burner if he's had time to light it.

The deck of Jonah's boat is festooned with pots of herbs and vegetables, a tangled mass now of the last wrinkled beans scrambling up bamboo canes, tomatoes splitting at the end of drooping stems, bright nasturtiums, mint and thyme and basil lacing the air with their pungent scents.

I tell him a little about Amy and my concerns about Yannis.

'He's reluctant to talk. Either that or he doesn't have good enough English, but I haven't managed to get a word out of him. He's a lorry driver, away a lot, doesn't seem engaged. Amy's fixated on the fact he went to the shop one evening and left the child home alone, asleep. She thinks he put his need for a beer above the child's safety. Wonders if she can trust him any more. It's hard to ignore the pain in his face when she says this . . . but what if I allow a safe-guarding issue to slip through the net . . . ?'

'You got his side of the story, I take it?'

'Not all of it, I don't think. Like I say, he's monosyllabic. Doesn't speak much at all.'

'And you're taking notes?'

'Of course.'

'I'd just keep stringent records for the time being. You're not their social worker, Renee.'

'No, I know. But I don't want to get it wrong. I care about them.'

Jonah smiles. 'Is there anyone you don't care about?'

From somewhere in the far distant past a voice speaks to me. *You give everyone time except your own family.* Who said that? It was probably my mother. She has a phrase she started to trot out each time I saw her, when Irena had first become estranged: *The cobbler's children are always the worst shod.*

'Anyway, I didn't actually come to talk about those two.'

I lean forward and loosen my scarf and let the cool wind lap around my neck.

Jonah takes a sip of his coffee and gazes out over the water.

A curlew's plaintive rising call sounds over the estuary.

'That's such a mournful sound.'

'Really? I always feel as if it's kind of hopeful, that rising note . . .' He pauses and a few moments go by before I feel that Jonah's looking at me. 'What *have* you come to talk about?'

Something seems to press painfully upon my clavicle. Is that what it's called? The soft tissue between the collarbones, that feels as if it's being compressed when an unhappiness rises up, gets too much to hold. My eyes prickle and I have to wipe a stupid tear away. I pretend it's the brisk wind off the tide.

'Take your time,' he says.

'It's Irena's birthday,' I tell him.

It's ironic that this subject, the one that Tobias and I should share, is easier to talk about with someone who only met Irena a few times, before she left, never knew her well, probably never will.

'Twenty-four. She's been gone for six years now. I can't help hoping, on these occasions, that she'll get in touch. Christmas, our birthdays, Mother's Day, Father's Day, a little bit of me continues to hope, and when she doesn't, it's like going through it all again. The fact she's gone for good. I'm so stupid, as if she didn't make it clear when Tobias had his stroke.'

'I remember.'

I lean forward, put my hands over my face.

'Hey,' is all Jonah says.

We sit for a while and Jonah is silent. I turn the mug around in my hands. The pressure between my collarbones intensifies. I shiver. I'm afraid I'm not going to be able to contain it. I pull my scarf up tighter again.

'I understand that Mia and Tobias can't forgive her for refusing to come home when Tobias was so ill.' My throat

24

is dry; it hurts when I speak. 'But she must have her reasons for leaving in the first place.'

I think again about the last weekend Irena came home, having left school. I often wonder if something happened at school that had traumatized her. But I didn't have the chance to ask her. And at first she seemed happy, excited, chatting about her plans to join a swimming team. To apply for a degree. She stayed for a couple of days, then went, without saying goodbye even, and we haven't seen her since.

*

Tobias and I had been against Irena going to boarding school. I wanted all my children to go to the local school. And Tobias, who would have considered paying fees if he felt it was worth it, was nevertheless reluctant to do so for Irena. He said she didn't have the academic calibre for the school she had her sights set on. But I could see it was something she needed. She was going through a difficult phase at the local school. She was something of a loner as she'd not made a good group of friends the way Mia had done, and the other children often taunted or teased her. And at home she regularly fell out with Tobias, who constantly picked up on her faults, her tendency to break things, knock things over. She told him she couldn't wait to get away from him.

It was as a result of one of their arguments that he finally gave in.

'OK then. If you really believe it'll do you good, Irena, I'll pay. But you'd better make it worth it.'

And she had. The school she chose allowed her to excel at things; she passed her exams, made some good friends, and one very close friend, Hermione.

'I thought she had found her niche at that school,' I say, remembering. 'She was doing so well. I mean, you know what it was like for her at the local school; I told you at the time how she was relentlessly bullied, especially once George started and the other children asked about why half his face was scarred. But . . .'

I swallow.

'Although that accident left George disfigured for life, literally, I always felt that it scarred Irena more, psychologically.'

'How old were they when that happened? You told me before, but remind me.'

Jonah doesn't need reminding but he senses my need to talk about it – something I can't do at home.

'George was a baby and Irena was only three. So she was not to blame. As we've tried to make absolutely clear to her throughout her life.'

'Of course.'

The scene I normally try to extinguish from my memory comes back to me, raw.

The children playing tents under the kitchen table. Stretching the cloth from the table over the chairs to pretend it was a house. On this occasion, Tobias had left a pot of freshly made tea on the table, boiling hot. George was only five months old, in his bouncy chair. Irena must have been trying to stretch the cloth further than it would reach, to make another 'roof', and the teapot came with it, off the table and onto George. I still find it hard to envisage this, the moment the boiling water hit him, the pain he must have felt. But I remember the cry, the ear-splitting wail that I could hear even where I was, in my room at the top of the house. I knew instantly something horrific had happened. The guilt is still there too, the fact I was upstairs at the time. I should never have been so intent on my work. I should never have let Tobias take his camera with him whenever he was in charge of the children. Tobias phoned for help the minute he realized George had been scalded. But George's burns were almost fatal. The hospital told us it was touch and go. That night was the worst night of my life.

'We treated it as an accident, which it was. It was no one's fault. Certainly not Irena's. And any other accident might have been forgotten, but George's facial scars were a constant, visual reminder. People were always asking, *how did that happen?* They still do. You know what kids are like; Mia would say, *Irena did it*, and later George learned to say the same. So the story that Irena caused the scars came with us, with her, followed her throughout her childhood. When George started school, a couple of years after Irena, the other children gleaned that Irena did it. George used to tease her that she was possessed. They all did. It was cruel.'

And even though Tobias and I never blamed Irena to her face, we had kept her away from George for the rest of his babyhood, as far as we could. Because Irena was, from the year dot, more un-coordinated than her sister, and more likely to act without thinking.

'You know, Irena might have *wanted* to hurt George. She used to drop her toys on him when he was newborn. Accidentally on purpose.'

Jonah smiles. 'What child hasn't done that to their new sibling?'

'But knowing that, we probably should have kept more of an eye on her that day.'

'Tobias should. He was in charge at the time.'

I wonder whether Jonah is thinking as I sometimes do: that Tobias was ultimately the guilty one for putting a pot of hot tea on the table to start with. And then leaving them unattended, even if only for a couple of minutes, instead of watching them.

'Tobias believes it was Irena's impetuous character that made her pull that cloth off the table in the first place. But she was three! I sometimes think it was the other way around: that accident somehow came to define her. I wonder if that's why she needed to get away to boarding school.'

'The perennial nature/nurture debate.'

'Yes. Who knows?'

I take a sip of the coffee.

'Anyway. What I wonder now is whether something happened to her at the boarding school? Something unspeakable? Because she came home after sixth form and left us again without a word that very weekend. It doesn't make sense.'

I put my face in my hands for a moment, then look up, take a big breath of salty air.

'I wish I could talk to her, Jonah. I wish Irena would at least let me ask her what made her reject us all. I am supposed to hold my family together. I am the mother, and yet I cannot heal the rift at the heart of it.'

Jonah nods, then pats me on the wrist. He gets up and goes into the cabin for more hot water and the jar of coffee, but I shake my head as he offers me another cup.

He sits down beside me again.

'You have no idea where she is now?'

'Still in France as far as I know. She gets a friend to send me a message once every couple of months to tell me she's OK. But she never responds to my emails.'

Jonah doesn't speak for a bit.

'The problem is,' he says after a while, 'it's ambiguous loss. For you, I mean. There's no closure. It means there's nowhere for your pain to go.'

I almost wish Jonah would stop being such a good listener, because I'm afraid it's going to make me cry in front of him, which would be mortifying.

'Sounds as if Tobias and your other kids have dealt with it by deciding for themselves they don't *want* to see her. They've told themselves they've rejected *her*, to disguise the fact she rejected them. An effective defence mechanism. It's harder for you because you still have hope.'

'Do you think I should stop hoping, Jonah?'

'I'm not going to grace that with an answer.'

I remember then, Jonah relating to me how his mother, a Jewish refugee, had come over from Nazi Germany as a young woman in the forties. How she'd had to find and build a home for her children alone in a strange country where she didn't speak the language, and how she had somehow found the resilience to create a life here. If she hadn't had hope, Jonah would not be here now.

'Do you know' – I look at Jonah. He's gazing straight ahead over the water – 'You're the only person, outside my family, who knows that Irena's estranged from us?'

Jonah is silent for a few minutes. I want to explain, but then he says, 'I'm going to get us some rugs, it's getting cold,' and the moment passes.

'I need to go.' I stand up. 'I'm picking up Xav from school.'

3

By three fifteen I'm in the playground waiting for the children to come out. They look barely out of childhood themselves, many of the mums and dads and childminders. They're laughing, making plans for get-togethers, watching their younger children clamber over the bright play equipment. The horse chestnut tree casts a green shade, its branches weighty now with conkers. Deliberately standing a little apart, not wanting the parents to feel they have to include me, I count the ones who have been to me as clients. Amy is there, talking to another mum, a little way off, her back to me. I think of her concern that her boyfriend is incapable of taking on the parenting of her child, wonder again what the truth is. Remind myself that as a therapist I have to take everything at face value. A worm of discomfort, anxiety about getting it wrong and somehow putting a child at risk, dissolves as Xav appears.

He's shoving his newest work of art into my arms, clutching my hand, tugging me along the street beneath the canopies of horse chestnuts. Chattering about finding 'something called an owl pellet' in the playground, how it was full of tiny bones and fur and seeds.

'Theo was going to eat it.' He pulls a face. 'I told him it's owl sick and he said it isn't because it's dry. But I know it is.'

'Were they mouse bones?'

'Miss Walker said shrew. The owl can't digest the bones

so it throws up. You can see what it's been eating, but *you* couldn't eat it. You'd be sick yourself.'

Digest! I'm blown away by my six-year-old grandchild's brilliance.

'Can we go out on the nature reserve before tea? Although I'm starving. Could we go to Suzy's and then go to the nature reserve, then have tea?'

'Of course.'

Mia says I'm unable to say no to Xavier and she's probably right. She says I should uphold her rules and boundaries. I argue that it's a grandparent's prerogative to spoil their grandchildren and she says it's different when you're in loco parentis, as I am three afternoons a week. That I shouldn't let Xavier dictate to me when I'm looking after him. But Xavier is such a pleasure to be with. I *want* to take him to Suzy's, I *want* to take him out on the mudflats and the nature reserve. It's for me as much as it is for him.

I buy Xavier a lolly from Suzy's, a cafe-cum-shop on the front, and get a takeaway tea for myself.

'What's your favourite ice cream ever?' Xavier throws this at me as he runs ahead towards the shore.

'Ooh, I don't know. Something called an *affogato* perhaps.'

'Ugh, what's *affogato*?'

'It's Italian. A delicious ball of vanilla ice cream with a strong espresso coffee poured over the top.'

'Hmm. Mine's this Nobbly Bobbly. What's the longest time you've ever stayed under water?'

'Not that long. I'm not an underwater swimmer.'

'I can stay under for a minute. What was your happiest day ever?'

He's always asking these questions at the moment. Some are easier to answer than others.

'Hard to say, Xav. Perhaps it was the day you were born. But then also the days your mum and Uncle George and Aunty Irena were born.'

'I don't think I've had mine yet,' he says. 'It could be today even.'

'Really?'

'We're going to the nature reserve. *And* I know the way.' He turns, runs backwards a few steps. 'I told Poppy I can get there by myself. I want to sleep out there one night and spot nocturnal wildlife.'

Nocturnal! He's practically a genius!

I trot behind him, trying to keep up, trying to keep him within sight. Xav might be clever, he might want to go on his own to the nature reserve, but he's too young, even if he knows the way. I follow him down to the shoreline to where the land turns to marsh and, further out, melts into the sea.

On this late summer afternoon the water in the creeks is shallow. We can walk out across the boardwalks and I point out the swallows swooping for insects. The tiny islets of land are covered in samphire, small pointy leaves of sea purslane, and dotted with the last pink flowers of marsh daisy. Closer to the water are fleshy leaves of floating arum. The plants are festooned with the tiny white husks of crabs left stranded by a retreating tide, and the banks of the creeks are strewn with strands of seaweed dried into dark drapes. I stand for a minute and breathe, taste salt on my tongue, feel the wind in my hair. Yes, I am happy out here. The impression when you screw up your eyes is of a burgundy and gold tapestry reaching to the far corners of the horizon, but when the tide comes in later, the carpet of flora will disappear entirely, as if it had never been. Xavier knows this about the place.

'I'm in the middle of the sea,' he shouts, one arm above his head. 'I'm a whale.'

'Or a shark,' I suggest. 'You look like you have a fin.'

'No, a whale, it's my blowhole.'

He runs across the boardwalks and squelches back through the mud, his hand in the air as he makes a blowing sound, while I stoop to pick samphire, the fleshy green stems that Xavier says taste like worms. I, on the other hand, am thinking how delicious they will be, lightly steamed with fresh fish from Bert's hut tonight.

After filling my basket with enough samphire for supper (and Tobias devours the stuff), I suggest to Xavier we go back to the village and to the little man-made sandy beach so he can play for a while longer.

I find a bench and check my phone while Xavier tips buckets of sand into a pile. There's a message from Mia saying she'll be late back from London this evening. And one from a client who says she needs to change her appointment this week.

I send a hasty reply to the client apologizing, saying I'll be in touch properly when I'm home at my computer and have my work calendar available.

When I glance up, a little girl has come to join Xav. Together they kick the sandcastle down. Xavier seems to have made friends with this child, an ethereal-looking girl with skin a similar shade to Xav's and locks of honey-coloured hair in a halo around her pretty face. After a while the girl runs over to a woman sitting on a bench. The mother, her skin a shade darker than her daughter's, is tall, slim, with short white hair, dressed in a Breton striped jersey dress and pink saltwater sandals. She looks up at me, and then comes over, holding her daughter's hand.

33

'Go on then, Poppy,' she says to her daughter. 'Ask Xavier's mum if he can come and play after school one day.'

'Granny.' I smile. 'I'm Xavier's granny.'

Something plays about her lips as if she wants to argue. Eventually she says, 'Anyway, I'm Harriet. I've seen you at the school gates. I assumed you were Xavier's mum.'

I don't know what to say. I feel I should apologize. In the end I say, 'My daughter Mia had Xavier young.'

'He's all Poppy talks about.' Harriet folds her arms, and smiles at the children. 'Xavier this, Xavier that. Fascinated that his name starts with a kiss!'

My confusion must be obvious because she says, 'An X.'

'Ah! Of course.'

'Apparently he loves minibeasts and sea creatures as much as she does. Such a bizarre obsession.'

'Not bizarre to them. Perfectly sensible to them.'

'You're right. I shouldn't expect Poppy to like the things I like . . . Hey, I don't suppose you'd like a drink while they play? The Harbour View's open and I'm dying of thirst.' She waves a hand towards the white building with the terrace just above the beach. 'I'll pop in and get us something. What will you have?'

While Harriet gets the drinks I sit down on a bench on the terrace, keeping an eye on Xavier and Poppy as they play.

Harriet returns after a few minutes and places two glasses of cold sparkling water on the table.

'Thank you.' I smile up at her. 'I'm Renee, by the way.'

Her mouth drops open.

'Not Renee Gulliver? You're the therapist? I've heard so much about you. Good things. From the school mums.'

It's tricky responding to comments like this. Confidentiality is one of the first remits of my profession and when people want to discuss my role, I have to be on high alert not to reveal who has been to see me. Not to reveal what I know about their family circumstances. I perhaps should have thought of this before agreeing to drop off and pick up Xavier three times a week from the school where gossip, no doubt, abounds. Who, I wonder, of the many couples I have seen over the years, has talked to Harriet about consulting me? About what I have done, or not done, for them? For their relationships?

'And don't you live in that house with the pine tree? Overlooking the estuary? At the beach end of the road everyone wants to live on?' Harriet's looking at me intently. 'I know that sounds creepy, knowing things about you when we've never met, but I've seen you coming out when I've been down to Bert's fish hut. I've seen Xavier in the garden. I just never realized you were Renee Gulliver.'

'I do. Live there, I mean.'

*

From the outside, we, the Gullivers, appear to have it all. I know this because of what Charlie, the manager at the counselling centre, has told me. She says that clients specify they want to see me because of what they've heard, or read, about us.

Charlie had a friend, a journalist on an interiors magazine, and asked me if I'd be happy for our house – which once belonged to Tobias's parents and therefore has never really felt like my own – to be featured in the magazine. She said it might be good publicity for the counselling centre if I agreed.

It was a few years ago, when Mia, Irena and George were still teenagers. But I regretted allowing them to do that feature the minute it came out.

The Gulliver family, Renee and Tobias and their
two girls and a boy, inherited the double-fronted
shoreline house from Tobias's parents.

The opening sentence made me cringe. It made us sound
so privileged, inheriting a whole house. A house I didn't
even really like, since it always felt like Tobias's parents'
however hard I tried to put my own stamp on it.

Renee, with her sophisticated aesthetic, treasures
objets from her native France and North Africa
which are dotted about her carefully curated
home. Sofas are covered in fabrics from Designer's Guild, and she collects works of art from
the open houses they hold on the island every
year. She displays beautiful, resonant pieces that
have significance in her work as a relationship
therapist. One has to wonder how Renee styles
her therapist's room, but she is reluctant to
reveal this most intimate and private of settings
to us.

'I did not give them permission to talk about me,' I
wailed when the article came out. 'It was supposed to be
about the house.' My three children laughed at my naive
trust in the journalist who had prowled the house asking
me probing questions.

'They want a story, Mum, not just a beautiful interior,'
George had mocked me.

There was one photo of the three children leaning
against the kitchen island, laughing, as if that was a common
occurrence. Which in those days perhaps it was. Irena must
have been home from boarding school for the holidays.

In the picture, George's face is carefully angled away from the camera so his scars don't show.

The piece then went on about our garden, which can be seen from the road, how well stocked it was. I ended up feeling exposed and regretful that I'd ever allowed the photographers and journalists into our house, knowing I'd been seduced through vanity to show off our family. How wholesome and happy we were.

And the image had lived on, well past its sell-by date.

Charlie insists clients often ask to see me because I represent something they think they want. But they don't see the fault, the blip, the dark stain on our perfect panoply that no one even talks about.

*

'And . . . sorry, I'm being terribly nosey,' Harriet is saying. 'I just wondered, why does he, Xavier, why does he live with you rather than his mum?'

'He doesn't.'

'Oh. I assumed . . .'

'My daughter lives a couple of roads behind mine. I do the school run from Wednesday to Friday while she's in London. She's a teacher there. It's lovely for me. Having them so close.'

'Ah! That's why I haven't seen her. I usually only pick up from Wednesday to Friday too. Poppy and Cy go to a childminder Mondays and Tuesdays.'

We watch our children for a few minutes.

'Must be nice. Having your daughter nearby. I'd hate to think Cy or Poppy would ever choose to live so far away I couldn't see them regularly. They have every right to seek out their roots in Saint Lucia. But what if they decide to stay out there? So far away? I don't know if I could bear it.

That's another thing to worry about, isn't it? As a parent? Where they'll decide to live when they're grown up?'

'It is.' I shift on the bench, look over to check on Xavier again. 'But it's a small world, of course. Even Saint Lucia's only a day's flight away.'

Because it's true. *Distance* isn't the thing you need to worry about, I want to tell Harriet. Geographical distance is surmountable.

'I'm so glad I ran into you,' Harriet is saying, 'because I've been looking for a therapist. It's . . .' She lowers her voice. 'We're having issues. My husband and me.'

'I'm sorry, you need to see someone else. I can't take on friends.'

'But we're not exactly friends, are we? Not yet?'

'Ooh. I don't know how to take that!'

Harriet's fingers have left prints in the mist on her glass. She has an earnest, intelligent face, one of those women who want so badly to get everything in their lives right, they sometimes overdo it, over-worry. Over-push. I'm making assumptions, of course. Something I have to be wary of. Because people are never what they appear to be from the outset. There is always something that confounds your expectations, something that surprises you.

'Hmm. I do understand, Harriet.' I turn my glass around in my hands. 'But there is a boundary issue.'

'I see.'

'I can give you the name of someone who'll see you.'

I ask for her mobile number and ping her the number of a colleague.

'Try her, she's really experienced. Anyway, I'm sure, to answer your initial question, Xavier would love to come and play with Poppy after school one day. Perhaps one of the days I pick him up? My daughter's after-school schedule's pretty packed on her pick-up days.'

'Sure.'

The sun has gone behind a cloud and the wind has changed. The tide too has shifted, turned. It'll be coming in, filling the pools, covering the islets. Living here as long as I have, you get to know the signs, the movement of the boats, the change in the sound of the water in the creeks.

'It's been really nice talking to you,' I say, sensing a cooling off from Harriet.

'You too.' She stands up. 'Poppy, it's time to go,' she calls.

Xav runs along in front of me all the way home, and soon the sun comes out again and light fills the whole estuary. By the time Xav and I get home, ten minutes later, the last sliver of mud in the creeks has vanished under water. You'd never have known it was there.

4

'I know I'm late.' I can tell straight away Mia's stressed when she comes in at seven thirty.

'The queue for the Woolwich ferry was longer than usual this evening. I nearly turned round but it was gridlocked everywhere.'

She marches into the kitchen, frowns at Xav's dish in the sink.

'What did he have for tea?'

'Fish fingers and chips . . .' I steel myself for a reprimand that, luckily, doesn't come.

'Mia, I worry about you driving all that way after teaching. You must be exhausted.'

I go towards her, wiping my hands on a tea towel, kiss her on the cheek.

'I'm fine.' She brushes me away. 'It's easier than the train when I have a lot to carry.'

In the sitting room she puts her arm round her father, who is as usual at the computer with his photos.

'How are you, Dad? Have you done your exercises? Taken your meds?'

'I'm fine, Mia, darling one. How was your day?'

'Ooh. Actually, I managed to engage a girl who's driven every other member of staff to distraction. I got her concentrating on magnetic fields by showing her how to make her

40

own compass. It was the first time anyone'd seen Grace become engrossed in anything.'

Mia is one of the most committed teachers I've ever met, and takes her job so seriously I fear she's going to burn herself out. The kids she works with are not the easiest, but she's devoted to improving their lives. Her plan is to become head of the science department in the next year or so. To get more disadvantaged girls into physics and science in general.

'It was a eureka moment. I wanted to build on it. I told her she could become a physicist, and she said, *Yeah, I don't even know what that is!* But I could see she was pleased someone was taking her seriously. It's moments like that that make it all worthwhile.'

'I do admire you, Mia.'

Mia has always been Tobias's pride and joy. She is the most like him, conscientious, hard-working. And good at everything she does. Tobias needs to have everything – including his children – in neat, tidy and clearly defined boxes.

'Thanks, Dad.' Mia gives her father another hug, calls Xav over to her and gets him into his coat. 'We need to go. Got to get you to bed, young man.'

I follow Mia and Xav outside.

'Is Dad really OK?' Mia straps Xav into his car seat and I hand her his bag. 'He seems obsessed with sorting those photos.'

'He's fine,' I tell her. 'You mustn't worry about him.'

'If I don't, who will?'

'Well, he does have me.'

'You're busy.'

I'm rather taken aback by this rare acknowledgement that I have a lot to do.

She shuts Xav's door. 'And I worry about Xav too. He's still so unsettled at night. I hope he'll be OK while he's staying with you.'

'Ah! Yes.'

'Mum. You haven't forgotten, have you? I told you, I'm going to Amsterdam the week after next. You said it would be OK to have Xav.'

Although I love my times with Xav, right now I'm thinking, *Mia, you take me for granted, you need to find some paid childcare, you can't keep relying on me.* But I don't say this out loud. I would never say it out loud. Because Mia needs me. Needs me badly since she left Eddie.

'And you're OK for tomorrow morning?' She stuffs Xavier's coat into his bag, buckling it. She looks exhausted, I note, dark rings round her eyes and her skin looks pasty.

'Of course. Are you eating properly, Mia?'

'I'm fine,' she snaps. 'Stop fussing.'

When Mia's in this mood, I can feel a little nervous of her. Which astounds me. If you'd told me when they were children I would one day feel afraid of my own daughter, either of my daughters, I'd have laughed. But Mia can be exacting and impatient and certainly doesn't suffer fools, and sometimes when I'm with her I feel a fool. But what I'm afraid of isn't, of course, that she'll upset me.

It's that I'll upset her.

I'm afraid of losing her, because once you know that's a possibility, you can never quite stem the fear.

I'll soon realize Mia's mood has, in fact, got nothing to do with me, or anything I've done. It'll turn out there's something else on her mind. She probably didn't even know herself what was really worrying her.

She moves towards the driver's door, where she pauses.

'I spoke to Eddie earlier,' she says quietly over the top of the car. 'He was on duty. On the ferry.'

'I see.' So that's why she waited for the ferry despite the long queue.

'I only wanted to update him. He wants Xav to stay with him overnight. But Xav isn't ready for that, is he? Won't it confuse him? Seeing as I don't want to get back with him?'

'Don't you? Want to get back with Eddie?'

'How can you even suggest that, Mum? I haven't forgiven him for what he put us through. And how will I trust him again? Once a liar, always a liar.'

Mia reminds me of her father when she makes blanket statements like this. As if people are absolutes, unable to change.

'But I don't want Xavier to suffer as a result,' she goes on. 'It's easier if Xavier doesn't spend too much time with Eddie now he's got used to living with just me.'

It seems to me that Xavier is coping perfectly well with the fact his dad and mum live separately. After all, they haven't actually lived together for the last three years. The little boy has spent more of his life with them apart than together. But Xavier has a right to spend time with his father, and in fact, I think it would be good for him. In addition to this, I'm aware of what Eddie must be going through, prevented from spending quality time with his little boy.

'It was over three years ago now,' I remind her. 'Eddie's done his time. He's taken his punishment.'

'For gambling our money away maybe. He hasn't done his time for betraying me and his son.'

'And you really don't want him back in your life?'

She hesitates before replying this time.

'OK, OK, of course I do! But how would we manage? If

he moved out here, he'd have to give up working the ferries, and I'd be supporting both of us. It isn't really what I had in mind when we met. It wasn't the life either of us envisaged.'

I laugh.

'What, Mum? I don't see what there is to laugh about.'

'I'm sorry. I was just thinking that life rarely turns out as we envisage. As we planned.'

'It's all right for you. You and Dad haven't exactly had it hard.'

I bite my lip. There's no point in going down this route, bewailing the fact Tobias can no longer work or walk properly. That I've lost touch with Irena. That I worry about my mother. Mia can only see as far as the edges of her own world at the moment. She doesn't need or want to hear my woes.

She's speaking again.

'I told Eddie Xav's not ready to stay over with him. But if Xav asks to stay at his dad's, I'm going to have to come up with a reason for why he can't.'

'Well, whatever you do decide to do' – I lean through the open window as she starts up the engine – 'be as honest as possible with Xav. It's never good to lie to your children.'

5

Tobias is already at the computer on Saturday morning. He's been working backwards from the present and has now reached the year of Xavier's birth – on the screen is a spread of photos where all our children, and Mia's husband Eddie, are here, at home together.

The photos show a summer's evening in our garden. Six years ago.

Eddie is holding Xavier, his newborn son, in his arms. Xav's body is tiny inside its babygrow, his face only just visible within a too-large hat, scrunched up against the light.

In another photo, George is helping Tobias pop corks from champagne, and Irena stands to the side, brooding, a frown darkening her forehead. I wonder if those photos will make it into an album, but I know the answer.

My two daughters look alike; they've both inherited my Moroccan father's dark hair and my French mother's features, unlike George who got Tobias's almost translucent pale skin, fair hair and blue eyes. In this picture, however, Irena has had her hair cropped and dyed it purple, as if trying to look as different from Mia as possible.

Then there are several photos of me, clutching Xavier to my chest, my eyes half-closed. The feeling comes back to me, visceral: the overwhelming, instinctive drive to protect this child at all costs. I never wanted to let him go. I swore I would be a better grandmother to Xav than I'd been a mother to my children. I would never allow any kind of misadventure to befall him the way I'd let George get injured when he was such a tiny, vulnerable baby.

That day – or most of it, at any rate – six years ago was one that remains golden in my memory. The garden was at its finest, our children were all home, as well as Eddie who I was fond of, congratulating myself that I actually liked my son-in-law. (Maureen always complained about her children's partners, as if no one was good enough for them.)

Best of all, we had a grandchild.

And, of course, Irena was back from her expensive boarding school for good. Tobias and I had been to pick her up in the car. I'd been so excited to see her, to hear about her last year at school, to be bringing her home. I'd missed her. I'd missed having everyone under one roof. Irena was happy, too, wasn't she? She'd talked of her success in the latest swimming competition, the fact her coach had told her to join a local team when she got home. She was still friends (I guessed lovers) with Hermione and was considering applying to university, but wanted a bit of time out to think about what course to do. She was going to base herself here for a while, try and get a job if she could, save some money. She seemed to have grown up a lot since the last time I'd seen her.

Then there are a few photos that show us in a pub garden. Me and Tobias, Mia and Eddie, George. Irena had stayed at home. Perhaps I should have realized then that something was wrong, but I was so besotted with my beautiful grandson. In the picture, we're all toasting George, smiling at our son, and I remember it was that same evening he announced he'd got a leading role in his first TV series. I'm holding Xavier, can remember rocking him in my arms. Brimming as I was with pride at this new addition to our family, I'd wanted to show him off to our friends and acquaintances who were also out on that idyllic summer's evening.

It felt significant, and not only in retrospect, because of what came after. Our children were all here together, we had a grandchild, we were content. As if we'd arrived some-where. I had a sense of quiet satisfaction. The Gullivers, what a wholesome, successful, happy family we were. Just as the interiors magazine had portrayed.

And all of it was due to my and Tobias's well-balanced relationship. Tobias with his defined views, his absolutes, his clear boundaries. *You misbehave, you lose your privileges. You get a good grade at school, you deserve a little prize.* Me with my child-centred approach to parenting. If my children did something that seemed thoughtless, I talked to them about what was going on for them. I didn't believe, as Tobias did, in punishment and reward. I prided myself on teaching them to become emotionally literate. Tobias and I were, I thought, complementary to one another. And it worked. Or I'd believed it did. It's true Irena had wanted to go away to school, but that was to get away from the chil-dren in the village, at the local school; not us. And she, Mia and George had always got on well together, apart from a brief period when George was a very new baby, and the girls used to find his crying intolerable. Mia would cover her ears and make loud 'la la' noises to drown out his cries. But then Mia had been devoted to Irena as a small child, and they found George, the new baby brother, an impediment to the games they loved to play together. I worked hard, though, to allow Mia and Irena to express any frustrations they felt and, as a result, I thought, our three children were close to each other in a way many people's weren't.

Tobias and I had always been a little smug about this.

We'd secretly looked down on friends who said their children fought tooth and nail. I remember times in their childhood when my three children would sit intertwined on the sofa playing some game, or watching something together, laughing, and I'd think how successful we'd been at bringing them up.

Tobias, who saw George's scars as a flaw, something that might hold him back, offered to pay for him to have plastic surgery. But I encouraged George to talk about what his injury meant to him. And he came to the conclusion it was part of who he was. That in a way it made him the person he was. He used his face to his advantage, gaining friends, eschewing the bullies who tried to tease him for it. And now getting a prime acting job at the age of sixteen!

'This is who I am,' he'd argued. 'No one is perfect looking, it's our imperfections that make us who we are. And my scars make me who I am.'

Apart from George's accident, I thought I'd done a pretty good job as a mother, and I prided myself as a mother-in-law, as a grandmother, as a daughter and as a wife. I thought I was a pretty damned hot relationship therapist as well. Although I knew the theory that when you think you've made some astute observation in the counselling room, it's time to take a step back, I still felt a quiet glow of satisfaction at knowing I'd earned a reputation at work, locally at least.

I had no idea that that evening, six years ago, this would all turn out to be an illusion.

An episode that does *not* make it into Tobias's family album is the one that occurred when we returned from our family meal. We got home to find Irena had smashed a tray of antique glasses (ones she'd saved up to buy herself for

48

Tobias's fortieth birthday) that I'd left on the table after our celebratory toasts earlier. There were shards of glass on the wooden floor, and she hadn't bothered to sweep up. Only one of the glasses remained intact.

'How do you manage to destroy everything you touch?' Tobias yelled at her.

I told her not to worry, they were inanimate objects, it had done no harm.

'Unlike what I did to *George*,' she'd glowered. Then she'd turned and left the room, slamming the door.

In bed that night Tobias had turned to me.

'That school has done nothing to improve her. I knew it! It was a waste of money.'

'Oh, come on, Tobias. It was the right thing for her. She was miserable here. Have you forgotten the bullying she endured? It did her good to have a fresh start, where she could explore different identities, be someone different. You offered her that fresh start.'

'Only because she – *and* you – put me under pressure. I might as well have thrown the money down the drain.'

'That's unfair. We discussed it. We both agreed she needed something different from Mia and George.'

'It seems to me that what she had at home wasn't good enough for her.'

I looked at my husband with surprise. It was as if he'd interpreted Irena's desire to go to boarding school as a personal affront. 'If anything,' he muttered, 'all that money seems only to have made her *more* disruptive. More dissatisfied with everything we provide for her.'

I tried to reassure Tobias that Irena was still a teenager, her moods still volatile. 'She's going to get into a local swimming team, and she would never have had the confidence to do that or to apply for university if she'd stayed at the local school. It was money well spent. Even if her behaviour can sometimes be a bit of a puzzle.'

I wanted to explain away what she'd done that evening. But I was beginning to wonder whether Tobias might be right. Irena had spoiled our perfect day. And as I lay awake, an element of fear wormed its way through me that there was something amiss in Irena which made her smash a tray of glasses for no reason. A fear that had begun when she had scalded her baby brother with boiling water all those years ago, a fear I'd tried to ignore, but which now reared its ugly head again.

When I came downstairs the morning after that family celebration of Xavier's birth, and George's success, Irena was standing in the hall with a rucksack packed, in dungarees, trainers and with a beanie pulled down to her eyes.

'I'm off,' she'd said.

'Where? Where are you going?'

'To find Hermione, like she asked me to.'

'I don't understand, you didn't mention this yesterday.'

'I hadn't decided yesterday.'

'But where is Hermione? How long are you planning to be away?'

'Who knows?'

A car had pulled up outside.

'That's my taxi, I need to get to the station before I miss my train.'

She turned and gave me a quick searching look before she walked out of the door.

I followed her, calling, 'Irena, Irena, wait.' But she was throwing her rucksack into the boot, getting into the taxi. She didn't look up again, didn't say goodbye, didn't wave.

The car pulled off down the coast road and I watched my daughter vanish.

No warning. No explanation. Except for a brief text from Hermione saying Irena had joined her in Paris and didn't want to be in touch.

And that was the last time I saw her.

Now, when I look back at the screen, I see Tobias is pressing 'delete' on the photo of Irena. The picture that sparked my memory of the last time I saw my middle child vanishes into the ether to join the other images of Irena in the dark labyrinth of cyberspace.

*

There are four of us left in the group I meet every other Saturday morning for a cold-water swim. At one time we were six but people gradually peel away. Not for any dramatic reasons, just because life, as they say, gets in the way. But today it's just me, Maureen and Sunanda who gather at the shore with our towels, swim hats, neoprene gloves and socks.

We used to call ourselves a book club. We'd meet in a bar in the evening and order bottles of wine and start off discussing the latest read but quickly move on to other issues in our lives, the concerns we had with our children, our relationships, our jobs, and our ageing bodies. We thought our bodies were ageing even when we were in our forties. Now most of us are in our fifties or sixties even, we've stopped worrying about it so much. It isn't that we've stopped caring. We occasionally discuss our favourite hair stylists, and our latest views on how long to go on dyeing. Or whether yoga is better for the back than pilates. Nat – who isn't here today – has even toyed with a little botox. But I guess you come to accept the loss of your youthful skin and hair and limbs after a while, and focus more on appreciating the things you do have. And perhaps, too, you get things into perspective. People die, and we're still here. Tobias nearly died. We're more aware of the precariousness of life and the preciousness of it.

We know we're lucky to be here.

So our conversations and activities have changed too.

As I pull on my swim hat, struggling to get the curls inside it, Sunanda asks me, quite innocently and reasonably, whether Irena got her birthday card.

'Oh . . . didn't she thank you?'

'Renee,' Sunanda persists. 'I don't want thanks. I just want to know she's OK? I haven't seen her for a long time.'

I search Sunanda's face for any hidden clues as to why she's asking me about my middle daughter but can only see her bright brown eyes, her unassuming expression.

'Irena's fine.' I pull on my gloves. 'She's absolutely fine. I'm sorry she didn't acknowledge your card – you know what they're like. She's incredibly committed to this green group. I'm afraid it takes all her attention.'

'She didn't come home for her birthday?'

'There isn't much opportunity for time off.'

'There isn't, when you're saving the planet.' Maureen is fastening the Velcro straps around her own gloves. 'Our climate emergency is not something you can put on hold.'

I feel a wave of appreciation for Maureen.

'Talking of family . . .' Maureen turns at the water's edge. 'I've got the whole bloody lot of them coming next weekend. It's Greg's birthday and I've got his mother and her husband and his brother's whole family and all my four and their children. Plus some of the foster children are coming back to visit. I'll be chained to the oven.'

She sounds as if she's complaining but really she is happy to be needed, happy to be the hub around which her whole chaotic extended family orbit. Including the children she

52

once fostered. We all admire Maureen. We think she should be given one of those awards for being a super-mum. Because she doesn't just embrace this big unwieldy family. She also childminds, taking care of other people's children from dawn till dusk, is a parent governor at the school, and chairs various committees on island matters, as well as volunteering for the food bank.

'Oh, well, *I've* booked a weekend in a log cabin in Finland.' Sunanda stands up and stretches. 'My kids are going to my ex's. I plan to spend the weekend alone in some woods. There's a sauna, and you can roll in the snow afterwards.'

'Brrr! Why go to Finland for arctic temperatures, love, when you've got the North Sea!' Maureen wades deeper into the water, dips her head in and comes up again. 'Ice cream brain freeze!' She dives under the waves.

I sit on a bench to pull on the neoprene socks that will stop my feet going numb with cold, then wade out to where Maureen submerged herself. I've learned to wait for a wave of internal heat before launching myself so that the cold comes as a blessed relief rather than a shock. I swim out after Maureen, waiting for the moment the sea's icy grip turns to a cooling embrace.

Sunanda's voice floats over the top of the waves. 'You're both so lucky, to have intact families. It makes weekends so much more straightforward. They're a bit of a shit-fest to organize when you're divorced.'

She brings up the subject of Irena again, telling me how impressive it is to have a daughter who is so committed to the environment she puts it before everything else.

If I were to tell her that Irena hasn't been home for six years now, doesn't email or text or communicate at all with me, and that Tobias, Mia and George have disowned her, she – and Maureen, no doubt – would be shocked. Perhaps more so because I make a living attempting to heal the rifts in other people's relationships and the fault lines in their families.

In my work, I see the aftermath of divorce all the time and know the pain and complications it can cause. But I've met no one who talks about the trauma experienced by parents whose child has divorced *them*. And I don't tell my friends the truth because the fact is, I'm ashamed. Not of Irena, but of myself. I'm ashamed of myself for failing at what should be the most straightforward role in my life. Being a mother.

After our swim, we wrap up in layers. Sunanda has a Dry-robe and Maureen and I admire the voluminous garment that allows you to get changed modestly and then snuggle under to keep warm. We order drinks from Suzy's and sit out on the platform overlooking the marshes. My skin fizzes after the cold, and my misery vanishes: the effects of the cold seawater are nothing short of miraculous.

The tide has already retreated, exposing grass tussocks and the muddy banks of the creeks. The samphire is beginning to fade, turning from its vibrant green to a wine red as it reaches the end of its season.

'Turmeric,' Sunanda is saying, 'but you must get it fresh. It looks like ginger root but thinner.'

'Do you mean you actually notice a result?' Maureen is drinking green tea, a new departure for her.

As they talk I glance round the coast towards where the houseboats and the mud berths are, and spot a figure walking over the flats.

'Do you think they know where they're going?'

They turn their heads in unison to look.

People who don't know the tides can quickly get cut off and often do, in spite of the notices everywhere warning them to take care.

'The tide's on its way out so I'm sure they're OK.' Maureen dunks her teabag in and out of her cup. The figure is of indistinct gender, wrapped in what looks like a black cape. They're almost close enough to see when they pull a hood up and turn to walk away from us towards the horizon again. For some reason, the vision sends a shiver through me. Or perhaps it's the chill from our swim.

'Ladies' – I drain my cappuccino – 'I'm going to love you and leave you. I've got a hair appointment and I have to visit my mother.'

Ella stands behind me as I sit in the salon chair and picks up my hair. Seeing myself in the mirror, I realize how much grey there is threaded through the chopped mass of dyed dark curls.

'I think you could add some burgundy lowlights,' Ella says. 'It will complement your skin tone.'

'Isn't that a bit young for me?'

'Hardly. Burgundy and green are complementary. It'll work perfectly.'

'Green?'

'Your eyes.'

I'm not sure about this, but she says it will give me a 'lift'. And it's a relief to put myself entirely in the hands of someone else. I'm still tingling from the swim earlier and there's something deeply soothing about letting Ella weave her comb through sections of my hair and paint colour onto it and fold it up in foil, while she chatters on about the holiday she recently took in Vietnam, how welcoming the people were, and how she collected recipes to cook when she got home for her children who all love noodles and Asian flavours – ginger and lemongrass and chilli.

When she's left me to attend to someone else, and while the colour develops, I pretend to flick through a magazine, but in reality I'm thinking of Irena again, flicking back through her life, obsessively searching for the catalyst.

As a therapist I hear how conflicts turn on the tiniest of remarks, the slightest of misunderstandings. A passing jibe, a momentary sense of injustice. But of course, these superficial tipping points are the pinnacle of a much deeper iceberg that will have been there for years. But what of Irena? What was the tipping point? What was the iceberg that lay beneath?

I try to think of anyone else I know who has become estranged from a member of their family. An old friend, Holly, stopped all contact with her sister after the latter insulted her late husband. Criticizing the husband Holly had just lost did seem harsh. But to cease all contact with someone you grew up with? The only person who shared your childhood, because of a fleeting comment? It seems so final, so brutal, to cut off completely, like severing a limb.

A school friend I met up with a couple of years ago told me her two siblings had fallen out after their parents died, that they could no longer agree on how to divide their family home and its contents. The two wouldn't speak to each other any more. Again, to me, the cost, losing all contact with your blood relatives, is not worth a house or a piece of land, however much attachment you feel towards it.

And yet here I am, in a similar situation. As if I've sleep-walked into the thing I most dreaded. And I cannot identify what I've done to cause it.

My thoughts are repetitive and obsessive and I'm relieved

when Ella comes back to check the colour under my foils and asks her assistant, a teenager called Suzanna, to take over, rinsing the dye out under the lukewarm shower. Her fingertips feel so small and light, massaging conditioner into my hair. I could lie here all day, my head back over the sink edge, the warm water running down my cheeks, Suzanna's gentle fingers easing all the tension out of my scalp.

Leaving a tip for Suzanna and Ella, I walk along the road towards my car. I run my fingers through hair that feels silky and light. When I catch sight of myself in a shop window, it takes me a few seconds to realize it's me.

My mother is in her usual wingback chair. I know these chairs have a purpose, to stop old people's heads lolling to the side when they fall asleep, I assume. But I loathe them with a passion. No one under the age of eighty sits in a wingback chair, do they? It feels as if they are a tacit message: 'Time for you to give up hope.'

My mum looks so small, nestled into the chair, clutching a magazine upside down.

She gazes up at me.

'What on earth have you done to your hair, Renee? You look like a beetroot.'

I should be grateful my mother recognizes me. I'm the only one. She no longer knows Tobias, Mia or George, and thinks Xavier, when I bring him, is her brother Pierre as a child. My mother never liked my hair. Hers has always been sleek and chic. She holds it against me that mine came out curly, as if I did it deliberately to upset her. Over the years I've tried every style to gain her approval. Before her eightieth birthday party, when my mother still lived in France, I splashed out two hundred pounds on a restyle and highlights at a London salon where they do the hair of celebrities, or so I was told. After spending such a generous sum I believed there would be nothing left for my mother to criticize. When I arrived at her house with my sharp bob and highlights she took one look and said, 'Renee, you need a good hairdo. If you really can't afford it, I'll *pay* for you to have it done!'

My mother gives off a delicate scent of the perfume she's worn all her life as I bend to kiss her. Guerlain, 'Promenade des Anglais'. I pull up a chair and sit in front of her and pick up her soft, old hand. The care staff like doing manicures and her nails are beautifully polished in a cherry red, her gold rings a little loose now on her slim fingers. She's dressed elegantly too, in a dusty pink silk blouse, grey cashmere cardigan and navy wool knee-length skirt. Her slender legs are crossed at the ankle and she's wearing brown leather buckle-up shoes. Her own hair, still naturally dark in the main, is, as usual, pinned up into a perfect chignon.

'They've moved me again.' She frowns. 'It's so confusing. They keep putting me in different rooms. They try to trick me, but I know what they're up to.'

I don't try to argue any more. I know the theory about going along with the delusions of a person with dementia.

'At least it's a nice room, Mum.' I gesture towards the window. 'You've still got a lovely view of the sea.'

'Ah, *oui. La mer. La mer.* But why is it that awful grey all the time?'

We chat while I sort through her clothes. Some buttons have fallen off one of her jackets. I pack it up to take home to repair. Two cardigans definitely don't belong to my fastidious mother – the labels tell me they are polyester – so I fold them up to hand back to the staff. The care staff are so good, doing the laundry for everyone, but it isn't surprising the clothes wander into the wrong residents' rooms at times.

'Of course' – my mother looks up sharply as I reach the door, about to go to the kitchen to make us some tea – 'Irena is looking much more like you these days.'

'What did you say?'

'Oh, Renee. Irena. Your middle child. She looks like you.'

'Mum. Irena's in France. You mean Mia.'

'Don't patronize me,' she retorts. 'I know my own granddaughters when I see them. And Mia hasn't been for quite some time. I know it's because she's busy teaching, but Irena came specially the minute she got back from Paris.'

My heart starts to thump hard.

'What do you mean, Mum? When was Irena here?' I move back towards her.

She looks up at me, frowning again now.

'This morning. Or was it yesterday? She brought me tulips. There – they're in the vase.'

She points at the windowsill, at the glass vase of white tulips that I brought her last time I was here. My glimmer of hope turns to disappointment as I cross the room and take the vase to the kitchen to refresh the water.

In the kitchen I bump into one of the weekend carers, Josie.

'I don't suppose you know who's been to visit my mother lately?'

'No one but you on the weekends I've been in.' Josie folds her arms. 'I don't know who might have been during the week. You'd need to ask one of the weekday staff. By the way, your mother needs pull-on bras. It's too complicated fiddling with fasteners now she's less mobile. Could you get her a few?'

I agree to do this, my heart sinking. Each incremental sign of my mother's deterioration brings a sense that I'm losing her, bit by slow bit. And the indignity too tears at my heart. If my mother knew I'd started to buy pull-on bras for her, when she used to wear only silk, she would be mortified. I take the tea back to the room with biscuits. She looks at the tea with disgust. My French mother despises the English penchant for PG tips with milk and has her tea black, but it still doesn't quite do it for her. Or perhaps her taste buds have changed because she's started devouring the digestive biscuits which she also used to detest.

'Mum, did Irena tell you where she was living?'

'Irena?'

'You said she popped in the other day.'

'I haven't seen Irena for years.'

'You said she brought you those beautiful tulips.' I sound impatient, which isn't fair. I try to calm myself, to speak more softly. 'You said she came the other day.'

'Renee! Stop having me on. You know very well you brought me those. I can't drink this tea. It tastes of soil.'

We make small talk after this, but my mother's forgotten the beginning of each of her sentences before she reaches the end, asking me what we were talking about.

I try to find something to engage her interest. We attempt a crossword but her attention span is so short I give up after the third clue when she begins to ask how long my father is going to be.

'He left hours ago,' she complains.

'He'll be back.' I turn her magazine the right way up, and hand it back to her before I go.

Leaving my mother fills me with a jumble of conflicting feelings, relief is there in amidst the grief. There is also guilt that I'm abandoning her in the room she thinks is somewhere else, with people who put milk in tea, believing my dad will be back to see her soon, such a long way from her real home.

She calls after me as I go.

'Do buy yourself a hairbrush, Renee.'

I can't face going straight home after this, to deal with Tobias and his needs.

I drive over the causeway to the harbour and walk around the headland and out to Jonah's boat.

He lets me in.

'What is it, Renee? You don't usually come on a Saturday.'

'I don't know.'

I sit on his sofa, which sinks in the middle. He's left a basket of wool on the floor and I see there are needles and the beginnings of some knitting.

'Men who knit,' he grins. 'It's a thing. They're all over Insta.'

'Insta? Since when did you have an Instagram account?'

'I'm a man of surprises,' he smiles. 'I'm making a blanket. Look at this.' He holds up a few rows of chunky knitting, in shades of dark blue and green like the sea. It's a bit wonky, and I see he's dropped a few stitches.

'It's impressive,' I smile back.

'It's a bit of a mess. But you've got to start somewhere. Are you OK, Renee? What is it?'

'I thought I saw Irena today.'

'Oh?'

'But it can't have been. I thought I saw her out on the salt flats at low tide. Then my mother said Irena had been to see her. And I wanted to believe her. And for a moment I did. But then I realized she was imagining it; she said she'd brought her tulips, but I'd taken her those last time I was there.'

'Wishful thinking. It's getting the better of you.'

'You're right.'

He frowns down at me.

'Renee, are you taking enough care of yourself?'

'I'm fine. Been for a swim today. It's such a tonic. *And* I've had my hair done.'

'Yes, I like the colour. Aubergine. But are you . . . you know, *actively* looking after yourself?'

'You think I'm losing it.'

'I think you have a lot on your plate.'

I look up at him.

'Let me sort out this knitting for you,' I say. 'You've dropped a few stitches, Jonah. I'm going to pick them up for you.'

When I get home, I take my coat off and Tobias looks up at me.

'Ooh, you've gone red,' he says. It takes me a second to realize he means my hair.

'Aubergine,' I correct him.

'You look like . . .' He stops himself in time but I know what he was going to say.

I look like Irena in her purple-haired days.

6

'Renee, could I have a word?' Xav's teacher, Christina, comes out into the playground and indicates she wants to speak to me out of Xavier's earshot. Xav obligingly goes to climb on the play equipment.

Christina was friends with Mia when they were younger. She's Mia's age, small, dark-haired, with the kind of pale white skin that reddens easily. Xavier loves her.

'His dad was up at the school today. Thought I should let you know. He didn't come in, was at the fence at afternoon playtime, trying to catch Xavier's eye. We haven't got any guidance as to what access he has. Could you ask Mia to let us know?' Her cheeks flush pink, as if she's a little intimidated by me, which takes me aback.

'Of course, but that's worrying. Eddie doesn't need to come to school without telling Mia or me. What's he playing at?'

'Exactly, that's why I thought I should tell you.'

'I'll talk to Mia about it, but from what Mia's said, she isn't comfortable with him collecting Xavier. Not yet anyway. Thanks for letting me know.'

'Do you want to make cupcakes, Xav?' At home, in the kitchen I get flour, eggs, butter and sugar out, and little cupcake cases, and we spend the next hour mixing and dolloping. By the time I'm bringing them out of the oven there's the rattle of the key in the front door and Mia marches in, brisk, in a print shirt in two shades of pink and a pencil skirt, her hair sleek even after a day in a classroom full of unruly teenagers.

'Wish I could wear things like that.'

'Like what?' She looks down at herself.

'That shirt.'

'But you can, Mum. You could.'

'Is it cotton?'

'It's recycled, I dunno, something or other. What did you do at school today?' Mia scoops up her little boy and gives him a hug.

'Would you like some supper, Mia? I can warm you up some lasagne.'

'I'm fine. I need to get Xav home. Come on, Xav, we've got to go. It's almost bedtime. I take it he's eaten?'

'Of course.'

'I'm still a bit hungry.' He eyes the cupcakes.

'You can have a bowl of Weetabix later. Come on, I'm tired and I need to get home. Is the ice pack for his lunchbox in the freezer?'

She marches to the fridge. 'I don't know why you do that. It's masochistic.'

'Do what?'

'Keep that photo on the fridge. It's like if I were to keep a picture of Eddie by my bedside, reminding me of how he screwed me over.'

The photo is of Irena, one I rescued from Tobias's print-outs. A rare moment when she was laughing into the camera. Mia removes the magnets and takes it down.

'Mum. You've got to let her go. Remember what George said? You're in denial. It means the wound will never heal.

She's made it quite plain. It's been six years since she left us. Best to forget she ever existed.'

I struggle to find a response to this.

Mia's words feel cruel, but I understand she doesn't mean them that way. They come from a place of hurt.

Six years, though. Six years in which Xav has grown from a tiny babe in arms to a child who thinks he knows his way to the nature reserve and discusses the contents of owl pellets. Six years in which Tobias almost died and has turned from successful businessman to someone who wiles away his days with family photos and uses a urine bottle. We've moved into a world in which Irena no longer features.

I take the photo from Mia and stuff it into a drawer.

'You need to get home, Mia, eat, get an early night. You've had a long day. Let's have coffee at the weekend.'

I follow them out to the car where Mia straps Xav into his car seat.

'OK. Saturday?'

'Yes, good. Love you. Love you, Xavier,' I mouth to my grandson who is looking out of the back seat window.

'I'll bring him round at seven tomorrow and you're OK to do the school pick-up?'

'Yes and yes.' I mentally riffle through the clients I've got to see tomorrow within school hours and the one I have in the evening and wonder how I'll also fit in a long overdue supermarket shop as well as a visit to my mother. And at some point I need to get Tobias's medication for him.

'Oh and Mum, don't forget about next week. I know Monday and Tuesday aren't your usual days but you did say you can have Xav.'

Xav presses his lips on the glass, leaving a mouth shape in the condensation.

'Of course.' It will mean moving a few clients around, which is always a bit upsetting for them. But hell, Xavier comes first.

It's only when Mia's gone I remember Christina Walker telling me Eddie had been up at the school, hanging about. I should have told Mia. But she'll be in the middle of Xav's bedtime now, and I don't want to worry her. I'll tell her when I see her in the morning. I stand for a bit, watching the last streaks of pink in the sky fade over the marshes, before I turn to join Tobias for my own long-awaited glass of wine.

7

Tobias doesn't look up from the screen when I go in with his glass, so I return to the kitchen and tidy up. I miss his companionship. Once upon a time we would have sat and chatted at this time of the day while I cooked, maybe listening to some music. Now he occupies his own little world and it's impossible to penetrate his thoughts. It makes me feel alone. Lonely even.

We'd agreed, when we married, that in addition to the fact we were attracted to one another, we were first and foremost companions. But the companion bit of me, the partner, that bit vanished when Tobias had his stroke and the man I married became someone who required me to lift him into bed and feed him pills and bring him wine in a particular glass and tolerate his unpredictable moods and silences.

I shouldn't resent it; he can't help it, I know this. In sickness and in health. We did make those vows. But he is different to the man I married and it makes me different to the woman he married. The things that drew us together – going out together to concerts, eating at nice restaurants, sailing round the coast, discussing the political situation, even if we did take different stances – have vanished since his stroke, and we've had to find something else to keep us together.

And that something else is Xavier. Mia and Xavier are

the little sticky bit in our family that keeps it hanging on by a thread.

And Irena? She's the bit that nearly tore us apart. We all, more or less, accepted her abrupt departure and subsequent absence – but it was the fact she didn't come when Tobias nearly died that sealed it for my husband. And for Mia. It hurt them irreparably.

I called the children straight away the day Tobias collapsed on his way back from his tennis club. Mia came from London, where she was still living with Eddie and Xav. I think they had begun to have problems by then, but I didn't know it.

George got the first flight he could from LA, where he was filming at that time. We took it in turns to go to the hospital and sit by my husband's bedside, in the early days, unsure at that time whether he would pull through.

We waited, too, for Irena to come back from Paris. Because although she'd been silent for three years by then, I was certain she'd want to see her father before he died.

Apparently she didn't.

I tried to ring her, but her number was unobtainable. I'd had texts from Hermione, the woman Irena was living – and, she insinuated, in a relationship – with, so I pinged her a message asking her to tell Irena to get in touch urgently. Hermione's reply was brief, saying Irena was busy, had no time to spare. I asked Hermione to tell Irena her dad was critically ill. I said I understood Irena had a new life, but this might be her last chance to see him, that she would regret it for ever if she didn't come. When my texts elicited no response from Irena or Hermione, Mia grew angry.

'I won't be able to forgive her if she doesn't come,' she said.

George tried to contact Irena too. He even offered to go

out to Paris on the Eurostar to try to find her and bring her home.

'How will you find her?'

'I'll just look up all the environmental protests happening in Paris.'

He shrugged when I questioned the logistics of this. 'It's possible she simply can't afford to come home if she's a full-time activist.'

'She's too up herself to come home is what it is!' Mia said. 'Her father's dying! Why can't she give up her principles for one day to see him?'

George did as he'd suggested.

He managed to trace Irena's protest group; they were campaigning on one of the link roads outside the *périphérique*, and he went all the way out there to pick up his sister. For a day or so I was hopeful. But he returned without her.

'Did you see her? Did you find her?' I asked, running to meet him the second he arrived in a taxi in front of the house.

'I found her,' he said. 'She told me to leave her alone.'

'But how was she? What was she doing?'

'She was looking pretty grungy, sleeping in a tent on the hard shoulder.'

'Didn't you tell her Dad might die? That this might be her last chance to see him?'

'I did what I could, Mum,' he said, 'short of dragging her bodily into a cab. I told her Dad was critically ill.'

'What did she say?'

'Hermione was there. She said Irena couldn't afford the time to come home. She said the campaign was too urgent to abandon. She said the environment comes first. That her dad might be dying, but the world is dying too.'

'That's inhumane,' Mia cried.

'Irena just agreed with everything Hermione said.'

'My sister's been brainwashed.'

'She's got her priorities wrong, that's for sure,' Eddie said, putting his arm around Mia.

'There was something different about her,' George said. 'It was like some light had gone out in her eyes.'

'If she's not eating or drinking properly, no wonder,' Eddie said.

Tobias didn't, of course, die, but we were told his rehabilitation would be long and slow and he would need extra support at home. The demands of getting him out of hospital and installed at home, the organization it took, the conversations with physios, with occupational therapists and speech therapists, took up every spare moment of my day. I was also concerned about my mother, who was struggling to settle into the care home we'd finally found for her.

Yet when I look back at that period, I think, why didn't I go straight out to Paris and beg Irena to come home? When we knew where she was? When George said a light had gone out in her eyes, why didn't alarm bells ring? My only explanation is that I was so preoccupied with sorting out Tobias, my mother, my clients, I just didn't have the time or energy to set out on a course of action I was pretty certain would end in failure.

Mia offered to take the rest of the year off to help at home with Tobias. I told her she mustn't. She was establishing herself in her first full-time job, and it would have been detrimental to her to leave it. Eddie was still earning his big bucks in the city back then – or so I thought – and they were still in London, so it felt wrong to disrupt the life they had created with Xav, with their lovely Victorian house and garden, and the friends they'd made.

George offered to come and live at home as well, but that would have meant giving up the part he'd been filming in LA. 'I can cope,' I told them both, with a breezy confidence I didn't feel. And so I ushered them both back to their young adult lives.

Before Mia left, she turned to me.

'I will never forgive Irena for this,' she said. 'If she asks to see me now, I'm not speaking to her. I'm having nothing more to do with her.'

'Please don't say that.'

I looked at her and saw she was crying, quietly.

'She's let you and Dad down so badly. She's let me down, too. She's supposed to be my sister.'

'You know when people get caught up in these movements, they become very blinkered. She'll change, she'll come back to us.'

I didn't wholly believe my own words, but I couldn't bear hearing Mia saying she'd never forgive her sister. I couldn't bear witnessing her pain. Neither could I bear to believe Irena was estranged from us for good.

'Mum, we've given her a million chances. Dad might've died and she couldn't make the effort to see him. There's something fundamentally lacking in her, like she's psychopathic or something. I've read up on the characteristics and she ticks many of the boxes.'

A shiver went through me at Mia's words. Was it because I feared there might be some truth in them? The little child who spilled boiling water on her baby brother? The child who had dropped things and broken things and lost things and shown no remorse? The young woman who had come home from her expensive boarding school and smashed a tray of glasses for no reason? Then left without telling us she was going? Had all that been a sign? I thought of my mother's words – *the cobbler's children are always the worst shod* – and wondered why I'd not seen it before; taken more care of Irena, maybe even sought some treatment for her.

'What do *you* think, George?' I asked, desperate for someone to make sense of all this.

'I think Irena's shown us she's given up on us,' he said. 'I think what she's telling us, Mum, is that she *wants* us to let her go.'

When Tobias recovered from his stroke – as much as he was going to recover anyway – he said we ought to renew our wills. They were out of date and we had to make sure they included Xavier. By then we had also learned Mia and Eddie were splitting up and Tobias wanted to make sure he would no longer be entitled to half of whatever Mia stood to inherit.

We pored over the documents for some time and Tobias told me the changes he wanted to make in the wording to cover various different eventualities.

Then he said something that hit me like a blow in the solar plexus.

He told me he was wondering whether Irena should be a beneficiary in our will any more. I immediately argued that of course she should; what was he thinking?

I put his suggestion down to the change of character that can come over a person after a major life-changing illness such as a stroke. Because it *was* a catastrophic change. Tobias had supported Irena in her youth, just as he'd supported the other two. He'd even paid for her expensive education once she and I had persuaded him it was what she needed.

'How can you turn on her now, abandon her, as if she doesn't belong to our family any more?' I asked, still unable to believe he could mean it.

'Because she's made it very clear she *doesn't* belong to our family any more,' he said.

8

That day

Xav and I stand at the window on the morning Mia goes off to Amsterdam and wave as the Uber disappears along the coast road carrying her off to the station. Xav seems happy enough to let her go. He turns to me the minute she's gone to ask if we can have Coco Pops for breakfast since he's not allowed them when he's at home.

'Cupboard, love.' I wink at Tobias.

We eat our breakfast together, the Coco Pops for Xav, followed by boiled eggs and toast soldiers for all of us.

'It'll be good for Mia to have a night away, even if it's work-related.' I wipe the milk Xav's spilled on the table. Tobias levers himself up as Xav runs off to play in the sitting room. 'She works such long hours and puts herself under so much pressure.'

'She takes after me.'

I glance at him; this is another thing that's changed since his stroke, the fact he can't work any more. And the fact he seems sometimes to forget this. But Tobias is right. Mia is conscientious and driven. Just as Tobias was, before he fell ill.

'I wish she could relax more, though. Let others take the strain. She was asking me whether I thought she should let

Eddie have more contact with Xavier. He's desperate to be more involved.'

'He should've thought of that before he gambled their life savings away.'

'Tobias! I think he's taken the punishment for that. He's learned his lesson. He won't do anything like it again.'

'He was a fool! He earned all that money in the City. He should have invested it in something low risk as I advised him to do.'

'He thought he could make money for them. He made a mistake, Tobias. We all make mistakes.'

'Not as stupid as that.'

'Well, anyway, what I'm saying is I think Mia could allow Eddie to have Xav to stay from time to time. For his sake, but for hers as well so she can have some time off.'

'Eddie's made his bed. Now he has to lie in it. Bring me my tea, will you, Renee, I need to set up the computer.'

This is what happens, our conversations stopping abruptly, Tobias closing down just as I feel we're beginning to talk again, properly.

I drop Xavier at school and he gives me a wave and runs off to play with Poppy.

By nine thirty Amy and Yannis are perched on the sofa opposite me. Amy talks for the first part of the session, while Yannis sits with his arms folded and his legs crossed, his head tilted away as usual as if he resents being here.

Amy tells me when Yannis is at home he spends his whole time watching football and drinking beer.

'He could show a bit more interest in Sasha,' she says. 'I feel so alone. It's like I'm a single parent.'

'Try to say it to Yannis,' I suggest, 'rather than telling me. Try and express to Yannis how you feel.'

'I feel like a single parent,' Amy says shortly to Yannis's cheek.

Yannis refuses to look at either of us and talks to his hands, folded in his lap.

'You make me feel like I can't do anything right. I take Sasha out and she's in the wrong clothes. I put her to bed and it's the wrong pyjamas. I read her the wrong books. I watch a film with her and you say I should be doing something else. I give up.'

'It doesn't take much,' she says, 'to know when you're in charge, you're supposed to *be* there with her. You're not supposed to go out to the shops while you're looking after her.'

Yannis does look at Amy now, a scowl on his face.

'Why bring that up again? We talked about that. I told you why I went to the shops. I thought we'd finished with that.'

'I just wonder how committed you are,' Amy insists.

'I've had enough of this.' He thumps the sofa with his fists and Amy flinches. 'I try to be a good stepfather to Sasha but it's like you block me at every turn. It's as if you don't want me to learn.'

'You shouldn't have to learn!' Amy cries. 'It's not a degree, Yannis. And I'm not your teacher. You're her step-dad! It's supposed to come naturally.'

When they've left I go into the reception area to get a cup of coffee.

'You OK, Renee? How's your mum?' Charlie is behind the desk, taking calls, booking appointments.

'Good, thank you.'

'Well, we all want the best for our loved ones.'

I still appreciate Charlie for recommending my mother's

care home. So I don't tell her it breaks my heart to see my mother in her one room, thinking they've moved her.

'While you're here, Renee, I should tell you, I'm having to fend off clients requesting to see you. I don't want to put you under undue pressure. But you've only got a couple of spaces in your calendar as far as I can see. Perhaps we can have a chat later about whether any of your current clients might be ending at any point?'

'Sure. I've got the Ollards now, though, and I'm off this afternoon. But I'll take a look later. Thanks, Charlie.'

Before returning to my room I pop outside to get my reading glasses that I'd left in the car. A man is leaning against the wall round the side of the building. It takes me a moment to realize it's Yannis. He's smoking, his face crumpled into an angry frown. Why's he lingering here? Why hasn't he gone home with Amy? He insisted he wanted to be a good partner, a good stepfather, so why is he avoiding her?

The vision comes back to me, his fist landing on my sofa, and for a horrible second I wonder if he might ever hit Amy. Or worse, the child?

As I retrieve my glasses from the car I wonder again about Yannis leaving Sasha to go to the shop and whether he is to be trusted with her. It's a fine line we tread as therapists at times. We're here to listen and not to judge but when alarm bells ring, we're not supposed to ignore our instincts.

The Ollards couldn't be more different to Amy and Yannis. They are both dressed in Barbour jackets that they take off simultaneously as they sit down. They are slender, their faces have an outdoorsy pink glow. I've been seeing them for some time now. About a year ago, Justine was going through the laundry when she found a receipt in

Ralph's trouser pocket, for a meal in a restaurant. The date and time were printed at the bottom. Her eye ran over the itemized list and she saw there was lobster and champagne among the other dishes and drinks listed.

It was such a clichéd way to discover an affair, Justine could hardly believe Ralph had been so unimaginative. She wondered if he was deliberately misleading her. Or, as we later discussed, whether he wanted to be found out.

Because Ralph had indeed been having a relationship for six months with (another cliché, Justine called it) a work colleague. They'd been dining out in Michelin star restaurants on evenings Justine had been led to believe Ralph was working late.

'That old chestnut,' she'd sighed. 'All so pathetically predictable.'

Justine had been shocked, she said, not so much by his infidelity, as by the banality of the details. 'Working late at the office', leaving receipts around. And what had upset her more than his seeing another woman, she said, were the meals he'd splashed out on.

'We *never* eat out,' she'd said. 'The meals he'd been buying hurt me more than his sleeping with her. I know that sounds ridiculous. I can't explain it to anyone else.' She looked at Ralph. 'My friends think I should kick you out for cheating on me.'

'And what do you think, Justine?' I asked.

'For some reason, I don't think of it as cheating. Because if that's your way of cheating, Ralph, you're pretty fucking lousy at it.'

'Gee, thanks,' Ralph muttered.

'What do you think of it as?' I asked her.

She'd leaned back, staring at the ceiling for a moment. Then she'd looked back at her husband and said, 'It's as though you're even more naive than I ever realized. It's weird but it makes me feel rather sorry for you.'

And so I'd been working with this couple for several months, unpicking what Justine felt about her husband's affair, and how her reaction had, Ralph said, 'taken the wind out of my sails'.

'I think I needed a little life outside the humdrum public repetitiveness of marriage and family get-togethers and childcare and responsibility,' he said. 'But now the secret is out, the incentive has gone.'

'Odd.' Justine's voice was curt. 'That makes me feel rather sorry for your floozy as well.'

They were reaching a stage where Ralph was admitting he had discovered a different side to Justine since she had found the receipt. 'One who is more open-minded and exciting and unpredictable than I ever realized.'

Justine, however, had begun to wonder whether she still respected Ralph when he could so easily be found out. 'His cleverness was one of the things I found sexy about him, now it seems that was an illusion. Your manner of carrying out an affair, Ralph, was just so . . . so dumb it makes me wonder if you have any brains at all.'

Today, they admit their pain is turning into a kind of learning experience and their relationship seems stronger now than when they first came, shell-shocked, into my room. I feel a tiny glow of triumph that perhaps, this time, the therapy has had a good outcome.

As I leave later, intending to go to the supermarket, my phone pings. It's a text from Jonah, asking me to visit him on the boat as soon as I can, but to please be discreet, not to tell a soul, not to let anyone know.

My heartbeat speeds up.

Should I text Tobias, let him know I wasn't coming

straight home, even if I didn't tell him why? Sometimes, after a counselling session, life seems to imitate what was going on in the room. In this instant, the feeling Ralph was trying to describe – the adrenalin rush at doing something no one else knows you're doing – hits me full force. And I realize I've been desperate for this. To make my own decisions, to do my own thing, to take a risk and step outside the humdrum, everyday life of my marriage. Jonah's message invites me to do something no one else – Tobias in particular – will know about, and this in itself feels exciting and heady and impulsive. I get into the car, fasten my seat belt, check myself in the mirror. Do those burgundy highlights really work? Have I aged? What ridiculous vanity! Why should it matter? I drive fast, away from the counselling rooms, my head down, round the coast to the harbour village.

I park in the visitors' car park and half run, half walk along the coast path to the mud berths. I have the rest of the day free. I don't know what Jonah has in mind, but I can spend the whole afternoon here if necessary. The food shop can wait. I'm alarmed at the secrecy of what I'm doing, but a brisk easterly wind rushes in from the sea, pushing me along from behind as if encouraging me, and though my stomach fills with butterflies as I draw within sight of the boats, I can't wait to get to them.

Later, when I leave the boat, I look around furtively, before hurrying back to the visitors' car park, taking the footpath, though the full spring tide is already half covering it in places. Then I drive to town to pick up Tobias's medication. I will come to hate myself for this. Because the truth is, going to town for my husband's prescription wasn't really necessary. I could have got it from the chemist on the island.

But I was covering my tracks. If I'd gone straight home, I would have skipped the tide, I would have seen the parents outside the school, I would have remembered: Mia was away on a course in Amsterdam, and even though it was a Monday, I was supposed to be picking up Xavier today.

9

Paul Kicks has found a room with a kettle. He puts a cup of tea in front of me and presses numbers rapidly into his phone. He turns to me, mid-call.

'Zoe, a teaching assistant, was on duty at home time. According to her, she thinks Xav said you were there for him.'

'But I wasn't. I wasn't. And Mia's in Amsterdam.'

'Hold on.'

He speaks back into the phone, his words jumbled. Then there's a pause. 'Ah, yes, yes, true, yes, I'll tell her.'

He switches the phone off. Turns back to me. His words sort themselves out.

'OK. Zoe's not sure he said *you* specifically. Now she thinks about it, she isn't sure. But Xav said *someone* was there for him. She's beside herself, blaming herself for not double-checking who he meant. In tears, afraid she's going to be disciplined. She put me on to his teacher, Christina Walker. Christina says his dad's been hanging around a lot at the school. She thinks he might have collected Xav today. And they say Xav is a child who would never leave unless he was sure there was someone there for him. They say he always comes back to class if you or his mum are late. So he wouldn't have gone without you.'

Things fall into place.

'Of course. Why didn't I think? Eddie's desperate to see

Xav. He knows Mia was away this week. It makes sense he might have been there at home time.'

'Do you want me to call him? Have you got his number?'

I take a deep breath. My heart rate slows a little.

'It's OK. I'll call him myself. You've been so kind, so kind, Paul. I think I need to be at home. Well, of course I need to be there. Eddie will be bringing Xav back at some point.'

Already I can hear Mia, her fury with me. *I told you I didn't want Eddie collecting Xav from school. And if you'd have been there like you promised, he wouldn't have had the chance.*

I put the cup of tea down on a small table in front of me and stand up.

'Are you sure there's nothing else I can do?' Paul looks at me with concern.

'For the moment, yes, I'm sure.'

I move towards the door.

'Call me the minute you hear he's safe with his dad.' Paul holds the door open for me. 'Please.'

I don't know if I answer. I press in Eddie's number as I hurry towards home, cursing out loud when it goes to voice-mail. Phoning Mia again, I tell her we think Eddie must have taken Xavier.

I steel myself for her vitriol.

'I *know*!' Mia sounds fazed rather than angry. 'Stupid of me. Stupid stupid stupid. Why didn't I think of that first? I've rung him but it's going to voicemail. I'm getting a flight. I'll go straight to Eddie's.'

'Mia, why don't you let me go? To Eddie's? This is my doing.'

'No, I have to see him. I'm going to kill that man for not telling me. And you need to be there in case he brings Xav back to yours before I get there.'

*

I arrive at home, where Tobias is watching some crappy quiz show on the TV. My husband, the man who should still be working, striking deals, booking restaurants and city breaks for us – *it keeps the spice in our relationship*, he'd say ironically, mocking something he believed I advised my clients in my counselling room – is switched off to me. The old Tobias would have leapt up, made rapid phone calls, known what to do. Now, however, I realize I can't even tell Tobias Xavier's missing, because it will cause him stress that isn't good for him.

The house feels emptier than it's ever felt.

The silence buzzes in my ears.

In the kitchen the sauce I'd been making when the phone rang is blackened around the edges and the sweet potato has thickened and is sticking to the bottom of the pan. Later I'll see I tipped it all into the bin, unaware of what I was doing, my mind stuck on a helpless loop. I forgot to pick up my own grandson from school and he's gone!

If he's not with Eddie, where is he?

I *will* the phone to ring, for Mia to phone back and tell me Eddie has been in touch, that yes, he has Xavier. That he took his son home with him. But why he didn't text one of us? He clearly has issues with Mia. But to take their son without telling her? That's cruel.

Of course it's possible Eddie only took Xavier home out of concern, seeing he'd been left at the gates. Eddie was desperate to spend time with his son, poor man. And today he realized no one had come to get his boy so he'd done what any dad would do, and taken him home himself. He simply hadn't managed to get in touch with us. After all, Mia was on her course all day. And I often forget to put my phone back on when it's been on silent for work. This thought calms me for a minute.

But then why isn't there a voicemail or a text from

Eddie? And anyway, I wasn't at work this afternoon. I'd moved the clients I normally had in order to pick up Xav, so my phone was switched on. That's how Jonas got hold of me. And why didn't Eddie tell one of the teachers?

My mind swings from one explanation to another, avoiding the obvious, that we *have no idea where Xavier is!*

Whatever's happened, it's because of me. I've put my own grandson at terrible risk by failing to be there at home time. Now I clutch at straws. Could Xav's disappearance possibly have something to do with who I was with this afternoon? We swore to keep our meeting secret. Taking a child uninvited from school would be like blazing a spotlight on the fact we'd been together. And the timing's not right. There wouldn't have been long enough for someone leaving the boats just after I did, at three o'clock, not on foot anyway, to get to the school in time. I dismiss this theory, which, for a second, felt like a glimmer of hope, because the tide of really frightening thoughts I've been trying to hold back are about to flood in.

What if Xavier decided, when he saw I wasn't there, to try to come home alone?

I want to go to the nature reserve on my own, he'd said only a few days ago. *I know the way!* In spite of the teachers' assertion that Xav would never leave school on his own, I can't stop the scene unfolding. The way Xavier drags me with him to the nature reserve, chanting over and over again that he knows the way. I see him in my mind's eye, running ahead of me, asking me what my happiest day ever is, his young limbs moving with such abandon, dancing out across the boardwalks, black hair blown upright in the wind, being a whale with his blowhole in the middle of 'the sea'. Because it *is* the sea when the tide's in.

Xavier's too young to understand how the tide fills those

creeks so fast, the way the water deepens in random pockets, so while you might have your feet on dry land, it doesn't mean you can reach the shore. If he had left school at three thirty, telling Zoe someone was there for him, and had gone out – and I was the one who had shown him the way; oh, the irony – down to the shore and out onto the grass tussocks as the creeks began to fill, between school home time and the time I arrived at the causeway, if he were out there squatting to peer into pools, imagining all the beautiful sea creatures he might identify, he would have been cut off in seconds. He could be out there in the retreating tide now . . . A colder wave washes over me. It was a spring tide today. The waters came up at a ferocious pace.

I cannot wait any longer. I pick up my phone to dial the police, only pausing when Mia's name flashes up again.

'I'm at the airport. Eddie's still not picking up. The bastard. He must have Xav! I'll kill him for not telling me.' Mia's silent for a beat. Then she says, 'This is unbearable! I can't really believe Eddie wouldn't have texted me if he had him. Has something terrible happened to him? Mum where is he?' She begins to sob.

I clutch the phone, feeling the sweat pool beneath my palm, and try to think straight. I am the mother here. I have to make things right. That's what a mother's job is. To make things right for her children, for her grandchildren. My knees feel weak. I cannot stop the squeezing sensation in the pit of my stomach. I don't want to utter the next words but I know I have to.

'Mia, I don't think we can wait to hear from Eddie. We have to phone the police.' I don't say the coastguard. I don't want to put my fear inside my daughter's head.

Her voice is dry when she next speaks. 'Mum, could you do that for me? I don't think I could bear it.'

10

Our instinct, as we take in something sudden and catastrophic, is to say no, this isn't happening to me. These things only happen to other people, those sad faces that appear on the television news, desperate, pleading for information.

We repel shock, denying it, giving our bodies time to recalibrate before we are able to acknowledge the truth. This was supposed to be an ordinary evening, playing with Xav, cooking, eating. My ability to mentally absorb what is actually happening is limited, dull, slow, even while my legs turn to jelly, my breath shortens, my stomach clenches.

When I've called the police, I can protect Tobias no longer. I go into the sitting room, lean over his shoulder.

'Toby, something terrible's happened.'

He looks up at me, slowly, still half focused on the television.

'You're saying what?'

Within half an hour of telling Tobias, the police arrive at our house to question me and Tobias about our grandson. I know it's protocol, I know the relatives are always the first to be investigated when a child disappears, but this feels such a waste of time.

They need to be out there, looking for our grandson. Not here asking us pointless questions.

When they've taken the obligatory statements they say

they're going to send colleagues in the Met straight round to Eddie's. They'll contact the head teacher at the school and ask what happened at home time. They'll set up road checks on the causeway. They will go everywhere, they tell me, their faces a blur as they explain; they will be all over the island questioning, searching.

I follow them to the door, leaving Tobias swallowing his painkillers in the sitting room.

At the door I tap the policewoman's shoulder.

She turns. 'Is there something else?'

'It's . . . I was the one to fail to pick him up. I wasn't thinking straight. I was in town, getting my husband's medication.'

I still can't bring myself to say where I spent the afternoon. I am still afraid of what saying the words out loud will do to me, to my family.

'You mustn't blame yourself.' She puts a hand on my shoulder. I look at her, wondering how she can sound so trite. But she is about twenty-two, only just older than George. Is she really capable of taking this on, I wonder? As if hearing my thoughts, she reassures me that they'll leave no stone unturned, that a missing child is top priority.

I watch the blue light disappear down the coast road and return to stand with Tobias at our front window. A mist has come in and sits over the marshes. Searchlights sweep across the estuary.

The police are insistent that they don't want members of the public, and that includes me, attempting to search the estuary when the tide is so treacherous. They want us to leave it to them and the coastguard, the experts. But being a passive observer when I was the one to cause this feels counterintuitive. I need to move, to search, to scour the island until I find Xavier, to wrap him up, to tuck him into the little bed I have all made up for him in George's old room, waiting. Eventually Tobias says he has to take some sleeping pills; he can bear the waiting to hear from Eddie no longer.

In automatic mode, I help my husband up the stairs and into bed, lift his legs so he can swing them in under the covers. He turns over, away from me, and falls asleep almost instantly, his medication allowing him relief from reality.

He leaves me to face the harsh facts on my own. Mia must be on a flight by now. We are both waiting to hear from the police that their colleagues in London have tracked Eddie down, that he has Xavier.

Once Tobias is asleep, I go back to the front window. The helicopters and police boats continue to beat about out there, lights swinging over the saltings. Tobias's bottle of sleeping pills stares up at me, temptingly. He's managed to enfold his fear in drugs. But I have to stay alert. And tolerate the horror, the guilt that whatever's happened to my grandson, it's due to my actions.

Looking out at the darkness isn't doing any good. I pace the house. Try Eddie's number again. It goes to voicemail. I feel like hurling my phone across the room. I try Mia's and get the same.

In desperation, I phone George.

My son does pick up and I bawl down the phone, telling him I forgot to pick up Xavier, that he's lost. That if he isn't with Eddie, we've no idea where he's gone.

'Mum,' he says, his voice calm, 'Mum, it's going to be OK.'

'How's it going to be OK? I forgot to pick him up from school! He's only six, George. He wanted to go to the nature reserve on his own. He thought he could. He thought he knew the way. If he went out there and got cut off by the tide . . . he can't swim, George, not without armbands.'

I want to tell George where I was this afternoon, to explain why I was distracted. But it wouldn't be fair to drag him into a secret I can't even divulge to Tobias.

Or to Mia.

'And it's all because of me. He's out there, George, I'm sure of it.'

'OK.' George speaks slowly. 'You don't know that. You think Eddie has him. That's much more likely.'

'You think?'

'I know. And Xavier isn't stupid, however much he loves the nature reserve.'

'I can't bear that I forgot to get him.'

'Mum, one thing at a time. Let's see if he's with Eddie first of all. And I'm guessing the police are searching the coast; they don't hang about if there's a child's safety at stake.'

'Oh George.'

'It's going to be OK.'

'Honest to God, George, I swore I would be a better grandmother to Xavier than I was a mother to you. I swore I'd never let him come to any harm, the way I let Irena scald you when my back was turned. And now look what I've done . . .'

I hear George sigh down the line.

'Now's not the time to go there,' he says. 'Like I say, one thing at a time.'

I long for George to be here, with me, reassuring me that everything will be all right. I want to ask him if he'll come home, but stop myself. George has a life to lead in London, rehearsals to attend, filming to do.

The new coat is hanging by the front door. When George

has said goodbye I pull it on, wrench on some ankle boots, wrap a scarf around my neck, and head to the shore in the dark. I stare out to where the marshes become the sea, to the inky indigo line of the horizon. It's almost black now, and far away, cloud shadows move over the surface of the water, separating, then joining together again. The tide is far, far out, but it will be on the turn by now, and as I walk down our front drive to the esplanade, and cross over the road, the slow gurgle of water in the channels, normally pleasing to me, fills me with dread.

As I stand there, the clouds part and a vast blood orange moon appears on the horizon. What they call a supermoon. It creates a path of broken light across the marshes. Xav would love this, I think. I hear his voice: *Wow! Look at that moon. It's the biggest I've ever seen in my whole life.*

The night air smells briny, with an undertone of sulphur, the stench the tide leaves when it's snatched what it wants from the land and retreated with its swag. I try not to think about Xavier as a part of this haul, his beautiful, delicate body, still barely out of babyhood. I push the insistent image, his small body flailing in the depths, out of my mind's eye, but it floats back.

I'm the one who showed him the way down to the shore. I took him there every week even when Mia told me she'd prefer it if I didn't. I was leading him into danger. My insistence on giving him freedom against his mother's wishes has led to his demise. I wish I could stop the image. It's an intrusive thought, I would tell my clients, if they described such a sense of irony, if they made spurious links like this.

Don't give it power, don't feed it.

The thought that slipped in and out of my mind earlier comes back. Maybe the timing was wrong, but I have to check. The alternative is too awful. And anyway, I need someone to talk to, now Tobias has left me to sleep off his own anxiety. I go in to fetch my car keys, checking myself automatically in the mirror, then chastise myself for my ridiculous vanity. But it's important on a certain level. I want to feel in control, I don't want to look as if I've lost it completely. I close the front door softly and then get into the car, and reverse out of our driveway.

There are a couple of young police officers doing checks on cars leaving the island.

'I'm sorry, but we're not letting anyone on or off the island without taking their information first.' A young officer leans towards my window as he takes a furtive look behind me. 'We'll need to do a quick search of the car as well.'

His colleague, another young man in a hi-vis jacket, moves over to the car, asks me to open the boot. I wonder if I should tell them I'm the grandmother of the missing boy but something stops me.

They don't ask when I show them my driving licence.

'I'll just get a photo of this.' The man's breath rises in a cloud as he takes a picture of my registration plate, and as his eyes also pass over the interior of the car. At last he and his colleague wave me on.

Once I'm over the causeway it's a short drive round to the harbour. I pull into the visitors' car park so I can take the coastal walk to the boats, away from the road. I use the torch on my phone to guide me. The visibility is still poor out here at this time. I can hear the sound of the water moving in the channels that I can't see, the popping of the mud as air bubbles are released. I know the way, but the paths are slippery after the spring tide of earlier and I have to go carefully.

The clouds part again and the massive orange orb of the

moon appears. The houseboats are stark against it. This moon feels supernatural. It's too big, too strange, too beautiful and sinister. It tells me, *you are insignificant, the universe doesn't care.* Passing Jonah's boat, in darkness now, I reach the one I'm heading for. My heart's racing as I bang on the boat door. It will be a relief to be able to talk, to cry, not to have to hide anything.

I knock again, but still there's no answer. I try the handle. To my surprise, the door is unlocked so I push it open and go in. There are dishes on the table, a half-eaten meal. A pile of conkers on the rug.

I push back the curtain that divides the living space from the sleeping quarters.

Although it's gone midnight, there's nobody here.

PART TWO

IRENA

11

They don't play conkers any more. It's a shame because I'd gathered a bagful. I liked to imagine him in the playground, his brown nut on a piece of string, whacking his mate's as if his life depended on it. I'd hardened one for him in my wood burner, the way we used to put them in the oven when we were kids, and bored a hole in it with a skewer to thread the string through.

I didn't believe I'd ever give it to him, but sending him presents, preparing things for him, kept my nephew real for me.

The conker had been in my pocket for days now. Five days to be precise. The other conkers I'd collected would stay in a pile in my boat until they had wrinkled and shrunk and someone would toss them away. They were everywhere at the moment, their prickly green cases hanging among the leaves over my head, just begging to have sticks hurled at them, to be smashed to the ground. Kids today, though. They aren't interested in conkers. It's all PlayStation and YouTube and virtual this and that. Anyway, I didn't get to play with Xav. Never have.

I'd been coming up to the school every day at home time since I'd moved onto the boat next door to Jonah's. I wanted to catch a glimpse of my nephew. I had even developed a kind of superstition around it, that if I didn't see him, something bad would happen to him. I was also curious about my sister. I wanted to know what she looked like now she was the mother of a school-aged child.

I couldn't imagine what we'd say to each other, if Mia did spot me. But by observing her from afar, I thought I might be able to intuit what it was in Mia that meant she had so unquestioningly taken our father's side, and disowned me, with no apparent remorse.

I didn't know if Dad was well enough to pick up Xav from school from time to time these days, but I was terrified of bumping into him. Dad and Mia had told me I was dead to them, and it still kept me awake at nights. George, too, had stopped contacting me since he tried to persuade me to return with him from Paris. If I lingered on those words, 'dead to me', they still had the capacity to make me cry. So I took extra care to keep out of sight, hiding behind the horse chestnut tree over the road from the school, among the conkers on the ground.

Hermione had said the way my family treated me was a kind of emotional abuse. That I had every right to reject them. That I occupied the moral high ground. But it didn't make the hurt any easier to bear. When your dad and the sister you were once close to say you no longer exist, when your whole family act as if you no longer belong to them, the pain goes very deep. It's a physical pain, a kind of constant squeezing sensation in the chest and throat.

I had missed Xavier the most in the years since I'd left, which was ironic since he was the one I knew the least. I'd missed seeing him grow – my goodness, I'd missed the whole of his babyhood, from tiny newborn to little boy. I hoped my presents had kept me alive in his mind – because he was blameless. I'd made sure to send him postcards from time to time, too, messages from his mysterious Aunty Irena.

My dad and sister had told me I no longer existed as far as they were concerned. George hadn't said as much but had kept his distance too. Mum, admittedly, had kept on trying to make contact. She'd replied to the texts I'd asked Hermione to send, just to let her know I was alive and well. But Hermione suggested this was obviously motivated by maternal guilt rather than any sincere attempt at reconciliation. And when Hermione had had to go to America, and my paid work in Paris had dried up, I'd had to come back to England. I found a room in a pub near the island to stay in for a few days, and in desperation, contacted the only person in England I could trust, an old therapist friend of Mum's, Jonah, to ask him if he knew of anywhere I could live, just for a while, just until Hermione came for me.

Jonah replied, saying he looked after some of the other houseboats in the mud berths on the saltings. He reassured me he would be discreet and said there was a boat I could live in until Hermione came back; it was next to his and the owners would be glad to have it lived in, in return for some basic maintenance. He said he would have to let my mother know I was there, though, as she was so worried about me. I begged him not to. He said it was a condition of my living there, that he would feel treacherous, letting me move next door to him without telling Mum.

Something about hearing this – and realizing my mother was genuinely worried about me – shifted things for me a tiny bit. And so I said OK, as long as she didn't tell anyone else in the family and didn't try to come and see me until I felt ready.

I moved into the houseboat – the first place I had ever lived entirely alone. I wouldn't be there long, I explained to Jonah; I was waiting for word from my partner, Hermione, before I could make any plans as to what to do next. But the minute she got in touch, I'd be going again. In the meantime, though, I felt safe, knowing Jonah was next door.

The day I moved into the boat, Jonah came over to see me. We sat in my cabin, with the little door open and the curlews calling over the salt marshes, and the sound was familiar – I'd heard it from my bedroom as a child – and comforting. For a short while, I had a glimpse of what it might be like to be living back here, for good. And it surprised me: I thought I could grow to like it. I realized I'd missed this landscape, the saltings, the tides.

Jonah told me that he understood I didn't want anyone to know I was here.

'But Irena, your mother has suffered badly over your estrangement. Don't you think it might be helpful to talk to her?'

I couldn't quite form the words I wanted to.

In the end I could only manage, 'My parents should have thought of that, before they betrayed me.'

'Betrayed you?'

I looked at Jonah's kind face, the question on his brow.

'That's how it feels. They don't want me to be part of the family any more.'

'I can't speak for your father, but Renee,' Jonah said, 'never disowned you, Irena. She doesn't understand why you left. She doesn't understand why you won't reply to her texts. She's desperate to see you. She has been grieving for you.'

I stood up and went to the cabin door and breathed the salt marshy air. Again, I had a momentary feeling that this, not Paris, was my true home, but at the same time, I was overwhelmed by a horrible sense of the impossibility of it all.

Then I turned.

'But don't you see? It isn't as easy as just saying, "OK, Mum, here I am." Not after six years. Not after being told I'm no longer a Gulliver. I've accepted it now, but it was agony. Pulling away. It hurt.' I put a hand on my chest. 'It still does. I only came to you for help because I had nowhere else to go. I'm going back to Hermione the minute I hear from her.' Saying those words out loud was odd. They sounded hollow. I wondered if I even believed them myself. I wondered whether I knew, deep down, that Hermione and I were over.

'There's all kinds of stuff to work through. Stuff you don't know about,' I said. 'It isn't as simple as you think.'

'Oh, don't worry.' He smiled. 'I know nothing is ever as simple as it might appear on the surface.'

Jonah obviously spoke to my mum a lot and knew her well through their work. Although I was sceptical about some of the things he believed about my mother, such as how devoted she was to me, and how she didn't understand why I'd ever left, I trusted him in every other way. He had a wisdom about him as if he'd been through a lot in his life too and could separate out what mattered and what didn't.

I asked him to wait, told him I'd speak to my mother the minute I felt ready, but warned him that if he told her before that point, I'd go away again for good, 'even if it means sleeping rough until I find Hermione,' I added.

The next few days on the boat did something to me. Perhaps it was the sea air, the close contact with the seabirds and the tides. But I began to feel calmer. Less angry with Hermione for leaving me, perhaps reconciled to the fact that the relationship was over. Maybe it was the way Jonah seemed to accept me. I realized I hadn't ever felt accepted before, not truly.

But then, as if in response to my own mental shift away from her, Hermione texted me, telling me she was in London and giving me her address there 'in case I was passing'.

That made me think it might be my last chance to do as Jonah had begged me, and talk to my mother. So on the same day I got Hermione's text – it was a Monday, my seventh day on the boat – I asked Jonah to text Mum and ask if she could come over without telling anyone.

'Only Mum, though, Jonah. No one else.'

I couldn't write to her myself: I couldn't think how to frame the words. Jonah said he'd contact her at lunchtime, when he knew when she'd be leaving work; she often only worked a half day on a Monday, he said.

Mum arrived in the early afternoon. I'd seen her from afar, of course, in the last few days, but not close up like this. She looked older, which isn't surprising, given it was six years since I'd seen her. It was difficult to define what exactly it was about her that had aged, a kind of thickening of her face and neck, I think, although she was still as slim as she'd always been, and her hair was shorter, bobbed, and she'd had some deep red lowlights that suited her olive skin tone. But her face was so sad, so drawn. There were dark circles under her eyes and lines around her mouth that hadn't been there before.

Seeing her like that, I felt a tug in my heart, and I was swamped suddenly with a feeling of terrible doubt about the decisions I'd made over the last few years.

Was it possible, after all, that my mother was an innocent party in my family's rejection of me? As Jonah had implied?

That thought hadn't occurred to me before. I'd always grouped Mum together with my dad. Mum and Dad, almost one beast. There's an age you reach when you see your parents as separate beings, and I asked myself: had I only just arrived at this point? As incredible as it seemed, it was probably true. I had never seen my mother as independent from my dad before. Now, as my mother stood in the doorway to the boat and there were tears in her eyes, I thought, *She is her own person.*

She isn't the other half of Dad.

And I have hurt her.

She held out her arms and I let her hug me. I had to be careful not to let myself get too emotional, because although my mother may have wanted a reconciliation, my sister and father *didn't*. My sister's words still rang through my ears, that I was dead to her, that I was dead to my father. That I was no longer a Gulliver. But my mother *was* still a Gulliver, and I didn't want to make things difficult for her, forcing her to choose between us.

It was awkward at first, almost as if we were strangers. We tiptoed around the big issues, making small talk. I asked Mum how George was. I had always loved my little brother and had missed him over the years. The hurt that he seemed to have rejected me too was still very raw. Mum's face lit up with that pride she'd always felt in him, and despite my love for him, I experienced a stab of jealousy that she'd never felt that same pride in me.

'He's filming on location at Tower Bridge.'

'Tower Bridge?' I'd had the idea he was in America, for some reason – perhaps because he had been the last time I'd had any contact with him.

'On the south side, opposite the Tower of London. They're there for a few weeks, it's a costume drama. He asked me to visit him if I was in London but I simply haven't had time.'

*

As a child, you're always labelled, there's no getting away from that. Of the three of us, Mia was the high-achieving and perfect-looking one; I was the misfit at school, non-academic and accident-prone; and George, our brother, well, he was the boy, and I think Mum would have adored him whatever he did, however he'd turned out. Perhaps part of this was a result of his burns.

George was a beautiful baby, blond-haired and blue-eyed. He got my dad's genes, while Mia and I got Mum's. But whereas Mia got dark green eyes and glossy black hair from our French grandmother and Moroccan grandfather, I got an odd jumble of mismatched features – a lopsided mouth, eyes that were neither blue nor green like my brother's or sister's but a kind of pond brown. I always felt I was the disappointment.

I sometimes wonder whether the fact George would otherwise have been so handsome made my parents feel even worse about what happened to him. Made them angry with me and unable to truly love me. Because it was a really terrible accident, and left half of his face utterly ruined. For a long time, I couldn't bear to see the result of what I'd done; as a small child, I would shut my eyes whenever the puckered side of his face came into view. It became a kind of phobia. I flinched at the sight of his scars. And then it became not just his scars, but a fear of seeing *anyone* who was visibly injured or sick or – although this wasn't on the cards until Dad had his stroke – anyone who might be dying.

I was ashamed of my phobia. It was hard on George. It was rough on anyone who had suffered a visible injury. But I couldn't help it. I cringed and went dizzy when George came up close to me. And of course, part of my horror was because it was my fault. My parents had never once blamed me, but I grew up knowing that I'd caused the accident, caused George's disfigurement, in the same way you know your name or recognize your reflection in a mirror. And even if my parents were careful not to hold me responsible, my brother and the other children taunted me about it.

And yet George *never* complained. He refused my father's money when he offered to pay for plastic surgery that would pretty much have eradicated his scars. George was a credit to my parents. As was Mia. Only I had let them down.

So I swallowed my jealousy as my mother's face lit up when she told me about George. She told me about Mia, too, that same pride in her voice: she was a successful teacher, going for head of department. Apparently, she and Eddie had split up after Eddie made some financial errors that had cost them their London home, but now Mia lived around the corner and Mum had got really close to Xavier.

Then she stopped talking, almost as if she'd exhausted her news. There was a silence and then suddenly she blurted out, as if she could no longer keep the words in, 'Won't you come home, Irena?'

'Home?'

'Back to us. To Dad and me?'

I laughed. 'How can I? Dad's told me I'm not one of the family any more. So, no, Mum, I can't come "home". That part of my life is over.'

A look of misery crossed her face. Then she said, 'I want to make up for the time I haven't been able to be a mother to you.' She begged me to forgive her, for not being there for me. She said the time I'd spent away had broken her heart. 'Your not getting in touch, Irena, has given me endless sleepless nights. Wondering where I went wrong. I need to understand.'

Both of us then had been lying awake, haunted by our estrangement.

'I want to go back,' she said. 'I want to do things

differently, so you never, ever feel you don't belong again. I am going to do all I can to understand why you left and to make it up to you.'

I stared into her eyes. They looked back at me, and they were so wounded and full of hurt and I wondered again what she knew, if I'd been right to blame her as well as Dad these last six years.

It struck me anew that it was possible she did love me, in spite of George, and that maybe, maybe, she was in the dark as much as I had been for most of my life. I felt a strange sense of things shifting again. If my mother was innocent, how cruel my actions must have seemed to her. But it didn't change what my family had done to me, the way they had ostracized me.

'Mum, I'm only here because I am homeless, temporarily, and desperate. I'll be gone again as soon as I can. No one needs to know I've been here.'

'Sweetie, what happened to Hermione? Have you split up?'

'She had to go to New York, to help her mother with a flat. I'm waiting to hear from her.'

I didn't tell Mum about Hermione's text, nor that I would be going to London as soon as I could.

Mum sighed. Then she said, 'I won't tell anyone, of course. Not unless and until you're ready. But I need this one-to-one time with you, in order to understand. And we need to rebuild our relationship. There's a lot of healing to do between us.'

I gave another little laugh at this.

'What?'

'You're sounding so like a therapist.'

She smiled. Then she said, 'We need to heal before we deal with the others – Dad, and Mia, and their feelings.'

'Mum . . .'

'What?'

'I'm not sure I'll ever be ready to deal with the others. They said they'd disowned me. I've come to accept that now. It's taken a lot to get to this point and going back would be like undoing everything I've gone through.'

She searched my face, with her big sad eyes. 'OK. I won't mention anything to them. And Jonah knows to keep quiet too. But I do want to visit you again, to continue to talk.'

Before she left she rummaged in her bag.

'Irena, I want you to take this.' She handed me a debit card. 'It's one I keep for my personal account that I hardly use. I want you to have it so you can buy food, or pay bills, or anything.'

'Mum, I—'

'I insist,' she said. She took my hand and wrote a number on my palm in pen.

'That's the PIN, if you need it. Now I'm going to get Dad's medication from town. I've thought about it. It will provide a good alibi if he, or anyone for that matter, asks where I was this afternoon. I'll say I've been shopping in town and picking up his medication. No one needs to know I've seen you. No one needs to know you're here.'

'Thanks, Mum.'

'Not until you're ready,' she added. She still didn't seem to understand I would never be ready.

It was already three o'clock. I didn't tell Mum, but I needed to leave too if I was to get to school in time to see Xav as I liked – needed – to do. I waited until she'd gone, and then I left the boat. Jonah had lent me an old bike, a rickety green thing with three gears and a rack on the back. I loved it. I cycled straight over to the causeway. The tide was high, the road almost covered, but I got across and onto the island before it was too deep.

I was later than usual to the school gates, but luckily Xav's class hadn't come out. I stood, as I always did, apart from the mums, in the cool green shade of the tall horse chestnut tree where I couldn't be seen. I would wait for Xav, I told myself, make sure he was OK, and then I would go to Hermione.

A couple of months ago, Hermione had come into our Paris kitchen where I was making coffee. 'I have to go to New York,' she'd said. 'My mother's flat there's empty and she needs a flat sitter. I'll be gone a couple of weeks.'

She didn't ask me to go with her. Neither did she ask for my opinion, the way I'd asked hers when I'd wondered about coming back to see my father after his stroke.

I'd always sought Hermione's opinion, and listened to it too.

I saw Hermione as my saviour. I had tried to end things with her, after I left school, deciding I wanted a fresh start. But that first weekend at home – my final weekend at home – confirmed for me I needed to go to her as she'd been begging me to do. She was strong and single-minded and worldly.

And I'd learned over the years I'd been living with her in Paris that it was easier to let Hermione make my decisions for me. Because often I didn't know what to think. What I felt. I needed Hermione to tell me.

Occasionally we would get into arguments, but I could never win. Hermione was quick-thinking, intelligent, three steps ahead of me. And if I pursued a line of thought she didn't agree with, eventually she would accuse me of betraying her. Of hurting her feelings. I learned to give up, and to agree with everything she said. It was easier that way. So I didn't question the fact she was going away for two weeks without asking me to go with her.

Hermione's 'couple of weeks' in New York had turned into a month. She texted to say she was sorry, she had to stay a bit longer to help out her mother, and I couldn't remain living in the Paris apartment without her. I had to be out by the end of the following month. She said she'd call me as soon as she could leave New York, that she would be going to London in a few weeks and we could meet there.

It was the French school holidays and my work teaching English had tailed off as families left Paris in droves to go to their Mediterranean villas. By the end of the summer I had run out of money and had nowhere to live.

It was this that eventually drove me back here. I began to wonder if Hermione had left me and was too cowardly to tell me.

Then, today, out of the blue, her text arrived. She'd given me her address and said I should go and see her. I thought of the bank card my mother had given me. I had the money. I could go soon.

I spotted Xavier before I could see Mia. He was at the fence, his hands holding the railings, his nose pressed through them. I'd seen him from afar, of course, but today I had time to really take him in. He wore a little duffel coat and his gloves were dangling on strings from his sleeves. My heart went out to him; it was a physical feeling. He stood there, gazing into the distance as each of his friends walked off with their mothers or their fathers, or their grandparents or childminders, and soon he was left there alone. This was unusual. On the days I'd been before, Mia was always there, with the other mums, in plenty of time. Or, if it was Mum, she would have been standing there, a little apart perhaps, for several minutes before the school let the kids go. I knew it wasn't Mum collecting today because she'd gone off to town for Dad's prescription when she'd left me. So where was Mia?

I looked around. No sign of her.

'Xavier!' I stepped forward from behind my tree, approached him at the fence. It was the first time since I'd been coming that I'd dared to do this.

Of course, in the years Xavier hadn't seen me, I worried he might not have been told about me, might not know who I was. And yet there was a strong family resemblance between us. He had spirally hair like mine, though shorter; and skin a shade lighter than his dad Eddie's, a couple of shades darker than mine; and my mother's green eyes. He was beautiful to me, but it wasn't just the perfection of his features I felt such a pull towards. He was my nephew; he had my genes, my blood running through his veins. I felt it. Although he had grown since I'd last seen photos of him, on Facebook, when he was just two (Mia had stopped posting them in recent years), and although he had lost the pudgy cheeks of babyhood, he was still Xavier.

'Xav, I'm Aunty Irena,' I said.

'Oh! Aunty Irena!' he cried.

His response surprised me. He burst into a blazing smile, and I saw that his two top teeth were missing.

I assumed Mia never spoke of me, had tried to erase me from his life. But his *oh* felt like a recognition, an understanding. It must be the presents and cards I'd sent that had kept me alive in his mind. He went to the teacher in the playground, tugged at her coat, and she nodded, then he came shooting through the gates towards me. When I put out my arms, he put his around my waist, rested his head on my stomach. I felt so much love for him in that moment, I would have given up everything to spend time with him.

For a second I believed I was even prepared to wait until Mia arrived to get him and confront her.

I would plead with her to let me spend some time with her little boy. I would beg her to forgive me for everything, for not coming home to see Dad when he was poorly, for not getting in touch for so long.

But then reality kicked in. The things I knew. The hurt. Her text: **You're dead to us.**

*

When we were young, Mia used to do my hair for me. She would get out all the hair things in the house – we had quite a lot, as Mum put them in our stockings for us at Christmas. We had a wonderful selection of bobbles, clips, mini bulldog clips, beads, combs and threads. I'd sit on the stool in front of the mirror in the bathroom and Mia would get George to be her assistant. I would let Mia be as zany and imaginative as she liked. She could give me topknots and plaits, and backcomb my hair into a fuzz. She would give me a weird side fringe with loopy bits, or she would comb it all over my face and we would try to trick George into thinking it was the back of my head, and we would end up in hysterical giggles at the results – and then I would ask to do hers.

But Mia didn't want me messing her hair up the way I let her mess mine. She argued she knew when to stop, whereas I didn't. That's what everyone said about me, that I never knew when I'd gone too far. That I ended up causing chaos. I didn't know when to stop.

*

I let Xavier hug me, then he looked up into my face.

'Can we go to Suzy's? Can we get a lolly?' he said. 'Then can we go to the nature reserve?'

'You have to wait for your mum,' I said, ruffling his hair. 'And I need to go before she comes.'

'Mummy's in Amsterdam.'

'What?'

'She went to Amsterdam for a work thingy.'

'Then who's picking you up today?'

His next words were like gold dust to me. They were so innocent, but he said them with absolute conviction.

He shrugged. 'Sometimes Granny comes. But today it's you.'

I stood there a little longer as the last of the other mums peeled off with their children and I soon realized Xavier and I were standing there together and still no one else had come for him.

My mother hadn't mentioned picking up Xavier today when she had left me on the boat to get Dad's meds, and she would never have had time to get to town and back with the tide so high. It dawned on me, slowly, that she must have forgotten she was doing the school run today. Maybe it was all the emotion of us seeing each other again, after so long.

If I hadn't been here, no one would have come for my nephew. I looked around. The teacher who had been in the playground supervising the children as they came out had gone inside.

I felt, with Xav's arms round me, a kind of euphoria.

Everything fell into place.

All those years my dad and Mia in particular told me I went too far and couldn't be trusted, and yet right here, right now, I was the only responsible one.

The only one who was here at home time to pick up Xavier.

'Yes.' I let Xav slip his hand into mine and we began walking away from the school. 'We'll go to the nature reserve, as soon as the tide's gone out a bit, but first we can go and have a cup of tea, or whatever you fancy, at the cafe.'

I should have gone to the teacher, explained I was Xavier's aunt and would look after him because his granny must have been delayed. But it didn't occur to me then.

Xavier's face lit up at my promise. The whites of his eyes were so bright, almost the palest blue, while his irises were dark, almost navy, and his milk teeth, the ones he still had, shone out, reflecting the white of his eyes. I was giving Xavier what he wanted. It felt so good, being with him, his hand in mine, a bit like falling in love.

Xav and I sat at a table at the cafe, in the window, overlooking the estuary. The tide was really high by now, the water lapping at the stilts of the little hut that housed Suzy's cafe.

I couldn't take my eyes off my sister's son.

His black hair that was like mine, his tawny brown skin, lightly freckled. Limbs lengthening, waiting for the rest of him to catch up, fill out. He was suspended between the pudginess of post-baby, and the gawkiness of pre-puberty. As near perfect as you get. I felt a pang, an actual pain, that I'd missed so much of his babyhood and his childhood.

And then another, different kind of regret. Soon, this moment would pass. I wanted to hang on to him as he was, to retain this time for ever.

'What would you like?'

'Can I have chocolate cake?'

'Of course.'

'Really? Mum never lets me have cake. She says it's breaking rules.'

I put out a hand and stroked his smooth cheek.

'Well,' I told him. 'Breaking rules is what aunties are for.'

The tide was beginning to go out again when we left the

cafe, and the causeway was just passable. I sat Xav on the rack on the back of the bike Jonah had lent me, and cycled home, standing on the peddles, letting the water splash up at us.

'This is great,' Xav shouted.

On the hill down to the harbour I freewheeled and we both cried out *wheeeee*, with the wind in our hair, and I felt a happiness I had not known for a long time, barely ever known.

'What's the best day of your life, Aunty Irena?'

'This is,' I said, as we bounced over the track towards the houseboats. 'This is the best day of my life.'

'It's the best day of my life too.'

We got to my houseboat.

I thought of phoning Mum, telling her I had brought Xav home with me. But something stopped me. If my mother knew, she would insist I take him straight back to her. And she would have to tell Mia. And Mia would want Mum to take Xav away from me. I knew that for certain.

This was my opportunity to make up for all the time I hadn't been able to spend with my nephew over the years. All the time I'd been denied in the past. I'd show them, Mia and Dad and, yes, Mum too. I would look after Xavier until one of them realized who I really was, who I was capable of being.

12

Xav sat cross-legged on the floor in front of the wood burner on my boat, and told me how he'd always wanted to see a whale out there in the sea. He'd seen seals, and a porpoise, but his dream was to spot a whale. He said he knew there were minke whales in the sea around England, but he wanted to see a blue whale. He said it with great seriousness, a frown on his forehead.

An idea came to me.

'Xav, would you like to see a real blue whale skeleton? I know it's not the same as a live whale, but it means you get to see the whole of one, how big it really is.'

'A blue whale skeleton?' His eyes grew wide.

'I know somewhere you'll be able to see one up close. It's in London. At a place called the Natural History Museum. We can go now, to London, and see all the sights.'

Mum had just given me her bank card, telling me to get what I needed. And Hermione had texted and said I could visit, and the address she'd sent was really central. Mia and my mum had failed to pick up Xavier and I had money to spend and Xavier wanted to see a blue whale and I wanted to see Hermione. It felt as if it were meant, all these things coming together at once.

'What sights?' Xavier was asking. 'Like Buckingham Palace?'

I laughed.

'There are much more exciting things to see than Buckingham Palace.'

Xav looked more and more thrilled as I talked. 'We can stay the night with my friend Hermione. She lives in one of the poshest areas of London, and we can have breakfast in a cafe and then go to the Natural History Museum to see the blue whale skeleton. You can also see dinosaurs there, and the bones of ancient sea creatures and ammonites and fossils. We can go on a riverboat, and I can take you to the aquarium where they have real live sea creatures in tanks, or we could go on the cable cars over the river. We could go on the London Eye, or over the roof of the O2, or there are tours through haunted castles, or there's the dungeons, and the zoo, where we could watch the gorillas and the penguins. We can sit on deckchairs in the parks and watch the pelicans, or go up the Shard, or drink tea in tearooms and I can take you to the biggest toy shop in the world. Or, if you prefer, we can go to the Tate and look at the river from the balcony. Or there's Shakespeare's Globe, or . . . or . . .'

I was getting carried away, but a little bit of me was thinking, *Hermione will approve of this stand I'm taking. She will think I've at last done something assertive, that will show my family how capable I really am.* And another little bit of me was thinking, *Now I've come this far, I might as well go the whole mile for Xav. In for a penny, in for a pound.*

'Really, can we really do all that?'

'Of course we can. We just have to get an Uber to the station and a train to London. We can go right now.'

It was only when we got off our train at Liverpool Street with its hordes of city workers in office dress moving as one wall, a tide of bodies hurrying towards the trains and ignoring my expression of indignation as they pushed against us, that I began to wonder if I'd gone *too* far, that the city was too big for us. Xavier looked so much smaller in the crowds than he did on East Lea island. It was getting dark by now. No one was interested in us, a woman and a small boy trying to find our way through the tube station, trying to find the line we needed to get to Hermione's, to her address in South Kensington. I clutched Xavier's hand tightly and told him not to move an inch from me, aware that within seconds he could be carried off in the crowd and lost, really lost. We squeezed at last onto a tube on the Metropolitan line and changed to the District line at Aldgate East.

Xav and I sat close together and I took his hand in mine. He'd gone quiet now. So I told Xav how Mia and George and I used to discuss as teenagers which our favourite tube line was. Mine was always the District line, this one, the green one. I liked that it went from east to west following the trajectory of the sun. Through the city's centre, Westminster and Victoria and Sloane Square and South Ken to Ealing Broadway that always sounded full of light. Though, of course, that was complete fantasy.

'I like the green line too,' Xav said, sweetly, though he had nothing to compare it to. I wondered if he was feeling (as I was, a little) that he'd rather be at home. I'd have liked to be on my boat, with my wood burner alight, Jonah popping his head in to see if I'd got everything I needed. Xavier probably wished he was on the island at his grandmother's. But she wasn't there! My mother wasn't there to pick up her grandson! And neither was my sister. And his dad had been banished from the family. Xav only had me.

We got off the tube at Gloucester Road. I followed Google Maps on my phone to the postcode Hermione had given me. Broad, tree-lined streets with terraces of tall houses, and expensive cars parked outside. Xavier was moaning that he was hungry and was missing something on TV that Granny let him watch. But we were almost at Hermione's address, and I felt a rising sense of excitement at how she'd feel when she saw me and the nephew I'd talked to her about so much over the years. And how she'd admire me for taking this stand against the family who hadn't let me near him.

'We're here now, Xav. Look, this is where we're spending the night.'

'I want to go home,' he said.

'Please, Xav, don't say that, we're going to have so much fun tomorrow. It might feel a bit strange now because it's dark but when you wake up you'll be glad you're here. You can choose where we spend the day tomorrow, I promise.'

We arrived in a beautiful square with a central garden surrounded by black railings, like something from a film. A little pub on the corner, its lights glowing softly in the dark. I rang the bell of the flat, on a brass panel, up steps beneath a wrought-iron porch on a house with tall white stucco walls stretching up to the night sky.

'Who is it?' Hermione's familiar voice floated out through the intercom.

'It's me! Irena!'

'Irena! Why didn't you tell me you were coming?' Did I imagine the hesitation before she added, 'Come in, come up.'

There was a click and the door gave to my touch. We entered a hallway so wide and grand and palatial I actually exclaimed. There was an atrium that reached up to a vaulted ceiling made of glass; plants filled the corners, and black and white polished tiles gleamed underfoot.

'Is this a palace?' Xavier asked, his eyes wide, his little hot hand clutching mine.

'Let's pretend, let's pretend we're a princess and a prince visiting a queen.'

I'd always known Hermione's family were wealthy, although she tried to play it down, especially amongst the activists we hung out with in Paris. We both used to wear second-hand ill-fitting clothes, dressing to keep warm when we were out on the streets stopping the traffic, and to sleep rough when we needed to, layers of vests and shirts and jackets and thick woollen men's trousers.

Hermione hid the truth about her apartment in the 16th arrondissement from the other activists, saying if anyone ever asked that it was just something her relatives let her use, not that it belonged to her mother and was one of several properties she owned. I'd sometimes wondered why she felt she couldn't be open about it. We were activists. We were all fighting for the same thing. We didn't judge each other's backgrounds. Now I wondered, was Hermione less sure of her own identity than I'd ever realized?

Hermione was standing outside the door to the flat. My heart rate increased the minute I saw her, looking so glamorous. She had changed and it made me feel uneasy.

'Irena.' She opened the door wider. 'It's good to see you. And who's this?'

She was wearing a tight black skirt, a leopard-print blouse with shiny pumps and gold bangles. I became overly aware of my own clothes, dungarees and old trainers, my hair probably a mess since I hadn't looked at it since this morning. She'd dressed like me in Paris, but now her hair was smooth as glass and up in a topknot.

'I'm Xavier.' My nephew held out his hand to her, and we both smiled.

*

When Hermione had left school, a year before me, she'd joined an environmental campaign in Paris, and badgered me to join her.

She insisted I should come, telling me I could live with her in her mother's flat. But I had other plans. I wanted to go home, shake off the Irena of the past, the one who scalded her little brother and left him with terrible facial scars. *The girl who tried to kill her brother.* That was what they'd said about me at the local school, before I'd left.

But George was becoming successful as an actor in spite of those injuries. I thought perhaps after all I could return to my family, become one of them at last. I wanted to see my brother, who I loved and had missed badly while I was at school, and I was keen to tell Mia all my news.

In the end, though – because of what happened that first weekend back at home – I had taken Hermione up on her offer. Crying, I told her everything, and she listened intently. Then she took my face between her hands and said, 'Irena, listen. That was abuse. I don't mean physical abuse; I'm talking about emotional abuse. To label you in that way.'

She began to sow seeds of doubt in me about my family. Or rather, to confirm the doubts I already had. The more I thought about it, the more I talked to Hermione about it, the more it rang true.

Even when Mum contacted me via Hermione, a few years later, to tell me Dad had had a stroke, Hermione reminded me they – Mum, Dad, Mia and George – were no longer my family; I had a new family now, in Paris. The activists who thought the way Hermione and I did, that we were here to change things. To disrupt traffic, to make people think.

The news about my dad hit me hard. My dad, my tall, strong, capable dad, had been cut down just like that. Mum begged me to come home. Then Mia texted to say I *had* to come.

For a while I was torn. I didn't want to let my dad die without saying goodbye. But Hermione insisted I stay strong. I owed him nothing, she reminded me. Going back to him now would let him off the hook for the way he'd treated me, and that wasn't right.

George came out to Paris, actually managed to track us down.

'He's dying,' George said.

'The world is dying too,' said Hermione, 'and I think that's a bit more urgent.'

I was so in thrall to Hermione. I thought her words were magnificent, courageous. And they let *me* off the hook: I was terrified of seeing my dad a shadow of his former self. Hating him when he was big and strong was one thing, hating him when he was weak and disabled quite another. If I didn't go, I didn't have to admit to my fear of seeing him so diminished.

I knew I'd ended any chance of reconciliation with my family, even when it became apparent Dad was going to pull through. But Hermione convinced me I'd done the right thing.

'You can't throw off the kind of label they've attached to you,' she said. 'The only way is to cut them off, reinvent yourself. Let me text, tell them you're OK, just to keep them quiet. Then you can get on with your life with me.'

*

Now, in Hermione's Kensington flat, we installed Xavier in front of Hermione's cinema screen, and she phoned for some takeaway. We gave Xavier a bigger choice than he'd probably ever imagined possible. Japanese or Vietnamese, Thai or West African. Lebanese or Moroccan, Italian, Brazilian, Jamaican. The foods Hermione chanted from her list were endless.

'Are there burgers?' Xav asked.

'All that choice and he wants McDonald's.' I looked at Hermione and she smiled and for a moment I thought perhaps things could be OK with her.

'I can do better than McDonald's,' Hermione said. 'Nothing but the best here, Xav, mate! We'll have posh burgers and chips, all three of us.'

While we waited for the delivery, Hermione poured me a glass of red wine and Xavier settled down to watch *Finding Nemo*.

'What happened?' I asked at last. 'You left. I didn't know if you'd come back.'

She looked awkward, not quite meeting my eye, brushing a stray hair from her face. Not like the Hermione I knew, who was always so self-assured. Her next words felt like a punch in the stomach. 'I've been wanting to talk. But I wanted to wait until I saw you, Irena. The thing is, I don't think it's working.'

I felt something drop down heavily inside me.

She turned and looked at me. 'Irena, things have changed. I'm sorry. I had a long think while I was in New York and I realized I can't go on campaigning. I'd begun to miss my creature comforts. But you . . . It suits you, the activist life. You can carry on without me, can't you? You mustn't be influenced by me.'

'You've met someone,' I said. I knew it. 'You have, haven't you? Why didn't you tell me?'

She sighed, stood up, went to the window, where she fiddled with the curtains.

'I didn't want to hurt you.'

'You didn't want to hurt me. So you went away without telling me how long you were going for?'

'No, no, when my mother asked me to go to New York I thought I was coming back to you, Irena. Honestly, that's the truth. But while I was there I realized how much I enjoyed living a normal, civilized life. In a comfortable apartment, with money and a social life. And then, OK, then I did meet someone, and he's . . . he got me a job here, in a gallery. It's what I need now. I can't go on beating the drum for the environment for ever, when there's nothing in it for me.'

'Nothing in it for you? What about your future? The future of the planet?'

'I still care about the planet. Of course I do. But I've discovered I like having conversations with grown-up people with grown-up ideas. Which I get at the gallery. I'm learning how art can change the way people think. And conversation. We don't all have to block roads to save the environment.'

'It wasn't fair of you just to leave like that, without telling me you weren't coming back.' My voice sounded weak, pathetic, as if I were a child complaining that her mother had gone out and left her alone.

'I thought I *was* coming back.' She came over and put an arm around me. I brushed her off. 'I did. But things became clear to me in New York. I realized I needed space. I suppose I've grown up.'

I was grappling to make sense of what she'd said. That I

mustn't be influenced by her. And yet I'd been influenced by her from the minute I'd gone out to Paris. Before, even. I'd been *happy* to be influenced by her. I'd thought she was helping me to become someone, someone strong and sure of herself instead of the lost child I'd been at home, in my family. The family Hermione had convinced me to turn my back on. If I didn't have them and I no longer had Hermione either, then who *did* I have?

'So, tell me the story,' she said, moving away from me. 'How come your sister's allowed you to look after your nephew?'

I walked over to the window Hermione had stood at earlier. She hadn't closed the curtains. There was a view over the square. An old woman in a bright orange headscarf idled along a path in the enclosed garden, smoking, her little dog trotting behind her, stopping to cock its leg every few seconds against a lamp post. I didn't want to tell Hermione the truth any more. I felt suddenly that if I told her the truth, she would take it and twist it any way she wanted to. As she had done with every confidence I had ever shared with her.

'My sister hasn't got time to take Xav to do the things he wants to do, like going to the Natural History Museum, so I offered to take him. I thought it would be good to stay here tonight, as it's so close, and then he wants to go to the aquarium, maybe. And . . . I wanted to see you, of course.'

'And, Irena, honestly, I'm glad you came to stay. It was a good idea. You know you can walk to the museums from here.'

'I'm making up for all my lost time with him.' My throat ached with the effort it takes to appear all right.

'Well, I'm glad your sister's finally seen sense.'

I looked at Hermione, and wondered who she really was. She had always argued my family had treated me badly.

124

She'd even used the term *emotional abuse*. Now it was clearly more convenient for her to believe they had taken me back, just like that – after all the misery, heartache and rejection she knew they had caused me – presumably because that meant she could get on with the new life she had decided she wanted for herself.

I was discarded.

She said nothing about the way my parents had labelled me, about how I should get away from them and reinvent myself. It was as if she'd forgotten she ever held those views – views that had had such an impact on me.

I turned to look at her but the doorbell sounded then and Hermione went into the wide hallway to buzz in the Deliveroo driver. I followed her into the kitchen with the boxes of food.

'Xav, dinner's here.'

Xav perked up after his burger, and by the time I got him into bed, he was almost asleep.

'We were both a bit lost in Paris, weren't we?' Hermione was sprawled on her enormous sofa when I went back to the sitting room.

'What?'

'We did what we could as activists. We had to move on one day. Find new ways to raise awareness. I'm glad we have. I went to the States, you went home, reconnected with your family. We'll look back and be glad, Irena. We can both start new lives.'

I couldn't face being alone with her, this new Hermione who I barely knew, so I pleaded tiredness and she led me to a vast bedroom next to Xav's.

'I've got to leave early tomorrow morning for work, so you can let yourselves out. Just lock the door and put the key through the letter box,' she said, and left.

I stood in the middle of the room, feeling dismissed all over again.

Hermione believed – or chose to believe anyway – that my family had taken me back, when the truth was, I'd only made a very brief and fragile kind of contact with my mother. And now I'd taken Xav without telling her, I had destroyed any chance of repairing my relationship with her.

I lay and stared at the ceiling. The bed was massive, the sheets smooth as silk and beautifully cool. So different from my bed on the boat with its crumpled sheets and heaps of old duvets and rugs. The sounds of the city continued all night, the distant rumble of tube trains, sirens, horns.

Thoughts circled through my mind. Had I believed Hermione would somehow admire me for taking Xavier without Mia's permission? Say I was showing Mia, who had so misjudged me, that I was perfectly capable of looking after the son she had failed to pick up from school? Perhaps. But I hadn't told Hermione the truth, afraid she would use it to her own advantage. Instead, she was using what I *had* told her to her own advantage. I was never going to win. Had I believed Hermione would welcome me and Xavier with open arms and tell me what to do next? If so I was deluded. I should have known. Everyone rejected me, eventually. Hermione. My sister. My own dad.

I couldn't sleep. Bringing Xavier here was a stupid mistake. One I couldn't just turn around and undo. For the first time, it occurred to me that people would have realized he was missing by now, would be worrying about him. Would mum have guessed he was with me? And if so, would she have told Mia? And how would Mia have reacted?

I lay awake, fretting, staring at the ceiling.

I don't know how long I'd been lying there, lost in misery, when the door creaked open. I looked up.

The Choice

Xavier was standing silently beside my bed.

I lifted up the duvet and he crawled in under it. He took my hand and tucked his arm against mine. It was as if he knew.

With his little warm body next to mine, we both finally managed to sleep.

13

The mosaic floor was hard and cold beneath us. Above us the ribs of the blue whale created an elegant white arc. The vertebrae from this angle looked like a string of white butterfly wings. 'Wow!' Xavier gazed up at it. 'It's the biggest animal I've ever seen in my whole life.'

'It's almost as if we're inside it, looking up at its backbone.'

'I'm a fish, keeping it company.'

We'd got to the Natural History Museum early, before the schools arrived. Hope, the blue whale, was suspended from the ceiling of the Hintze Hall, and I could see straight away we'd get a better impression of its size if we lay down on the floor. So that's what we did. Xav moved his arms and legs, pretending to swim on the floor.

It was OK. We were OK. This was better than Paris. At that moment, I would rather have been with Xavier than anybody in the whole world.

I hadn't told Mum Xavier was with me yet. Every time I picked up my phone, intending to text her, I imagined her disappointment in me, in the fact I'd proved myself the irresponsible one all over again, and I couldn't face it. If I didn't make contact, I could pretend it was OK. But I knew I'd have to face the music sometime. *I'll phone her after this*, I decided. *After I've fulfilled my promise to Xavier*. It felt important that I completed the plan we'd made together.

And then I'd have to confront the inevitable, and let him go, and get out of his life again.

Xav had been awake when I got up earlier, already sitting in front of Hermione's big screen again, eating a bowl of cereal.

'I've got to go, Irena.' Hermione came into the room dressed in a silky black jumpsuit, gold trainers, gold jewellery, her hair all straightened, black and shiny. 'You can help yourself to whatever you want from the kitchen. Then let yourself out. I'm honestly so pleased for you that you're reunited with your family.'

I stared at her.

'Thank you for having us,' I said politely. 'There was no need. But thank you.'

'Goodbye, Irena,' she said, with a glance at Xav. 'This is hard, isn't it? But I think a clean break is the best way to do it.'

I didn't answer.

'You can't lie down in the galleries.' I looked up. An elderly steward was looking down at us through his glasses. 'We've got school parties about to arrive. It's a safety hazard.'

'It feels safe on the floor.' I glanced at Xav and he giggled.

'*You're* the safety hazard.' The steward scowled. 'You won't be laughing when someone goes head over heels over you and breaks their nose or worse.'

'We'd better do as we're told.' Xav and I stood up.

'It's actually a teenager, that whale,' the steward called after us as we began to walk away. I turned round. His stern expression had softened.

'If you want to show your son how big an adult blue whale is, you can go and have a look at the model one in the room through there.' He waved his hand in the direction of an arch. My son! He thought Xavier was my son. It felt like being handed a small gift.

'What's your favourite water animal, Irena?' Xavier asked me as we left Hope and made our way to see the model whale. 'Mine used to be the pink river dolphin, but now it's definitely the blue whale. Poppy says hers is the duck-billed platypus, if we're allowed to include amphibians.'

Amphibians! How did he know such a word at the age of six?

'Are shellfish included?' I asked him. 'Plankton?'

'Everything,' Xav said, 'you can choose anything you like.'

'Jellyfish, then,' I told him.

'Noooo, yuck, they are the one thing I hate!'

I laughed. 'You said I could choose anything I liked.'

'Anything except jellyfish. They're taking over our oceans because we've taken too many fish. The jellyfish are eating all the plankton and multiplying. They are ninety-nine per cent water and have no useful role in the ecosystem.'

'Thank you, Xav, you've told me something I never knew.'

It was still only mid-morning by the time we left the museum. We'd walked through the galleries, taken the escalators into the volcano and earthquake zone, browsed the gift shop. Had a sandwich in the cafe.

Now we walked down to Chelsea Embankment and waited for an Uber boat.

As it swung out into the dark swell of the Thames, I told Xavier how whales sometimes swam up the river and got stranded, like the baleen whale that they had rescued and taken back to the sea. I didn't want to tell him about the more recent one that hadn't survived. He sat next to me, playing with one of the toy dinosaurs we'd bought him at the museum, and I glanced at my phone.

I still hadn't phoned Mum. The longer I left it, the harder it became. I was getting twitchy. I didn't know where to go, what to do. The boat picked up speed, the buildings raced past us on the banks: Westminster, Big Ben, the London Eye. I felt I was being swept along, out of control.

An uncomfortable worm of anxiety that had been in my guts all day seemed to get bigger, fiercer. We'd come too far, we'd been gone from the island too long. I didn't want Xavier to know how I was feeling but I wondered how long it would be before he said he was homesick as he had last night. I needed to do something, and soon.

The boat pulled in at the Tate Modern, with a clanking and a roaring, the water churning up beneath us. Maybe it was an unconscious choice, staying on the boat, but we did, we stayed on it as it pulled out again, and at last it pulled in at the Tower, and I told Xav this was where we were getting off.

We walked over the bridge to a green space dotted with benches. There was indeed a film crew, set up over by the river wall, opposite the Tower of London. I found a bench and patted the empty seat next to me. Xav came and sat beside me, leaning against me. I put my arm around him. We sat for some time, gazing across at the Tower of London.

'Aunty Irena,' Xav said suddenly. 'What is the best day of your life now?'

I looked at him, and saw he was gazing up at me, his eyes wide, clutching the plastic dinosaur I'd bought him from the gift shop at the museum.

'This is,' I told him.

'It's mine too,' he said.

It was simply that I didn't know how to bring it to an end.

PART THREE

14

RENEE

My eyes are dry, and I have that fuzzy-headed feeling left after a night of no sleep by the time I reach my car. I climb in, drive around the headland, over the causeway and along the coast road. At home I don't bother to go to bed.

There's a message from the police detective in charge of Xav's case telling me she's had no luck so far, but they're continuing with their enquiries. I ring her back, tell her about Irena, that her boat was empty, that I wonder if she has Xav. That I can't get hold of her. She takes Irena's details, those I know, thanks me, says she'll be in touch the minute they have news.

I pace the house until dawn, then return to the window. Irena's mobile goes to voicemail. Where is she?

That's when Mia's name finally flashes up on my screen and I snatch up my phone. She's going to tell me Eddie has Xavier. I feel a lifting, a sigh, and I can barely speak as I press answer. But she's telling me the opposite of what I want to hear – that she's with Eddie, they're on the way home, but they haven't got my grandson.

The first early-morning dog-walkers are strolling along the esplanade outside my window. A van driver unloads crates of beer outside Bert's fish hut and he helps put them into piles. The early-morning risers of the island are going about their business as if it were any ordinary day. I try Irena's phone again and again it goes to voicemail. My voice

135

is hoarse as I leave a message. 'Please, *please* Irena, will you ring me?'

At last I spot a black Prius approaching down the coast road. This is when I begin to shiver. I shake so much I feel I'm going to break a bone. I drag a throw off the sofa and pull it around myself and go to the front door. The car, an Uber, pulls up outside and Eddie gets out, and he helps Mia out. They walk, Eddie's arm around Mia, her head bent, towards me, waiting in the open doorway.

The lack of sleep, this anxiety that has taken hold of my body, it seems to have stalled me for the moment. I can't speak. I stare at them. The Uber is already disappearing back down the road.

Eddie's arm is tightly around my daughter.

'He isn't here, is he?' His face is etched with fear.

Mia reads my expression then starts to sob. 'I never should have gone away. I won't ever go away again. Where is he?'

When Mia and Eddie have gone back to Mia's house, to see if Xavier might have gone back there, Tobias comes quietly into the room and stands behind me, looking out over the estuary.

'No news?' he asks, redundantly.

The sun is up. There's a cloudless sky. The daylight feels too harsh. I should have told Mia my suspicion. That Irena has Xav. I know what stopped me. Fear of losing Irena again. But I can't hold it in any longer.

I turn to my husband.

'Tobias. I have to tell you where I was yesterday afternoon.'

'Oh?'

'When I failed to be at school at pick-up time.'

I put out a hand, hold on to his wrist.

He pulls his arm away.

We don't touch any more. It's been a long time and I miss it. For some reason I only register this now. Now that I need Tobias's support. Because we need to be a team, a husband and wife team who both want the same thing: an intact family.

The only way of achieving this is to be open. I have to be honest with Tobias, in spite of what Irena begged. But for this I need physical contact. I need him to hold me in his arms as he used to, ten, twenty years ago. We could never really communicate any other time: when there was physical space between us, Tobias could not acknowledge feelings, whether mine or his. Everything had to be rational, ordered. But once I was close to him, I would be able to speak, and he to listen. So now that I have to tell him what's on my mind without his closeness, it's like speaking across a great abyss, my voice barely audible by the time it reaches him. He stands two metres away from me holding on to his walking frame and stares straight ahead out at the estuary.

'She didn't want you to know. But Irena's back. She's been back a week, nearly – living on a houseboat. And that's where I was yesterday afternoon, talking to her, trying to understand what made her leave. What stopped her from coming home.

'She wouldn't tell me, she seemed unable to explain. But that's why I forgot to pick up Xav from school. And I now think . . . I now wonder if she might have something to do with Xav's disappearance. I don't know why, and I don't know how. But he's gone and she's gone and . . .'

Tobias frowns.

'What do you mean, Irena's gone?'

'Gone from her boat. I went to look last night and she had gone. But she'd been there in the afternoon.'

'She'd been in touch with you? I don't understand.'

'She . . . didn't want to contact me. She needed money, a place to live. She contacted Jonah. He persuaded her to see me. Tobias, you told her she was dead to you. She couldn't get in touch with you. Or Mia. She . . .'

As I predicted, Tobias reveals nothing, no feeling at this news.

His face remains expressionless. When he speaks, it's with calm rationale.

'I assume you've told the police your theory? That Irena has abducted our grandson?'

His voice is so cold it actually sends a shiver through me. Or perhaps it's his use of the word 'abducted'.

I feel like a child who is about to be in big, big trouble for something they never intended to do.

'I told them she's gone but that I wasn't sure if it was related.' My voice comes out faint, almost a whisper. 'I was waiting to hear from Mia, we thought Eddie must have picked up Xav from school. That was what both Mia and I thought, believed . . . hoped. But now we know Eddie never had him . . . I do wonder . . .'

'So, Irena is intent on destroying this family one way or another after all.' Tobias turns his back to me. 'We have to tell the police, Renee, that Irena is unpredictable. Unstable, even. For Mia's sake – and for Xavier's. We should do it right now. We should make it clear that she can't be trusted to keep him safe.'

He doesn't mention George's burns, but it's clear to me that's what he's thinking about.

'Tobias, I've told them it's possible his aunt is taking care of him. They are looking for her. But we don't want them to arrest Irena. Not after everything she's been through. Not after she's been estranged from us for so long and there's a possibility of reconciliation. Do you think we can talk, about the fact I've seen her? Talked to her? How you feel about it? Where we go from here if . . . if . . . she *has* taken Xav?'

He swings round, swiftly for him, with his poor balance.

'If Irena has taken Xav, then there's nowhere else to go,' he says. 'She's already disowned us. Now she's tormenting Mia as well. Phone the police and tell them she's not to be trusted. She abducted a child. Do the right thing, Renee. Then will you please give me some peace?'

I stare at my husband's hunched back as he walks out of the room, leaning heavily on his frame.

15

IRENA

There was a steady stream of red buses, cars, cyclists and pedestrians crossing beneath the arches of the towers on Tower Bridge. People lounged along the river wall with coffee cups, with headphones. Beneath the bridge, a little way away, were some lighting rigs and vans and people milling about in costume. Beyond them, boats ploughed up and down the river, tugs pulling barges of cargo, Uber boats, lifeboats. Police boats.

'I need to check the map on my phone,' I told Xav, and he snuggled up close to me, and looked about him.

There were twenty missed calls from my mum. I deleted them. I considered putting Xav on a train, texting Mum his arrival time, and disappearing for ever from their lives again. But something had been restored between me and Mum and, most of all, Xavier that I couldn't bear to break and lose again. I should've done all this properly. Like a normal, responsible aunt. I could have at least called Mum and said, 'Xavier's with me, I'm spending a couple of days with him.' Perhaps she would, after all, have trusted me? But I hadn't called, and as a result I was in a trap of my own making. I had no idea how to get out. Just as Mia had said, when we were children, when she did my hair for me but wouldn't let me do hers, I always went too far. I never knew when to stop.

And so I was going to hand the problem over to my little

brother. I simply couldn't think of any other way out. At last I plucked up the courage. I took Xavier by the hand and led him over to where the film crews were set up near the bridge. I scanned the people in costumes, looking for George.

'Xavier!'

An actor in breeches and thick stage make-up walked towards my nephew, smiling, pulling off his curly wig. He bent down, took Xavier's hand and Xavier put his arms around the man in the same instant, trusting way he did with me outside school.

'Uncle George!' Xavier said, letting my brother pick him up and swing him around.

I instinctively moved over too.

'Irena!' George gazed at me for a few seconds, over Xav's head, trying to communicate something silently. 'Well, this is a surprise. My long-lost sister and my nephew, come to see me filming. I'm afraid we've just finished.'

He put Xavier down again and ruffled his hair.

I stared at my brother. He was older, of course, a man now, rather than the teenage boy I'd left six years ago. The oddest thing, though, was that in stage make-up, the facial scarring that I'd always found so upsetting had been covered, and George looked as he would have done if he'd never been scalded as a child. He had a scarf around his neck covering the place where the skin was puckered. And somehow, this felt significant, as if the terrible accident that had haunted me all my life had never happened. It felt for a fleeting second as if this really might be a chance to press a reset button and start again.

'Do you want me to show you the set, Xavier? Come over here, come and look.'

George took Xavier by the hand. We moved towards the

group of actors in costume, chatting, laughing together, as if there was nothing to worry about in the whole world.

'You sit here and watch,' George said, indicating a bench for Xavier. 'And I am going to have a talk to Aunty Irena.'

Xav stared wide-eyed at the film crew, people dressed in Victorian clothes. I suddenly understood why George liked being an actor. In that moment, the thought of being someone else entirely felt very compelling to me. Putting on a costume and a wig and entering another world with a new identity. Casting off everything that had gone before. Emerging, unencumbered, as a different person, with no baggage or expectations or labels or recriminations.

The actors were all flocking around Xavier, shouting to George about how cute his nephew was. I looked back at my brother.

'Irena,' he whispered into my ear. 'What the fuck are you doing? Mum is beside herself. Let alone poor Mia. You know they've called the police?'

'What?'

'I'm going to have to phone home and tell them you're here. That Xavier's safe. But how the fuck did you get hold of him? Why didn't you tell them? Do you *want* to hurt them?'

'I didn't mean to, I didn't mean to take him.'

'They have no idea where he is.'

He was staring at me, his eyes wide and angry, full of disbelief. The thought crossed my mind that he despaired of me as well, that he had no reason to forgive me for leaving the family, any more than Mia or Dad did.

'I've been stupid. I hate myself, I have to leave, I have to go somewhere far away again now . . .'

'Shh. You're not going anywhere.'

He ran his hands through his hair. 'I'm phoning Mia and Mum. Then I'm getting you a coffee while I think.'

When he came back with the coffee, I held the cup between my hands, warming them. I hadn't realized how cold I'd got on the boat. I watched Xav, trying on bits of costume, surrounded by George's actor friends, laughing.

'I have to go. They'll never forgive me. I think I'll go back to Paris, find someone to live with out there . . . I have plenty of contacts.'

I felt George's hand on my arm.

'I don't know what the hell has gone on with you, Irena, but I'm not letting you disappear again. You're coming back to East Lea with me.'

'What about the police . . . ?'

'We'll tell them there was miscommunication. That Xavier was with his aunt and there was a misunderstanding. They'll say we wasted police time, but we can live with that. The main thing is to get Xav back to his parents. I've got a few hours free now, I'll call us an Uber.'

'An Uber? To the station?'

'To the island. I'm coming too. I'll get out of this costume. I can't risk losing sight of either of you again. We'll drop Xav at Mia and Eddie's. Then we'll sort you out. I'm going to ring them now.'

'I don't want to go home,' Xavier said as we crossed the causeway onto the island an hour and a half later. 'Aunty Irena and me had such a great time together. I don't want to leave Irena now she's sad.'

I took my nephew's hand in mine.

'It's OK, Xav,' I said. 'I'm not sad. I'm happy that I've spent this time with you. Making up for all the years I wasn't here.' We were already drawing up outside Mia's house on the island. 'You go now, your mum wants to see you.'

George took Xavier to the door. I could just see my sister as she reached to lift Xav into her arms. Eddie stepped out, shook George by the hand, thanking him, hugging him. I sank down into my seat in the car, and bent my head, trying to keep out of sight.

Trying, yet again, to disappear.

16

RENEE

Tobias and I have barely spoken to each other. I'm still reeling from his response – the starkness of his conviction that we should tell the police our own daughter abducted her nephew. When George called, telling us he had Irena and Xav and was bringing them home, Tobias simply said he needed to sleep. I helped him up to bed, handed him his medication. He was shutting down again, rather than confronting the situation.

I leave Tobias in his blissful repose. Outside, I bow my head against a light rain that's blowing in from the estuary, and clamber into my car. I'll be unable to concentrate on anything until I've seen Xavier, and checked on Irena.

'Renee.' Eddie opens the front door. 'It's good to see you. George has gone already, I'm afraid. He took Irena back to her boat. Then he had to get back to London, he's got an audition. But we're beyond thankful to him for bringing Xav all the way home.'

'Of course. Is Xav OK?'

'He's actually fine,' Eddie smiles. 'Says he's had the best time of his life. It's me and Mia who are complete wrecks.'

'I'm sure you are. I won't stay long. I know you need to be alone, together.' It's going to take them some time to process the fact their son is home and safe and happy and in one piece.

I follow Eddie into their kitchen. There's a bottle of wine open, half drunk, plates unwashed, food left in dishes on the table. The signs of an attempt to act normally, and of failing to do so.

'Sit down,' Eddie says. 'Coffee? Tea?'

'No thanks, I suddenly feel rather shaky.'

Mia comes into the kitchen. She stands still when she sees me. Turns away. Then turns back and folds her arms.

'I've put Xavier down to bed. He was exhausted. He was out like a light.'

I put out a hand to take hers but she shakes me off. We're a close mother and daughter duo in many ways but physical affection has never been one of our strengths so I shouldn't be surprised, but it hurts nevertheless. She's still angry with me for not being there for Xavier. Of course she is. I look up at her and her eyes, when they meet mine, are filled with hurt and recrimination.

Eddie explains briefly what they gleaned from George. That Irena had been at the school gates – she'd been regularly, apparently, just to catch a glimpse of Xavier, but yesterday, she realized Xavier had been forgotten. And so she'd taken him, intending to ring one of us, but somehow ended up going all the way to London with him. Then, afraid she'd gone too far, and not knowing how to turn back, she'd found it impossible to call, to admit to what she'd done.

'My fault, of course, that no one was there for him,' I interject. Mia doesn't say anything, she just shoots me that accusatory look again. 'I was concerned about getting Dad's medicine in time, and it went clean out of my mind.'

Why do I say that? Why embellish my part in the story? Why not tell the truth now it's going to come out anyway?

'So apparently one thing had led to another' – Eddie's

146

voice is calm – 'and she ended up staying overnight and taking him to see the blue whale at the Natural History Museum. Which he hasn't stopped talking about.' Eddie smiles, hesitantly, glancing at Mia. 'Luckily Irena then had the good sense to find George who brought them home. The main thing is that Xav's safe. I think it's going to take a while to come to terms with this. And the implications. In some ways, his teacher is to blame more than anyone, for not checking who he was going home with.'

'His teacher's my friend,' Mia says coldly. 'Christina or her assistant Zoe would never have let him go unless they believed he was safe. I am not blaming them. And anyway, they would never have been in this position in the first place if you, Mum, hadn't failed to be there.' She gives me another hard stare. 'I don't know what to say. What to think. I'm going to have a lie-down with Xavier. I need him near me. Has someone informed whoever needs to know to call off the search?'

'I've done that,' Eddie says.

'We can talk tomorrow when I've taken this in.' And she goes off up the stairs, her feet a slow, weary tread.

Eddie lets me out. 'Mia's been in a terrible state, we both have. But she'll be OK. We'll get through this. Thank you, Renee, for coming. I've called the police, explained his aunt was taking care of Xavier. That there was a breakdown in communication.'

'Thank you, Eddie. Thank you so much. I have to go to Irena now. I don't want her to be alone. And I have to understand what possessed her to take Xavier without telling anyone.'

'We'll see you tomorrow.' Eddie begins to close the door. 'Let's trust Mia will have forgiven everyone by then.'

*

It's almost dark by the time I get to Irena's boat. She's crouched over the wood burner, wrapped in a rug. When she looks up at me her eyes are full of fear. It's this I find the most upsetting, that my own daughter might be afraid of me.

'Irena.' I move over to her, sit beside her, put my arm around her. She flinches away. 'Will you come home with me, stay with me tonight?'

'How can I? I've messed everything up, all over again, haven't I?'

I think of Tobias. She's right. Now isn't the time to take Irena home.

'OK. How would you feel if I spend the night with you here?'

Her face relaxes.

'OK. Yes. I'd like that.' She gives me a small smile.

We don't speak a lot, and as it grows properly dark, I watch her as she slowly stands, puts on a couple of lamps, moves over to a pile of clothes.

'Here.' She pulls out an oversized T-shirt. 'You can sleep in this. And there's a spare bamboo toothbrush in there. I get them in packs of six.'

I feel a flicker of warmth as I realize she actually wants me to stay, isn't just humouring me.

'OK. Thank you, Irena. I'll sleep on the sofa.'

'You can have my bed, Mum.'

'Don't be silly. I can sleep anywhere,' I lie.

'I insist. Do you want anything to eat?'

'I'm fine. I'm not hungry.'

'Me neither, but I'll make us some fennel tea if you like?'

Later, once I'm in bed and after she's handed me my mug, she looks across at me from where she's lying under a quilt on the sofa, a pile of assorted cushions in the place of pillows. She's left the curtains that separate her living quarters open so we can see each other and the light from the wood burner casts an orange glow on her face and forms shadows under her large eyes. She looks back at me and a memory comes to me that is so bright and clear it's as if twenty-four years hadn't passed since the moment.

When she was a newborn, after all the visitors had left, after I'd introduced Mia to her little sister, and my mother had been and gone, and Tobias had taken Mia home, I at last had time alone with Irena. I picked her up, glad for the quiet, and she looked at me with the deep, wise gaze of an old person, and I felt she could see right inside me, right into my soul.

She held that gaze for quite some time.

I felt she was trying to tell me something. Or beg something of me.

It was as if she'd been here before, and she needed me to know, and to somehow understand or forgive something in her.

I chose the name Irena, a name I'd always loved.

'It has the first three letters of my name slap bang in its middle,' I told Tobias, who couldn't fathom why I liked it. But it was my way of making sure this daughter was protected by me, because I felt she needed my protection more than Mia did.

'Irena means "peace". It's got a gentle ring to it, like the word "serene".'

'Serena's a nice name too,' Tobias suggested. But already, my baby girl was Irena to me.

How have I come so close to losing her? Looking into her eyes now she's a grown up, I wonder if she's communicating a need for some kind of protection again.

I wonder all over again, what happened to her? What

made her leave us for those six long years? And now she's back, will she stay? I still don't know the details, I still have so much to learn.

'Tell me what happened, Irena?' I murmur, after a while. 'How did you manage to take Xavier to London, without telling anyone?'

'I . . . it's complicated.'

'Of course it is.'

Where did this impulsive side to her come from? The side that I don't understand and can't fathom? The carelessness that made her drop boiling water on her baby brother, and smash things, and disappear, or now, take Xavier without telling us?

There will always be an aspect of our own children that we will never fully understand, I realize, and this thought fills me with a kind of despair. There is always a part of them we never really know. They come from us, but they also come from somewhere unique. They are part of us, but they are also apart from us.

It's dealing with this constant, slow separation, without losing them entirely, that I – all parents perhaps – find so challenging, so perplexing.

'Irena. One day, not now, can we talk about what made you leave us, what meant you became estranged from us? I need to understand.'

'You really don't know, do you?'

She thinks I know? She thinks I understand why she disappeared for six years?

'I've thought about it,' I tell her. 'My God, I've lain awake at night obsessing over it. I've tried to work it out. Did something happen to you at boarding school? Something clearly went very wrong after you went there, because a child does not come home from her boarding school for

150

one night and then leave for six years without a very good reason. But I wish you could tell me.'

The light from the wood burner dims suddenly, as the last of the embers burn out. In the silence that ensues, I wait anxiously for what Irena is going to say. But she's silent for quite some time.

I realize I like being on the boat, just the thin wooden roof between us and the stars. I like the fact I can smell the outside air, and hear the water lapping around the hull as the tide comes in. It occurs to me that living in a proper house with central heating and double glazing seals you, not just from the elements, but from a keenness of feeling. Every sense is muffled by comfort. Being in our grand, double-fronted house with its carpets and curtains and soft furnishings seems suddenly to have buffered me from reality. From being able to really see and feel what's going on.

Or perhaps I just like lying here because Irena is here. It is as if a gap has been filled, a constant pain palliated.

'Mum,' Irena says at last. 'I'm sorry I didn't tell you I took Xavier from school. I do realize how stupid that was. I knew it, even as I was doing it.'

I don't answer for a few minutes. I want to hold the silence, see if Irena will go further, explain what she was thinking. Even perhaps explain what came before.

She turns onto her back, stares up at the roof.

'The thing is, I was *there*, at the school gates, on Monday afternoon, and no one came for him. So I thought, *this is my chance to look after him.*'

'How? How were you there? There wasn't time for you to get there without a car after I left the boat.'

'I borrowed Jonah's bike.'

'Ah. But how did you know Mia was away? I didn't tell you!'

'I didn't know. The fact is, I've been going to the school every day at home time, trying to catch a glimpse of Xav.'

Something suddenly occurs to me. 'Irena, had you been to see Grandma, the week you came back?'

'I did pop in, yes,' she says. 'Before I contacted Jonah, before he found me the boat, I stayed in a pub for a couple of days. Grandma remembered I lived in Paris. I was worried she'd tell you; she was more with it than I thought she'd be.'

So my mother was making sense! I'd missed Irena for six years, but this knowing I might have seen her sooner, even a couple of days sooner, fills me with a new kind of regret. On top of the fact I'd underestimated my mother.

'I made sure Mia or you didn't see me,' Irena continues. 'But I'd missed seeing him grow up. I missed him so much.'

The presents that had arrived for Xavier every birthday come into my mind's eye. Thoughtful presents, worth more than someone living Irena's kind of existence could probably afford. Things Mia refused to have in her house, because they spoke of the sister she had decided was no longer a sister. Things I had therefore kept at mine, telling Xav they were from his Aunty Irena who lived in another country.

How thrilled he had been. Xavier was always appreciative of gifts in a way I don't remember my own children being when they were small.

'Wow!' he exclaimed when, on his fifth birthday, Irena sent him the bike. 'This is the best present I've ever had. Thank you, Aunty Irena,' and he blew a kiss into the air. And I showed him again the photo of Irena I kept on the fridge – until Mia removed it – so she would stay real in his mind.

'So on Monday afternoon, when no one came for him,'

Irena is saying now, 'I went to the fence and told him I was Aunty Irena. And it was as if he knew me, as if he had known me all his life. He was super pleased to see me. He wanted to come with me. It was like he was expecting me. Like his teacher was expecting me – I mean, she just nodded when he told her someone was there to pick him up. She didn't even look round. So I thought, *I have been given this responsibility.*'

She turns, plumps up the cushions she's using as a pillow, sits up a little.

'Anyway, I didn't mean to bring Xavier all the way to the boat even, let alone to London, but each step I took . . . it kind of led to the next. The further I went, the harder it was to turn back. And I also thought Hermione would know what to do. That once I got to hers, she would tell me I'd done the right thing. Sort it all out somehow. She'd texted me. I thought she wanted to see me. She has a flat in Kensington. And Xavier wanted to see whales and I realized I could do this, I could take him to Hermione's, near the Natural History Museum, and I could show him the blue whale there. It seemed to make sense at the time.'

'I understand.' And I do. I do understand how Irena wanted to give Xavier things Mia hadn't the time or energy for. It's what I wanted to do for him too. Except that I often didn't have the time or energy either.

'But does Mia? Does Mia understand?' Irena asks, her voice anxious.

'She's still very upset. It's going to be hard for her to get over the fear, she – we – didn't know where Xavier was for a whole night.'

I need to weigh out each word, be careful not to frighten Irena into silence again when she's been silent for so long.

'Mia would've demanded I take Xavier straight back to

153

her. I didn't tell you, or her, or anyone because I wanted that time with him. She'd never let me look after him before.'

'Irena, you haven't *been* here. How could your sister let you look after Xav when you wouldn't get in touch with us?'

'How could I get in touch? Mia told me I didn't exist for her any more.' She pauses, letting those dreadful words hang in the air. 'She made it very clear Dad felt the same. She told me I didn't belong to the Gulliver family after Dad had his stroke.'

I want to ask her why she didn't come when her father was critically ill. Suggest that if she'd come back, for a day at least, this stalemate may never have arisen. Such a simple thing to do, such infinite repercussions when she didn't. But again, I caution myself. If I am too insistent, she might clam up.

'So anyway, you see why I couldn't tell Mia? Mia wouldn't let me *touch* Xavier. Right from the start. Do you remember? The weekend I first came home from boarding school, when Xavier was a brand-new baby?'

'She wouldn't let you hold him?'

'No. She wouldn't.' Irena continues to speak to the ceiling. 'And it hurt so much. There was my sister and her Cambridge boyfriend, Eddie. Eddie and Mia! The perfect couple. Everyone said so. And their perfect baby. I wanted to wrap him up and keep him safe for ever.'

'I felt that too.'

'Maybe, somewhere in my unconscious, he reminded me of George as a baby . . .' She pauses, glances at me. 'Before he . . . before he was damaged for life. When I was little, I loved George so much . . .'

Her words seem loaded, significant.

I remember how I, too, had seen Xav as an opportunity

to get it right. How I'd told myself I would never let any harm befall him the way I'd let George get burned. Were we placing too much expectation, between us, on Xav? But Irena goes on.

'I could see exactly why Mia had fallen for Eddie and why you liked him. I liked him instantly, his warm open face, his kind manner. The way he held his son so very tenderly. He even took an interest in me, the "little sister", asking me what my plans were now I'd left school, spending more time with me than anyone else in my family was prepared to that day. Do you remember?' she continues. 'You offered to take Mia and Eddie and George, and me too if I wanted to go, out for a meal and a drink in the evening to celebrate Xavier's birth. And I said I'd stay and look after Xavier, so Mia and Eddie could have some quality time with you, and I really wanted to. Mia just said, *I'm sorry but no.*'

She pauses.

'She was a new mother, though, Irena; new mothers are terribly protective of their babies.' I offer this hesitantly, not wanting to dismiss Irena's feelings, but also wanting to be fair to Mia.

'I'm his *aunt*! I promised I'd call her if Xavier cried or needed her in any way and she said, *You wouldn't understand. He's been in my body for nine months, I have to have him close to me.* I pointed out that it would only be for a couple of hours. And do you know what she said? She said, *But with your track record anything can happen in a couple of minutes, let alone hours.* And she nodded to George. So I said, *For fuck's sake, Mia. I was three years old when that happened*, and she said that George wasn't much older than Xav and she didn't feel happy about leaving him with me. She wouldn't let me hold him *because of what I did to*

George. That's when I went up to my room. *Fuck them all*, I thought.'

Irena stops again, waiting, as if wanting a reaction of some sort.

I can't think of a response. When I say nothing she goes on: 'I've never told you this before, but I've always had this fear . . . no, it was a terror . . . of injuring someone. Like I hurt George. What Mia said meant the terror came back. Supposing in a moment of madness I dropped Xav down the stairs, or threw him out of the window? Because when Mia said that, it made sense. I poured boiling water over a little baby in a bouncy chair. Why would she trust me with her newborn, even if he was my nephew, my flesh and blood?'

I get out of bed and move to my daughter's side, hold her hand. She's crying. Irena is actually crying, as she tells me this.

'Irena. You didn't "pour boiling water" over a baby. It was an accident. You were too young to know what you were doing and you had no idea there was hot water in the pot. It wasn't your fault.'

'You say that. You *always* said that. But think about it. George could've died. And he's been left with those terrible scars. Do you, a psychotherapist, believe that would have no effect on me? Do any of you think I could dismiss the fact I had it in me to do that to a baby?'

I look at my daughter with a new kind of awe, acknowledging for the first time her awareness of the long-lasting psychological effects of a childhood trauma.

And a wave of guilt washes over me that I was unable to stop the repercussions of that event for her, even though I'd tried.

'That weekend,' she goes on, 'you were all so busy congratulating Mia and Eddie. That's why I didn't come with you to the pub that night. The way you saw me, you and Dad and Mia, and George probably, I could *never* alter it. And it meant I wasn't even able to hold my newborn nephew when I most needed to.'

'Irena. That's why you smashed those glasses?'

'Not exactly. There is more. But I really need to sleep now.'

'OK. Yes, you must be exhausted. After your trip to London and after all this . . . I think you've told me enough for one evening. It's harrowing. We'll talk more tomorrow. You look so tired, Irena. And there's a lot to process.'

'OK. You're right, I'm knackered.'

She turns over and within seconds I hear her breath steady and realize she's sunk into a deep sleep.

I lie and feel the natural change in temperature as the air in the boat cools, taste the rain in the air, listen to the sound as the wind gets up, all things I know now I could grow to love. Perhaps, as Jonah said, it's a sign of growing old.

I try to take in what Irena's told me and realize it's what I'd always feared, that the incident with the boiling water had cast a long shadow over my middle child, far more damaging in some ways than the injuries George, the apparent victim, had suffered – and just as hard to shake off. But I still hadn't got to the heart of it.

17

RENEE

The next morning, I leave Irena early to be at home in time for Mia so she can get Xavier straight back into his normal routine. It's one of my Xavier days and I don't ever want to let Mia down again. Before I leave her, I turn to Irena.

'Promise me you'll stay a bit longer, so we can talk more?'

She nods, and lets me kiss her goodbye. I have the feeling things are improving between us. Yet I'm still acutely aware she could disappear again at any point.

Jonah's on his deck, trimming off the dried-up stems of plants as I go past.

'Renee, I don't usually see you at this time of the morning.' He puts down the secateurs, claps his hands together in their gloves.

'I've just spent the night with Irena.'

I approach him, ask if he has a minute. He nods and we sit and I tell him Irena's story.

'Is she doing OK?' is all he asks when I've finished.

'I think so. I wonder if you'd mind keeping an eye out for her, just this morning if you're around? I'll be back later but I need to check up on Mia.'

He comes down with me onto the path, pulling off his gloves. He squeezes my hand and tells me of course. He's got the morning free and he'll watch out for her.

I leave him, my hand still warm from his firm touch,

reassured at the thought of Jonah there, tending his plants, chopping wood for the wood burner. Sitting on his deck, drinking his instant coffee with water boiled on his tiny gas ring. A sentinel for my wayward daughter.

I've only just got in, and am changing into a fresh outfit, a loose navy cotton poplin dress with wide sleeves that only touch me on the top of my shoulders, when I see Mia arriving already, like any other ordinary school morning. It's such a relief. I'd taken for granted those humdrum days you barely notice. I should have cherished the regularity of days in which nothing out of the ordinary happens. Days in which I take Xavier to school, go to work, pick him up, cook, have those easy chats with Mia about nothing very much.

The only thing that makes this morning different is that Eddie is with Mia. They come across the garden, Xavier between them, laughing as they swing him up and let him down again. He's chatting away to them, bright-eyed, full of joie de vivre, happy to have his dad back. There is no evidence that he's traumatized by the time spent with his aunt.

Things can return to normal with Xavier today, then. And later, when I've finished seeing my clients, I'll go back to Irena and continue to work on regaining her trust in me, and eventually, I hope – I believe – she'll come back to the fold. If Mia and Eddie are also getting back together again, we'll once again be the Gulliver family, the wholesome clan of the magazine feature. There'll be nothing left to hide, to feel ashamed of.

Xavier runs in the minute the door opens. He goes through to the sitting room to get out the toys I keep for him here. I'm about to open my arms, hug Mia to me, sob with relief with her, but Mia stops in the doorway and her words are like darts, sharp and jabbing.

'We just spoke to Harriet. She called to find out if there was any news about Xavier. When I said you forgot to pick him up, she said that was strange because she saw you down on that boat again on Monday afternoon, just before school run time?'

'Stop it, Mia.' Eddie puts out a hand and places it on her shoulder.

'I won't stop. Isn't that the boat where Jonah lives? Harriet said she'd want to know if someone was putting secret meetings before the safety of one of her children, and therefore she thought I should know.'

'This island's a cesspit of gossip,' Eddie mutters. 'I know why I wanted to stay in London.'

Mia ignores Eddie.

'*It's never good to lie to your children*,' Mia quotes at me, her voice cracking.

'Stop it, Mia,' Eddie says again.

Mia continues regardless. 'That's what you said to me, Mum, only a week or two ago. And then you forget to pick up Xavier! I was about to forgive you. Because you were so concerned for Dad you *went to get his medication from the town*. But now it turns out *you* lied to *me*.'

I put out a hand to steady myself against the door frame.

'You need to come in. We can't have this conversation here.'

'Yup, let's sit down.' Eddie's voice is calm, measured. 'Come on, Mia, you're stressed after all that's happened, but this isn't helping.'

He leads her through to the kitchen. I follow them.

'Harriet saw you.' Mia turns to me. 'She saw you down there at the houseboat on Monday afternoon. And she's seen you there before. She says she asked to see you as a therapist. That you refused. Could that be because you wanted to leave time in your day to cheat on your sick husband, I wonder?'

'To cheat?' Such an odd word to use for something so full of heartache, I think, trying to remember who mentioned cheating recently; it takes me a while to recall it was my client, Justine, saying she felt what Ralph did was hardly 'cheating'.

'To have an affair, then, with Jonah.'

'I know what cheating means.'

My daughter frowns at me, and her face is so pale, so tired; she's been through too much lately. And of course, I am to blame. But not in the way she thinks.

'I'm not having an affair, Mia. I wasn't with Jonah on Monday afternoon. The truth is . . .'

I stop, turn my back to Mia, put the kettle on, get down some mugs, buying myself time to explain. I'd sworn to Irena I wouldn't tell anyone we'd met on the boat on Monday afternoon. But that's no longer relevant now Mia knows her sister is back.

'OK. The fact is, I was with Irena on Monday afternoon.' I spoon coffee into the cafetière.

In the moment, I assume Mia will more readily forgive me for seeing Irena behind her back than for what she thought I'd been doing: having an affair with Jonah, betraying her father. And failing to pick up Xavier as a result.

But my assumption is wrong. Visiting her sister, without telling her, means, of course, that I've betrayed *her*. I pour water onto the coffee. I look up and see Mia is staring at me, her frown deepening. There is a pregnant pause, a weighty silence freighted with so much unspoken feeling the air seems electrified. I wish I could push the words I've just spoken back into my mouth. For Irena's sake. For everyone's.

'I don't understand.' Mia looks at me with disbelief. 'You

knew Irena was here? When Xavier disappeared? You knew she was no longer in France?'

I swallow. I have a sense of things being about to slide again, to hurtle in a direction I can't predict and have no control over.

'Irena had been back a few days. Yes. But I didn't know at first. She only asked Jonah to text when she was ready to see me.' Why is my voice so querulous? Why can't I command it to sound confident, assertive? I need to convince my daughter I'm in charge, that I know what I'm doing, and yet I seem unable to. 'She didn't want us to know she'd had to come back. She'd only come because she needed somewhere to live, some financial help.'

Mia gives an ironic laugh.

'I get it. Irena leaves us for six years, then comes begging for money!'

'Mia.' Eddie puts a hand on her arm again. 'Hear your mother out.'

He gestures for me to go on speaking.

'Jonah has other boats he takes care of down there. He found one for her to stay in while she gets back on her feet. On Monday she decided she was ready to see me. I got a text from Jonah, he's our sort of go-between. And you know, I wanted to be a mother to her after so long. I wanted to cook for her, to take her food. And oh, Mia, I was glad I did. She was undernourished. And sad, so sad. I needed to help her! You must surely understand that?'

'I'm not sure I do. Not after what she's done to us. To you especially.'

'What do you mean?'

'Refusing to support you when Dad had his stroke, of course.'

There's a movement in the doorway and I look up to see Tobias is standing there, listening, watching.

'Would you all keep your voices down?' Tobias says. 'I can't concentrate.'

'Where's Xav?' Mia says.

'I've left him watching CBeebies.' He takes a step into the kitchen. 'But I've heard your conversation and I have to say I'm with you, Mia. Irena doesn't deserve your time or attention, Renee.'

'Irena's our daughter. I have to help her no matter what you think she's done. And I honoured her request for discretion because I want her to trust me.'

'I don't believe this.' Mia looks at Tobias. 'Can you believe what you're hearing, Dad? Eddie?' Eddie gives a helpless shrug. Tobias turns and hobbles away to be with Xav. 'You were with my sister the afternoon you forgot Xavier?' Mia's voice is cold.

'Yes. I was. I left Irena's boat at about three. I was preoccupied, I admit, by seeing her after all this time, and that's why it went clean out of my mind I was picking up Xav. Instead of going straight to the school I went to get Dad's medication from town.'

A shot of guilt bolts through me again at this last sentence as I remember how unnecessary that detour was. I was doing it to protect Irena, and forgetting Xavier in the process.

'Oh. So that bit was true, at least.'

'Mia, please. I can't tell you how sorry I am for forgetting I was picking up Xav. I will never forgive myself for that oversight.'

Mia paces about, her hands in her hair. Then she spins round. 'It didn't occur to you straight away that Irena might have taken Xav? When I phoned from Amsterdam and you realized you'd forgotten to pick him up?'

I know how implausible it must seem that it didn't. Not at first anyway.

'Mia, Irena *begged* me not to tell anyone she was back. I didn't think she would go near the school, where she might have run into you. Then we thought *you* had him, Eddie.' I turn to my son-in-law. 'We were convinced, weren't we, Mia? And we couldn't get in touch with you and—'

'Christ, Mum!'

Mia's face is distraught.

'So let me get this straight. Being with Irena, the daughter who almost killed her little brother and refused to visit her dying father, means you forgot you were supposed to be taking care of Xavier. Your six-year-old grandson. And it didn't cross your mind she might have taken him?'

'No . . . well, yes, but . . .'

I want to tell her I had a worse fear, that Xav might have gone out onto the marshes, that he might have drowned. That checking this hadn't happened was my priority. But Eddie is hugging Mia to him and she is sobbing now into his chest. When she looks up at me again her face is incredulous.

'Mum, don't you *see*? Irena could've come home any time. But *especially* when Dad was unwell. Instead – hey! She comes when she's run out of money. And steals Xavier away like a bad fairy. It's like you can't see how unstable she really is!'

'She thinks we've disowned her. Can you imagine how that must feel?'

'*She's* the one who disowned *us*. And now, when I need you most, she's manipulated you. Her behaviour is scary, Mum . . . it's psychotic.'

'She needs help,' I concede. 'She needs some security, a sense of routine.'

There's a silence. Mia looks at me again, her frown deepening.

'She didn't want me, or Eddie, to know where our son was? I think that's commonly known as abduction. Which as far as I understand it is a criminal offence.'

'You're going to press charges?'

'We haven't decided yet.'

'Mia, I think you should think very carefully before you do that.'

'That's what I've been saying,' Eddie chips in.

I take a deep breath.

'Mia, you need to know I'm suggesting Irena moves back home. I'm going to talk to Dad about it. She needs our support. She's been through a lot.'

Mia stands up, puts the strap of her bag over her shoulder and walks across the kitchen. 'Eddie and I will take Xav to school ourselves today. I've already phoned work and told them I'll be late in.'

The strength seems to drain out of me. I so need to spend time with my grandson after all that's happened. He needs time with me. But this isn't the last of it. Mia's next words send me reeling.

'You have a choice.' Mia pauses in the open front door. 'Irena. Or me and Xavier. Who's it going to be?'

'Mia, that's ridiculous. I am not choosing between you and Irena. I can't do that, you must realize . . .'

'It's up to you,' she says. 'But if you insist on maintaining contact with Irena, you won't be seeing me, or Xavier, any more.'

18

RENEE

Over the years of meeting clients in my office, I have often wondered how people get themselves into such monumental fuck-ups within their own families. How, I've asked myself, have they let their own petty jealousies or sibling rivalries or relentless grudges or unfair criticisms take precedence over their closest relationships? I've sat and guiltily wondered (guiltily, because I am supposed to be non-judgemental) why one or the other in a couple is not prepared to climb down after an argument. It's not that hard to reconcile. It can't be so difficult to reach out after one partner has 'cheated' or made a mistake. It's not impossible for a parent to forgive a child for not living up to expectations, or for being with the wrong partner, for moving to the wrong place or believing in the wrong thing. It isn't worth it, I've wanted to say. It isn't worth breaking up with the people you love and who you've invested a lifetime in, for the sake of money, or sex, for the way you raise the children, for a house, for a lifestyle preference, for a religious or political viewpoint.

Or for the way you sort the recycling.

Of course, these conflicts people bring to me in my counselling room mask what lies beneath, the tectonic plates that have been shifting and cracking for years before that final disagreement precipitates an earthquake. And yet all those years I've spent listening to my clients, trying to uncover

166

what lies beneath, my own tectonic plates were shifting, and I didn't see or sense how catastrophically.

What has happened to my family?

What are the underlying cracks that I can't see, can't identify, that have caused this break-up that would measure fairly damn high on a Richter scale of family break-ups, if there were one?

When Mia and Eddie have gone, taking Xavier with them, I don't know what to do with myself. This should be my Xavier time. I find myself staring out of the window at the estuary, blankly, aware only of a pale sky, that the tide is in. A trio of gulls sit on the waves, bobbing, before taking off in unison. That old image comes to me, Irena, Mia and George snuggled up on the sofa together, in this very room, giggling together at a teen magazine. They were close once upon a time. What happened? When did things change so dramatically? What happened that means my grown-up daughters and my husband have become strangers to one another?

Irena told me that Mia wouldn't let Irena hold Xav as a baby. How can I have missed how hurtful that was? OK, I was preoccupied by Xavier, and busy congratulating Mia and Eddie, but it's no excuse, not really; I should have paid equal attention to each of my children. If Mia were to know how badly Irena was hurt, I wonder if she might begin to understand and therefore forgive her sister for taking her son from school. But even that misunderstanding doesn't seem enough of a reason for Irena to leave us all with no warning and to reject her whole family for six years. There was more. Irena said there was more.

My thoughts pivot to Mia saying I had to choose between her and Irena. Irena needs my help. I have to protect her from any further uncertainty, from homelessness, from loneliness. And perhaps she needs a therapist to talk to, in order to untangle all the loss she's gone through. Losing Mia and Tobias, losing Hermione. Losing Xav.

I have to be there for her.

But Mia and I are close too. She needs me, yes, to help with Xav, but I need her to help with Tobias. I have leaned on her since he had his stroke, I realize, have welcomed her no-nonsense approach to his physical needs and her unconditional love for her father. And I lean on her for company; it mitigates evenings spent alone with Tobias. I can't lose her. In addition to which, how will *Xavier* feel if he can't see me any more? He's only six years old. I've been a daily feature in his life since he moved here at the age of three. He's already been through the trauma of losing regular contact with his dad. He will believe anyone he gets close to disappears.

I never envisaged that there would be anything so insurmountable that it would wrench my family apart for good. That I would be the catalyst for its final, irredeemable break-up. I never for a second foresaw myself in a position where repairing the relationship with one daughter would mean forgoing contact for ever with the other. And worse, with my grandson.

I get through the day somehow. I see three lots of clients in the morning – two relatively new couples, then Dan and Joe, the couple with the surrogacy issue. They are all caught in dilemmas, but none seems as pressing or as insoluble as mine.

There are two more couples in the afternoon. I don't feel I'm listening properly, which is a cardinal sin for a therapist. But Mia's words ring through my ears: *Irena. Or me and Xavier. Who's it going to be?*

How can I respond to such an ultimatum?

In between clients, I try to convince myself Mia will calm down; she was still in a state of distress when she gave me this choice. Can't she imagine how dreadful it would feel to be banned from contact with *her* child? But Mia by nature sees things in absolutes, like her father. When she says something, she means it. And she was so traumatized by Xav's disappearance, understandably, I can see why she doesn't want me to consort with the person who took him.

As I leave my counselling room I decide I have to talk to Tobias. He's their father. I need to discuss the situation, the ins and outs of our relationships with our daughters, as we might once have done, before his stroke. Even before he became disabled, Tobias was difficult to get through to at times. But he's my husband, the children are our shared responsibility. I want to ask him how I – we – can possibly choose between this one slim opportunity to rebuild our relationship with Irena, and the strong bond we both have with Xavier, and with Mia.

'Tobias, could we talk?'

'Hmmm?'

'Could you perhaps put that off for a bit? I need your full attention.'

Tobias closes down the window he's on online and swivels round in his chair to look at me.

'It's about this ridiculous ultimatum Mia gave me – well us, in fact. Her or Irena. I don't know about you, but I have come to need Xavier in my life more than Mia needs me to look after him.'

'Yes, me too.'

'And I obviously love having Mia nearby, as I know you

do. But I need Irena back in my life as well. And yet Mia says I have to choose. I need to find a way through this, I need Mia to understand, and I need your support.'

'Renee, it's a no-brainer. What Irena did shows us there is no way forward. She's put all of us, but most of all Mia, through hell.'

His face is set, and I wonder again whether the stroke means his thoughts have also become even more rigid, whether if he had never been ill, he might have been more elastic in his thinking. More willing to explore and understand what lies behind Irena's actions.

'Don't you want to make up with our middle daughter?'

'Of course I do! In an ideal world. But she doesn't want it. Irena has made her feelings quite clear. She does not want to be reinstated in this family. If she did, she would not be testing us all to our limits. Not to mention putting Xavier in danger.'

He turns back to the screen.

'That's ridiculous, Tobias! Irena didn't put him in danger. She was keeping him safe. She took him because I had forgotten to be there, she was taking care of him.'

'But she didn't tell Mia.' He swivels round again and his face, the half that isn't part paralyzed, is crumpled into an angry frown. 'She didn't tell us. Mia wants to press charges. And I have to say, I'm with Mia. Taking Xavier from school without telling her amounts to abduction.'

'Abduction! Really?'

'There's no question about it.'

'Come on, Tobias; Irena is Mia's sister. It's crazy of her to think of pressing charges. Irena's Xavier's aunt, for goodness' sake. She took better care of him than most people – including me or you – would have done.'

Tobias raises his eyebrow. I know what he's thinking,

that I *didn't* take care of Xav. I wasn't there for him when I should have been.

His voice is quieter when he next speaks, but no less hard-edged.

'Irena is no longer Mia's sister and she's no longer my daughter. I paid for Irena's schooling because that's what she begged me to do and she thanked me by vanishing and refusing to come home when I nearly died. Irena has shown us she doesn't need or want us. Mia does need us, she does want us, not to mention all she's done for us, both of us, ever since I fell ill.'

And now I see we are at an impasse. Tobias is not, and will never be, on my side.

Not where Irena is concerned. His hurt, his sense of rejection, and now his anger with her for what she's just put Mia through, run too deep.

'Irena neither wants nor deserves to be part of this family,' he repeats. 'Get me my wine, will you, Renee? I'm going through the next raft of photos and I could do with a drink.'

'OK. I see. The conversation is over.'

'Yes, it is.'

I stare at the husband I used to find so attractive and wonder what on earth I ever saw in him. It seems to me a layer that once overlaid who he really was has slipped away and now I can see the truth. He's more unforgiving than I ever realized.

I go into the kitchen and find the glass he likes and pour out his cold white, take it through, slam it down in front of him.

Why won't he try to understand our daughter? Something drove Irena away. As her mother I need to get to the bottom of what it is. Tobias, as her father, should want to know what made her leave us too. Something made her refuse to visit him when he might have died. But then I should have known, Tobias doesn't have the time or perhaps the capacity for anything that might prove difficult, or contrary to his way of seeing the world.

Irena, according to Tobias, was our impulsive child, Mia our responsible one. George the easy, charming success. Tobias had them labelled and in boxes and they had no room to change. And when Irena left, lost touch, then failed to do her duty as a daughter by visiting him on his sick – or, as we believed at the time, on his death – bed, he'd disowned her. He dealt with things in absolutes, black and white, as did Mia.

'I'm going out,' I tell him after I've put his wine in front of him. 'I need some air.'

He glances up at me.

'If you're thinking of seeing Irena, consider what you're putting at stake as regards Mia and Xavier. As I say, Mia's always been here for us, Renee. She put herself out when I was ill. She's been a stalwart member of this family. She has shown us how strong she is, supporting Xavier when Eddie let her down. While Irena puts herself first. Always has. The sooner you accept she isn't one of us, the better. If Mia has asked us to choose between her and her sister, it's obvious, isn't it? Irena's demanded it of us already. We stick by Mia.'

I'm smarting when I leave the house, and I gulp great drafts of sea air, wanting to wash the toxic atmosphere between Tobias and me from my lungs. I have no intention of putting my relationship with Mia and Xavier at stake. How can Tobias imagine I would do that? But I'd gone to Tobias wanting support, wanting him to acknowledge how terrible a choice this is for me. For us. Wanting a sign that he might talk to Mia, say we can't make such a choice, as parents. But he'd refused to give me that sign.

I get into the car and drive over the causeway and round the coast road towards the harbour. Tobias might be able to dismiss our middle daughter. He might be able to attribute her estrangement to her irredeemable personal failings. But I can't. I know we're implicated somehow. And I'm anxious to see her. No one will know where I've been. If they ask, I'll say I was visiting Jonah. I'm afraid that Irena might have heard through the grapevine – which I'm realizing is alive and kicking here on the island – that Mia is considering pressing abduction charges.

I'm afraid if Irena has heard, she might have slipped Jonah's vigilance and vanished again.

The boat windows are glowing in the failing light, little golden rectangles against the darkness of the sea and violet sky beyond. I pass Jonah's boat, where a thin coil of blue smoke rises from his chimney. Then I make my way along the path to the boardwalk where, to my relief, I see Irena's windows are lit up too, orange against inky clouds. I knock on the door. There's movement inside, and then the door opens.

There's a sweet smell of applewood from the wood burner as I go in.

'I was about to have a cigarette.' Irena doesn't seem surprised that I'm here. 'Do you want one?'

'No, thanks. I see living in Paris has influenced you!'

'Can we sit outside so I can have one?'

'Of course.'

We go onto the deck. Irena unfolds some deckchairs and finds a blanket to put round me and hugs her own coat closer around her shoulders.

She lights up her cigarette and blows smoke into the evening air.

'Are you OK, Mum? Is Xav OK now he's home?'

'He's fine. Back at school.'

'It's funny. I miss him. Even after a couple of days.'

I nod. A hollow feeling has opened up inside me, too, since Mia's ultimatum. How do I tell Irena her sister refuses to forgive her? That she won't let her see Xavier again? How do I explain that I can't see Irena either if I want to maintain contact with Xavier? Irena will see this as appropriate punishment; another thing that proves she can't be trusted. Tobias's words when she smashed the glasses, that night before she disappeared, come back to me: *How do you manage to destroy everything you touch?*

'Irena . . .' But then I change my mind. She doesn't need to know about the choice. Not yet. 'Last night, you told me a lot, and I began to understand how you felt that weekend you came home from your school. And I do regret that we were all too busy congratulating Mia and Eddie to pay you much attention. I recognize that was a failing on my part. No wonder you smashed the glasses!'

Irena sighs, takes a drag on her cigarette so it glows brighter for a second. A tiny red beacon against the darkening sky.

'I was eighteen, Mum. I was rebellious and angry. I didn't want to make things easy for you.'

'You said that wasn't all. That there was more. And while I understand you felt upset that Mia wouldn't let you hold Xav, I don't believe it was enough to make you disappear for six whole years, or to refuse to come home when your father was ill. I know there is something else significant that I am not aware of. And I need to know what it is.'

She blows smoke into the night air. The clouds part and

the moon emerges, lighting up the deck, and illuminating a pot of velvety dark winter pansies I hadn't noticed before. Irena is beginning to turn the boat into a home.

'OK.' She begins to speak. 'There is more. While you were out that night, I noticed there was a box of old print photos in the sitting room. I flicked through the photos, back to the ones when we were little children. There was an envelope of photos tucked away, ones I had never seen before.'

She pauses. Stubs out the cigarette into the pot of pansies. Pulls the coat still closer around her shoulders.

'The photos were of me and George and Mia sitting under a table laughing, a cloth spread out to the sides, forming a tent.' She looks sideways at me. 'A brown teapot on the table.'

'Oh God. That was the day. The day of George's burns.'

'Yes, it was.'

'I didn't think Dad ever developed those photos. He felt terrible he'd even been taking pictures, rather than watching you all properly.'

'Yes, so he says,' Irena goes on. 'We'd made a house under the table and it looked very cute; I could see why Dad wanted to take pictures.'

'Oh Irena, don't. Don't go back over it all.'

'Why, Mum? Why don't you want me to talk about it?'

'Because it was traumatic. For all of us. But it was most traumatic for you, I think, Irena. We never wanted it to be like that, we never wanted you to feel implicated in any way. We always wanted you to put it behind you.'

'How do I put something like that behind me?'

'You have to. You were only three. It wasn't your fault, you know it wasn't.'

Irena turns and gives me an intense, searching look and then continues.

'We'd put a miniature tea set on an old box, and had turned the underneath of the table into a perfect little house with its white tablecloth roof. It occurred to me the photo was taken on the very day I scalded George. I looked closer. George was perfect, his face unscarred, and I saw how beautiful he would have been if I hadn't pulled that cloth and scalded him.'

This time when she glances at me there are tears in her eyes. Her misery at what happened is still very present in her. When she next speaks her voice has a crack in it.

'There was George, my baby brother, sitting in his bouncy chair, grinning up at Mia. Blond hair, blue eyes, perfect features. He was so damn cute.'

'He was.' Now I, too, feel tears prickle my eyes. I wipe them away. My tiny third child, so happy and easy, and so adorable. He was a kind of picture-book baby with his huge blue eyes and fluffy blond hair.

'And in the picture *I* was so happy,' Irena continues. 'I was smiling at my big sister Mia who always invented these great games. I had no idea everything was about to change. I was only little, I couldn't have known what I was doing that day, as you keep telling me. Although I always thought, looking back, that even a tiny child knows if you pull a cloth off a table, the things on the table come with it. George was so tiny, so trusting, and he was sitting right underneath the table and the teapot was right on top of it. I must have known!'

'Stop it, Irena, it's only going to make you feel worse, going over it again. You were very young. We wanted you to forget.'

'OK. I'll stop. Going back to the day I found those

photos – that was when I smashed those glasses. After I saw those pictures. The champagne glasses were on the table, and I grabbed the tablecloth and pulled it, hard. I pulled out the cloth from under the glasses. I wanted to see and feel how it had happened. Now instead of the teapot, the glasses fell off and smashed with a loud crash onto your beautifully polished parquet floor. It felt good. It felt satisfying, and liberating.'

'But . . .'

'Mum! I broke those glasses because I was being Irena. The girl who pulled a teapot of boiling water off the table and scalded her perfect little newborn brother. I wanted to see how it felt.'

I grab her wrist.

'Irena,' I say, firmly. 'Please. I don't understand what you're trying to say.'

She pulls her hand away from me.

'When you came back in from the pub you all stared at the mess of glass I'd left on the floor. You remember what Dad said? He said, *You can't even keep a bloody tray of glasses safe!* That's what Dad shouted at me. *What's the matter with you, Irena? You destroy everything you touch.* I stared at him, absorbing his words. And then I said, *I did it on fucking purpose. I can't do anything right, as you all love to tell me, so I'm just living up to expectations.* And you, Mum, you said, *Irena, please, for once just stop before it's too late*, giving me a look. I turned to you, and saw your expression, and in that moment I knew why everything I did ended up a bloody mess.'

My mobile goes, its ringtone piercing the night air. Interrupting Irena's story again.

Tobias's name flashes up on the screen.

'I'd better get this. It's Dad.'

I press answer.

'Where are you, Renee? Mia's looking for you. She's here. She popped in to talk to us and wants to know where you are.'

'OK, Tobias, I'm on my way home.'

'But where are you?'

'Tobias, please, just tell her I'm on my way.'

I turn to Irena.

'Will I be able to speak to you again, later, tomorrow?'

She shrugs.

'The ball's in your court, Mum. I'm here now. I'd like to talk to you again. And I'm not going anywhere. I've got nowhere else to go and I like . . . I like Jonah. He's been really very kind to me. He doesn't know the Irena who fucks everything up.'

I put out a hand and stroke her face. 'You know you're not that person to me, either. But Jonah's a really kind man. He'll take care of you, if you need anything at all. He's been a very good friend to me lately. Irena, you know I love you, don't you? You know you broke my heart when you wouldn't get in touch.'

She looks up at me, gives me a quick smile. She still doesn't know about the choice Mia has forced me to make.

19

RENEE

When I pull back the curtains the next morning, there's a cloudless sky, every detail of the estuary sharply defined. The water is a glittering sheet of blue. It's a beautiful late autumn morning.

As I'd driven home from Irena's boat the evening before, my thoughts kept going over and over what Irena had told me about the day she found the photos. How they prompted her to smash the glasses when she was eighteen years old and home from school. What was she trying to tell me? Our conversation was left hanging, unfinished in the night air. But I had to get back home before Mia suspected where I'd been.

Mia was still there when I pulled up outside the house.

'I left Eddie at home with Xavier.' Mia looked drawn and pale. 'So I could come and see how you are, because I was concerned about you. But you weren't here. I see you've made your choice.'

'Mia, please, it isn't that simple.'

But Mia was already walking away.

Everyone's feelings were running high last night, I tell myself the next day as I gaze out over the estuary. Things will be easier this morning. I'll talk to Mia again and we'll smooth things over. It's impossible, of course, to choose between your children. Mia will soon realize this; she has to.

Downstairs I make a cup of tea for Tobias and take it up to him. Then I take my own cup of coffee to the sitting room and stand at the window and wait for Mia to arrive with Xav. We'll talk. Woman to woman. Mia must understand that you don't stop loving a person because they err, you don't give up on someone you love because they lose their way.

It's a Thursday and one of the days I take Xav and pick him up from school. I'm impatient to apologize to Mia, for her to give me one of her ironic, conciliatory smiles. To tell me she didn't mean to be so sharp with me the evening before, that she was hormonal or exhausted or stressed from work.

George phones. He tells me he got the part in the film he auditioned for. It's going to be filmed in America. It means going away for six months.

'It won't be starting for a while but it's an opportunity I can't miss. You don't mind, do you, Mum?'

'Of course not,' I lie. ' I'm thrilled for you, George. You have to go.'

'I will be back. I promise.'

'Thanks, George. That helps, you know it does.'

I look out for Mia and Xav coming up the path, to the front door, for Xav to run in, dump his book bag, heel off his shoes, to leap into my arms and then, when we've hugged, to sit at the table with me. The world is waking up out there, boats being dragged from or into the water, seagulls wheeling. Bert unpacking things from ice boxes and taking them into his hut.

I think about George, how successful he's becoming, how I mustn't let my need to have my children near hold him back. Because he's picked up on my sadness about not seeing Irena for so long. For a moment I miss him, wish he were here right now, next to me, gazing out at the sea. When he was younger he would have been keen to get out there in his dinghy, standing at the tiller on a morning like this. Why do things have to change? Why do children have to leave and go their own way?

I'll tell Mia how sorry I am for being at Irena's boat when she popped around yesterday and impress upon her that I hadn't chosen to see Irena rather than her and Xavier, not at all. I was simply ensuring she had enough to eat, was warm enough, was safe.

I get out the ingredients to make the breakfast Xav most likes, because Mia doesn't have time: flour and eggs and milk for maple syrup pancakes. We'll make the mixture together, drop it from spoons into the pan, hear it sizzle, then flip the warm discs over and catch them in the pan again. When he's eaten, we'll head off to school, and Xav'll tell me about the sea creatures he saw in London with Irena, and he'll ask me what my favourite underwater creature in the whole world is. I've missed him. I haven't had any time with him since George brought him home, and I need his refreshing six-year-old company.

At seven there's no sign of Mia and Xav. Mia has to get the seven thirty Liverpool Street train so she'll have to be here soon or she'll miss it. After another few minutes, I pick up my mobile and dial her number. A recorded voice tells me my number has been blocked. Mia is clearly still in a mood with me. There's no answer on her house phone either.

By eight thirty I know something's amiss. I've still heard nothing from Mia so I drag on my coat and boots and shut the front door behind me. It's only a ten-minute walk to her house. Taking the shortcut, the way I know she comes to me, down a short alleyway behind the houses, I make certain I won't miss her if she's on her way. It's a bright morning, and there is frost in the shadowy pockets of people's gardens, the skeletons of rose bushes dusted with light snow, and there's a thin layer of fragile ice over the puddles. I'm almost at Mia's door when someone calls me.

'Grandma, Grandma!'

Xavier is walking along the other side of the road with Harriet and Poppy. I stop still, shocked to see that my grandson's already dressed for school, his book bag and lunchbox clutched in his gloved hands. What's going on? He hasn't had his breakfast at my house. We haven't made his pancakes or brushed his teeth, or had our conversation about our favourite sea creatures.

'Xav, stay with me,' Harriet holds on to his arm.

I cross the road.

'Harriet, have you seen Mia?' I hold out my arms to Xav who pulls away from Harriet's grip, towards me.

She gives me a searching look.

'She went to work an hour ago. She asked me to take Xav to school.'

'But . . . I don't get it. I take him today. She didn't call to say she'd changed her plans.'

Xav leans his head against my side and I instinctively put a hand down to weave my fingers through his hair.

'She didn't tell you?'

'Tell me what?'

'She and I are doing swapsies from now on. She told me you weren't looking after him any more. She rang last night.' Harriet makes to walk away, Poppy dragging her by the hand. Xavier watches Poppy, as if unsure whether or not he should go with her or me.

'Could you ask Mia to ring me, please, when she gets back tonight then?' I speak to Harriet's back, keeping my voice natural: I don't want Xavier to witness me upset, to worry.

'Sure.' Harriet doesn't turn to look at me. 'I'll pass on the message.'

She takes a few steps and pauses, as if deliberating. The two children walk ahead. Then she does turn and lowers her voice. 'I have to tell you, Renee. Mia told me she doesn't trust you with Xav any more.'

'I don't understand. She didn't say that to me. She said—'

'I only know what she told me. She made me promise to take Xav right into school and make sure he goes into class, and to be there when they come out this afternoon. She's afraid of him going missing again, and you can't blame her. She doesn't want you to have anything to do with him.'

It's understandable, I tell myself. I turn round and head home and go upstairs. I'm suddenly far too hot in spite of the weather. In my room I rummage about trying to find something cooler to wear. *Layers*, I tell myself. It's cold out there, so I need layers. Things I can take off when I go into the centrally heated office. Mia's still distressed by what happened on Monday. She'll get over it, and things will get back to normal. It's understandable she doesn't trust me yet to take and pick up Xav after what happened. She needs time.

I find a cotton shirt and button it up. The buttons are in the wrong holes. I undo it and start again. I need a jumper to go over the shirt and a jacket to go over the jumper. But I don't want to feel too bulky. Heat rushes over me. I pull off the jumper, fling it across the room. Maybe a dress with tights will be more comfortable? I tear off the shirt and pull on a simple shift dress and tights but they feel too clingy. I barely have the strength to take everything off and start again. I go to the bathroom, lean on the basin. I run the cold tap and splash water over my face. I return to my room and put the first outfit back on: wide-leg trousers, shirt, jacket. However much I try to put myself in Mia's shoes, the hurt won't go away. Why didn't Mia tell me herself? That she wanted Harriet to take Xav to school? Why do it like this? Then it occurs to me, she's putting me through what she went through when she had no idea where Xavier was.

She clearly believes I have not suffered enough.

And though I don't realize it yet, this is only the beginning. Mia continues to walk past the house in the mornings, taking Xav to school or to Harriet's. Her chosen route, one that she used to take in order to drop Xav with me, feels deliberately cruel, a torment, both to me and to Xavier, who I know would prefer to stop, come in as he used to, empty his toys out all over the floor before devouring the breakfast I make for him or that we make together. But Mia doesn't stop or look up as she passes, her face set. One morning, I open the door, call out to her, but she doesn't answer.

Tobias suffers too. One of the routines that kept him going was Xav's regular visits to our house, his mornings before school when he would eat breakfast with us, or his afternoons and evenings when he would stay and have supper before Mia came to collect him. I can't bear to see Tobias's stricken face, his look of resentment for what he feels *I* have done to our family since Irena came home. And this in turn means we begin to argue in a way we never have before.

Our disagreements are over the smallest things.

'You know I don't like this mug,' he complains as I place his tea on his desk beside the computer one morning.

'I had no idea.'

'You did. I've told you a thousand times. I can't drink tea from a mug with a slogan on it. You know that, Renee.'

'You could perhaps try getting it yourself. Then you can pick the right mug!'

I storm out of the room.

'That's cruel, Renee. You're taking advantage of my disabilities.'

'You're deliberately exploiting your disabilities. Get up, put a bit more effort into your rehabilitation.'

Petty irritations that leave us silent and resentful. And underneath is this unspoken thing, the crack in the foundation of our family that caused Irena to leave us, that in turn means Mia has stopped speaking to me, that I cannot seem to identify, let alone heal.

A week goes by. Each morning, I consider going down to the houseboats to see how Irena is doing, but then I am stalled. If I'm seen down there again, I will only strengthen Mia's resolve not to let me see Xavier. I text Irena, explain things are very complicated, I'm not going to be able to visit at the moment but I'll leave the food I've promised her with Jonah until I can get away. I text Jonah too and ask him if he'll keep an eye out for Irena, check she's OK, that she has what she needs, until I can get down there myself.

In the meantime, I can no longer bear the silence in the house. Without Xavier's regular visits, without Mia and without being able to talk to Irena or to see George, and with Tobias remote, at his computer, silently sorting through the millions of family photos, I loathe being at home.

When another week has passed, I text Maureen and ask if we can meet up and she says they've just been for a swim, but I could meet them for a coffee at Suzy's where they are now. I feel vaguely hurt that they've met without me. I go anyway, and spot my friends from a distance, a tableau of three women. They are huddled on the decking of Suzy's cafe, heads bent towards each other, Sunanda's purple Dry-robe, a red scarf blown by the wind, a furry hood, a black puffa jacket, feet a jumble of boots and trainers.

Faces turn towards me in unison. Why didn't they tell me they were meeting for a swim today? Mixed with a feeling of relief at seeing my friends is a creeping sense of paranoia that they didn't invite me. I try to rationalize, I'm an adult, I'm responding like a schoolgirl. Friends do sometimes meet up and forget to include you. There's nothing that significant about it. But it stings nevertheless.

'How's it going?' Maureen is the one in the fur-hooded parka. She smiles up at me and pulls out a chair.

'I'm fine. You?'

'Did I tell you we're moving?' She grins. 'Dave wants to downsize, move to be closer to the grandchildren in Cornwall.'

'You can't go. I won't let you. I'll miss you too much!' For some reason, this news feels more catastrophic to me than I would ever have imagined. (Later I'll realize it's another separation, another leaving.)

'It's crazy, though, isn't it?' she says. 'You and I, I mean, we've barely seen each other lately, apart from for the odd swim. I hear Mia is back with her hubby and they're all living round the corner now? You must be over the moon. Although I hear they're thinking of relocating to London.'

Eddie's moved in permanently? They're thinking of going to live in London? This is the first I've heard of it and I turn my face towards the horizon, blinking away tears.

I want to tell Maureen, *I haven't seen either of my daughters for days, or my grandson, and my son is too busy to come home and Tobias is not the person I married.*

186

I don't, though.

I don't tell Maureen how desperate things have become. Something stops me.

'How's Tobias doing?' Maureen continues to chat on, unaware that the tears I'm wiping away are caused by misery rather than the brisk easterly wind. 'Nat says she's seen him walking on the promenade and he looks like he's recovered really well.'

'Yes, his walking's improved a lot.'

'It must be lovely that you two can do things together again.'

She talks about the house they've found, how it over-looks a river, how Dave has always wanted to move back to Cornwall, to his roots.

'I'm still in two minds, though. I mean you, Renee, you have that gorgeous grandson nearby, fulfilling work. If I could argue we have to stay here for my work, I would. But of course, I can do childminding anywhere.'

'Sounds like this is more Dave's idea than yours?'

'Oh, I don't know. There's the climate down there, those gardens! The other kids will come for holidays. It's a bit more of an attraction for them than East Lea. So all in all I think it's the right decision.'

'I hope so, for your sake.'

Sunanda and Nat, who have been deep in conversation about online dating, say they'll pop in and get us more coffees.

When they've gone, Maureen leans over towards me and puts a hand on my arm.

'Renee, you don't have to keep up appearances with me, you know.'

'What do you mean?'

'It's written all over you.'

I glance at her, at her kind face and sympathetic eyes. 'What?'

'We all realize how hard it's been for you becoming Tobias's carer. It's no mean feat at your age, when you've got your mum to look after, as well as your grandchild. Everyone needs you and that can be quite a burden to carry, as I know all too well. We know you've been too busy to come swimming any more, and didn't want to nag you to join us.'

I look back into Maureen's eyes.

I want to tell her how lost I feel. I'm hardly too busy. It's the opposite. What's more, I'm a relationship therapist who has failed at all the most important relationships in her life.

I still can't do it, though, can't bring myself to admit even to Maureen, such a dear friend, that I have messed up my own family. That I would love it if they still needed me the way Maureen imagines they do.

'You can't do it all.' She shakes her head. 'No one's perfect, Renee. It isn't surprising you forgot to pick up your grandson. It's actually a relief to me to learn that you're flawed like the rest of us. Thank God no one's perfect. Even Renee Gulliver. Ah! Here's Sunanda with the coffee.'

20

RENEE

'Renee, can I have a word?' Charlie beckons me over as I arrive at the counselling centre the following Monday.

'This is awkward.'

'What? What's awkward?' I pull out my desk diary, flick through, check who I've got coming this week.

'Renee, listen. You need to know. Some of your clients have asked to be referred to someone else. And, well, we perhaps need to have a chat about why that might be.'

'What do you mean?'

'There are too many cancellations for it to be coincidence.' Charlie folds her arms.

'*What?*'

'I know. It's odd. Given that you're usually the first choice of therapist for most clients. But I've been thinking. This is a small community. It's perhaps got something to do with what's been going on for you lately.'

'What?' It seems to be all I can say.

'Renee! Everyone knows you usually take Xavier to school and pick him up three times a week. School playgrounds are a hotbed of gossip. Word must have got out that you forgot to pick up your grandson and your daughter has stopped speaking to you. And that's why you're no longer doing the school run for her.'

A fire seems to have been ignited beneath my chest and the heat is unbearable. It intensifies, moving up towards my face. I need a jug of cold water to hurl over myself. If I could only explain. Feeling this hot is debilitating; I can't focus on anything, my brain has misted up. But I can't explain, and Charlie has no idea. I seem to have lost my capacity for speech. I yearn for the sea. If only I were out there now, in the cold water, my mind empty, only the scent of fresh salt air and the lap of the waves on my skin.

'A mistake I'm sure quite a lot of people make.' I put a tissue to my face, dabbing sweat from my brow. Is it a mistake a lot of people make, though? Do other people ever forget to pick up their grandchildren from school? The reality is, I know all too well, it was a mistake that could have had fatal consequences. Failing to be at school at pick-up time – that *does* happen to other people. But not realizing I'd forgotten for over an hour? That was an unforgivable error. During which time Irena had set off for London. And if Irena hadn't been there, if Xav had told the teacher I was there and she'd let him leave and he'd gone out to the shore . . .

'It wasn't my usual day,' I hear myself bleat. 'I'd double-booked. It's easily done.'

'That's the trouble.' Charlie gives what I think is meant to be a sympathetic smile but it comes out as more of a grimace. 'You know, people don't want a therapist who is getting forgetful, and—'

'I'm not getting forgetful.' The heat is unbearable. I wonder if my face has coloured. 'I've had a lot on lately.'

'Sit down. We need to talk.' Charlie shuts the lid of her laptop with a snap and takes off her glasses.

Reluctantly I pull out a chair and sit opposite her at the desk.

'Tell me,' she begins, 'what's going on for you, Renee? Because you've been looking . . . distracted recently. If you're feeling, you know, hormonal, if you're having a bad menopause, there are things you can take to help. I listen to a lot of podcasts. There's a lot of alternative stuff if HRT is not for you.'

Charlie is younger than me. I doubt she's had a hot flush in her life.

'This has not got anything to do with hormones.' I take a deep breath. 'But, OK, since you ask, there is some stuff going on for me at home . . .'

'Now we're getting there. Do you want to tell me more about it?'

'I'd rather not.'

'Well, of course, that's up to you. But I think you need to be aware that people are conjecturing. About why you forgot your grandson. Clients, I mean.'

She stops, looks a bit embarrassed.

'What have they been conjecturing?' I ask, coolly.

'It's . . . OK, well, I overheard someone saying they'd seen you down at Jonah's boat the day your grandson went missing. And, I know, I know, it's small town gossip, but how can I put this? Renee, they were asking each other how you can behave in this way when your husband is disabled. It all seemed a bit sordid. To them. *I* have no opinion. *I* don't judge. I want you to know that. But I think you ought to know. You may want to be a little more discreet. It's a small community and these things get about.'

I get up, cross the room, and do, finally, open the window. Then I sit back down again, still dabbing at the sweat on my brow.

'I'm peri, I get hot too,' Charlie says. 'At night. I know what it's like. Look, Renee, as you know, the bottom line is, people want a relationship therapist who they believe to be a role model. You have always been that person to our clients. Now they see you doing things they don't equate with that image, they're perhaps – and I'm making a guess here, remember – losing faith in you.'

'Christ!' I put my hands into my hair. 'For goodness' sake, Charlie, we're counsellors, not priests. You know that. Therapists have issues too, it's what makes us empathize with our clients' crap.'

I surprise myself with my own words. I pause, then decide I've come this far, I might as well let it all out. 'I'm human too, for goodness' sake. My family fucks up too. Clients don't have the monopoly on dysfunction! Am I supposed to be some saint? Am I not allowed to have my own skeletons in my own cupboard?'

There's something rather satisfying about letting everything out. As if a valve has been released. My God, I thought we'd refuted Freud's theory of the hysterical woman. How dare anyone imply what's happening in my life is down to hormones? On top of my needy clients, I've got a sick and disabled husband, a mother with dementia, two daughters who won't speak to each other and who I'm forced to choose between, a son who's about to move to the other side of the world and a grandchild who I adore and who I'm not allowed to see any more.

It doesn't take hormones to explain why I'm under quite a lot of stress at the moment.

'Of course.' Charlie remains infuriatingly calm. 'But this is different, Renee. In the locality, your reputation rests on the image people have of your family, your home, your lifestyle. Of course you have issues at home, we all do at times. But our clients see you as a mature woman with life experience. That's why you've always been in demand. Some people have waited months to see you. Now those very same people are asking for someone else. All I'm saying is perhaps you should consider keeping a low profile for a while? Take some time off? Two of your clients have cancelled this week.'

'Names?' I'm aware I sound abrupt, but I can't afford to lose clients.

Charlie lowers her voice. 'Amy rang, ranted down the phone to me. She says she can't put her trust in a therapist who did the very thing she believed her husband had done.'

'*What?*'

'I know, I know. She says – and I'm not breaking confidence here, because she told me quite openly – that she's been talking about her partner leaving her child home alone, and how you asked her if she thought his behaviour a safeguarding issue. As it turns out, Yannis had only popped out for five minutes for some Calpol because the five-year-old daughter had a temperature. He had no choice, there was no one to watch her. He had the receipt to prove it. He was trying to do the right thing.'

'He never told me. Why did he never tell me?'

'Apparently he felt he shouldn't have to. He expected Amy to trust him, he didn't see why he should defend himself. But *she* thinks you didn't ask appropriate questions in the session that would have encouraged him to explain. And now you're guilty of forgetting to pick up your grandson *and* he was abducted, she suggests what you did was worse than what Yannis did. Because you put your grandson's safety at risk.'

I feel my face turn even hotter now as Charlie's words settle and make sense.

Had I made that speculation about Yannis because of his silence, his bolshy body language? Had I failed to allow him to give his side of the story, to pay him equal attention, rather than focusing on the impression he made? If so, I'd

193

been guilty of a terrible sort of assumption. Stereotyping even. Not in the least bit professional. This is really bad news for me, and Charlie knows it. I can see it in her eyes, in the way she clearly didn't want to tell me.

'Email Amy and Yannis and tell them they need to have some ending sessions with me before they transfer, if that's what they want to do.' I barely recognize my own voice; it comes out impatient and authoritative.

'I'm afraid they've made up their minds,' Charlie says.

Reality kicks in at last. I'm losing clients, and work. I'm losing my identity. I've lost Irena already, and Tobias, the man he was anyway, and George is about to leave for LA. I'm losing Mia, and my son-in-law. But the most distressing of all is I'm losing Xavier, my grandson. This isn't temporary after all. My future flashes before my eyes, a future devoid of love. Who am I if I am not Renee, the therapist, the mother, the wife? The grandmother with the beautiful, welcoming home?

I thought I was putting my family back together again. Instead, it's shattered. It's like those shards of glass Irena left over my parquet floor the day before she disappeared. It's in a thousand broken pieces. After investing the last thirty years of my life in marriage, work and family, it has all come to nothing.

'Hey.' Charlie gets up and puts a hand on my shoulder. 'Renee, listen. You're obviously going through a lot at the moment. Don't you *want* to take a break?'

I look at her coldly, which later I'll regret, because she is only trying to help.

'Cancel my clients for the rest of the week,' I demand. 'Tell them I've got better ways to spend my time than listening to their troubles.'

'Renee?' Charlie looks really alarmed now. 'You don't seem yourself. Do you need to talk to someone?'

'I'm sorted,' I tell her. 'I have someone to talk to, thank you very much. If my clients want something to gossip about, I'll give them something.'

And I march out of the room.

21

RENEE

Jonah is on his boat, stoking up his wood burner, thankfully, since on some days at this time he's counselling clients at his own offices in town. He's wrapped up in thick clothes, boots and wool socks that he's tucked his jeans into, and a massive fleece. Protection against the wind that's turned fresh out here. I can hardly believe people – and again I wonder who started the rumour – think I'm having a relationship with Jonah, behind my disabled husband's back. That I put Jonah before the safety of my grandchild. And then I remember Mia telling me she'd bumped into Harriet, and how she had mentioned seeing me down here, mistaking my visit to Irena for a liaison with Jonah. So word had got around, as it does on a small island like this.

How wrong they were, though. I'd always thought of Jonah as my wise old man friend. A kind of guru figure. Even, in some ways, a father figure. Someone I looked to for advice and philosophical enlightenment. Everyone needs a wise old man, or woman, I'd told myself. And Jonah fits the bill perfectly. He's perceptive and clever and vastly superior to me when it comes to therapeutic experience. Although he started out as my supervisor when I first trained, we've since become friends. I've never thought of him as someone to desire; it hadn't occurred to me. And I assume that Jonah has never seen me in that way either. It's one of the reasons I've always felt relaxed around him, able to talk to him.

'Hey.' Jonah straightens up as I climb down the steps into the cabin. 'Renee. I was hoping you'd come by. Sit down. I wanted to tell you. I've got Irena some work up in the boat-yard. She's up there now. I hope that's OK. She seems really pleased. She's taken to it, according to Terry the boat builder, like a duck to water.'

'Oh, Jonah. I needed some good news.'

I sit on one of his armchairs, and he sits opposite me on his sofa.

Jonah tells me that Terry, the boat builder, has offered Irena five mornings' work to start with. It's given her a shape to her day. She enjoys the work. It's physical and practical and she sees instant results, something I know Irena would find rewarding. There's a glow to her, Jonah tells me. A lightness in her demeanour, as if a weight has lifted.

He wonders if she and Terry might be starting a relationship. I don't reply, I don't say I think Irena prefers women. It is not my place to comment on my middle daughter's life, her choices, or her relationships. Not when I've obviously got so much of it wrong so far.

'So she's OK, Jonah? As far as you can see?'

'She's better than she was when she arrived. Clearly enjoys the meals you've been bringing her.'

At least I'm feeding my daughter, then, even if I'm unable to speak to her. There is some satisfaction in this, some warmth knowing I am mothering her in one way at least and that she is accepting it.

After a while I ask Jonah if I can talk to him about what happened this morning. How I've been advised to take a break from work. I tell him about Amy, and her suggestion that my forgetting Xavier was as bad as her partner leaving her daughter alone to go to the shop. I put my head in my hands.

'I made terrible assumptions about Yannis. You remember? I mentioned him, the Albanian lorry driver. He was always very quiet in the counselling room. But I had no reason to wonder whether he perhaps lost his temper more than he admitted, at home with Amy or even with the child. Would I have thought that if he was articulate and middle class? Maybe not! I even put it to Amy that Yannis leaving her daughter home alone might be a safeguarding issue. It was a huge mistake.'

'Go on.'

'I learned today that when he left Sasha in bed at home alone, it was only for five minutes because he needed Calpol to bring her temperature down. He'd popped to the shop just next door. Maybe he got some beer at the same time, but basically he was being a caring, conscientious stepfather. Not neglectful. On the contrary.'

Jonah raises his eyebrows as he listens, and I wait for his reprimand.

When it doesn't come I go on: 'I know, I know it was dreadful stereotyping on my part.'

'He didn't tell Amy he was buying Calpol?'

'No. He didn't. Not at first. Apparently he didn't feel he should have to justify why he'd left Sasha. He thought Amy should have known he would never have put his stepdaughter in danger. He'd weighed up the risks and decided five minutes spent fetching Calpol was better than letting her run a fever. Whereas I forgot I was picking up my own grandson. I left him unattended.'

'Well, strictly speaking, the school are in loco parentis until a parent or carer picks up. So that's not actually even true. You didn't leave him unattended, his teacher should have been watching him. Checking who he went with.'

'I know. But from what I heard . . . through the

grapevine, as Mia isn't speaking to me . . . ' – I swallow back the hurt – 'Zoe, the teaching assistant on duty, saw Irena at the gates and thought it was either me or Mia. And Xavier told her someone had come for him. Anyway, Mia blames me.'

'Hmm.'

'She holds it against *me* for not being there. And I *am* guilty of not being there, Jonah, whatever anyone says. It's academic in the end who was legally responsible. Imagine if Xav had managed to leave on his own and had gone out there' – I wave my arm towards the salt flats – 'and got cut off by the tide. Imagine if he'd gone with someone else and been abducted . . .'

'Hey. Now you're catastrophizing.'

'Anyway, my clients know I failed to pick up my grandson and they see me as the most hideous hypocrite. And it seems like they've been spreading the word.'

'We all make mistakes as therapists at times,' Jonah says. 'We wouldn't be human if we didn't.'

'I bet you never made a mistake.'

'You're kidding me, aren't you?'

'Not at all. You always seem so level-headed and calm. I can't imagine you ever getting something wrong, professionally.'

I look at Jonah. He's staring out to sea, into the distance. I wonder what thoughts are going through his head.

'One of the reasons my marriage broke up was because of a mistake I made as a therapist,' Jonah says, not looking at me.

'Really?' I don't want to sound too curious.

'Let's just say I insulted one of my clients. And my wife wouldn't forgive me.'

He still doesn't look at me, it's as if he's talking to the horizon.

'How? How would you insult a client?'

'I called him a misogynistic prick. In the counselling room.'

I stifle a giggle. I cannot imagine Jonah, so measured, so calm, calling anyone a prick.

'He must have provoked you badly for you to insult him like that?'

'He was a complete dick,' Jonah says, turning his face towards me, giving me an intense look. 'The way he talked about women. The things he said! The way he tried to goad me to agree with him.'

'He sounds tricky.'

'He was. After I insulted him, he tried to have me struck off. It was fair enough. I'd overstepped the mark. It wasn't professional. But I couldn't help myself.'

'Some people just push our buttons.'

'We're trained to be aware of that, though, Renee. I should have contained it. Anyway, there was a hearing – I thought I'd lose my job. I was suspended for a while. And my marriage went down the pan. My wife said she couldn't respect me any more.'

'I would've thought that should have earned you respect.'

'Not in my wife's eyes. She thought it unprofessional. She saw it as a failing in me, a weakness. Of course, in hindsight, this was only the tip of an iceberg. I then stopped bringing in the salary she'd got accustomed to. By the time I was reinstated we were beyond repair as a couple. We weren't right for one another. Hadn't been for some time.'

He stops and looks at me at last. 'So, you see? None of us are perfect. I nearly lost my professional status, I certainly

lost some earnings, and my marriage fell apart. Hence . . . '
– he holds out his hands – 'I now live on a boat.'

'I appreciate you telling me that, Jonah. I had no idea
what was behind your marriage break-up.'

'Well, there you go, those are the bare bones of it. I just
wanted to tell you no one's perfect. Not even yours truly.
Now, what's the latest with you and your daughters?'

I glance at him. I'd like to ask him more about his client,
the details, why his wife was so unforgiving. But I realize
he's told me enough for now and wants to move on.

'You really want to know?'

'Of course.'

'OK.' I take a deep breath. 'Mia won't forgive me. Or
Irena. She thinks Irena taking Xavier away amounts to
abduction. That's why I haven't been spending any proper
time with Irena. If it gets back to Mia that I'm visiting her
younger sister, she'll stop me seeing Xavier ever again. She's
forced me to make a choice – her or Irena.'

'That sounds harsh.'

'Yes.'

The pain is there, the pain in my clavicle. I wait for it to
subside before I can speak again.

'It's kind of understandable, though, isn't it? After what
I did. Mia's stopped me seeing Xavier anyway. I'm afraid if
I'm seen visiting Irena, she'll make it permanent.'

Jonah speaks again, quietly.

'You don't really have a choice then, do you? Just as you
were connecting with Irena again.'

'Oh Jonah, I simply don't know how I've made such a
mess of my family.'

'I can see this is intolerable for you. I'd never be able to
choose between my two sons. Children can be so cruel at
times – even grown-up ones.'

'You think it's cruel?'

'I do. There are some things kids just don't understand – can't understand – until they're at that stage in life themselves.'

'Exactly. But Mia has a child, she knows the hell you go through when you're separated from them.'

'She doesn't equate having a small child with a grown-up one,' he says. 'She can't. She hasn't been there yet. But I'm here. I'll make sure Irena's OK. I'll let you know if she needs anything.'

'I'm so grateful you've got her some work with this Terry person. And that she likes him. At least if I know she's found someone, I won't feel so bad that I can't see her for a while. I have to say, though, I thought she preferred women.'

'Renee,' Jonah says. I feel his hand on one of mine. 'Renee, Terry *is* a woman!'

I look at him, and see that a smile is playing around his lips.

'OK, so yet again, I've made assumptions!'

'Easily done.'

'Well, I'm happy for her.'

'Of course you are.'

'But she has to know this isn't my choice, not at all. I need her to understand I'm lying low until I can clear the air. That I'm longing to spend more time with her.'

He gazes at me for a while. 'I think Irena knows now she's seen you that you would never be able to make a choice between her and Mia. She will still be here, I'm sure. Take the time away, Renee. Do something for yourself, have a change of scene or something. Go somewhere different. Switch off from all this.' He waves his hand in an arc across the salt marshes. 'Your children are grown up. You don't have to be there for them every moment of every day. You

have to let them make their own mistakes. If you remove
yourself, they may even find a way to repair the mistakes
they've made by themselves.'

It sounds tempting, the thought of walking away from it
all.

'I can't go away, though, Jonah. I have to be here for
Tobias, and for my mother. And however far away I go
geographically, this misery' – I place my hand on my
chest – 'this pain, that my children are estranged from one
another, will come with me.'

'You know,' Jonah says, 'it's important for all of us to
keep a little bit of our inner selves alive, even when we have
people who seem to need us and make demands of us.
Because in the end, we're all on our own.'

I listen to Jonah's words but I don't really hear what he's
saying. I won't really take in his words until a while later.

The stifling care-home heat hits me in the face. I go across
my mother's room and throw open the window. I place the
bag of pull-on bras on her side table, then I pull a chair up
opposite her.

'My goodness, Renee.' My mother looks up at me. 'Your
hair is like a bird's nest. You look as if you've been dragged
through a hedge backwards.'

'I feel as if I have,' I tell her.

'What is it?' my mother asks, concern on her brow. She
leans forward, looks into my eyes. 'What is it, *chérie*?'

On occasion you wouldn't know my mother was unwell.
I still get taken in by this at times. And now is one of those
times. I speak to her as I would have done before she began
to forget things. The way I would have done in the past
when I was upset. I want my mother to take the strain, tell
me everything is going to be all right as she would have

done, once upon a time, when I was a child. When it was her role to be the mother – and the grandmother – rather than mine.

'I'm having family troubles.'

I want her to tell me they will pass, that I can cope, that all will be well. She sighs, and then speaks.

'Well, you know what I always said, you should never have married Jacques.'

'You mean Tobias.'

'No, I mean Jacques.'

'My husband's called Tobias, Mum. Jacques was *your* last husband.'

I sound impatient. I'm not going along with her as I should do. But she doesn't seem perturbed. She continues: 'Well, anyway, Jacques was a terrible lover. And Renee, a woman should never put up with a terrible lover. Age is no excuse. If Tobias is not fulfilling you, you should leave him. I did warn you.'

I can't help smiling now at my mother.

'You're probably right.'

'I'm always right, Renee. You don't live for eighty-five years and learn nothing. And I can see it in your body, in the way you hold yourself, that he isn't giving you what you need.' She chuckles.

I smile again, because she is right in a way.

'I can't leave Tobias, though, he needs me.'

She leans forward, strokes my hair.

'You need to smooth this down,' she says. 'If you want to find a new amour. You're still very pretty, Renee, it isn't too late.'

'Thank you, *Maman*.'

I stay with my mother for an hour or more. Today I like sitting and letting her talk in this meandering fashion where she touches upon reality, then scoots away again into other realms. I find it soothing. It doesn't matter what the content of her words is, it only matters that she's here, and she cares. When she tires of the chatter, I suggest we put some music on her radio. I manage to find a station that plays the kind of mainstream classical music she enjoys these days. I leave her listening to Beethoven's *Emperor* concerto and go and make her some black tea and bring it back to her. We sit and eat digestive biscuits together, and she tells me about her lovers and who was the best and who was the worst. And when I leave, I feel a little better. And I think, knowing she's helped me, that she does too.

22

RENEE

Tobias is out when I get home. The house has the horrible stillness it's acquired since Xav stopped coming. A stillness, and a coldness, even when the heating is on. It's astonishing, I think, how quickly a house can stop feeling like a home. Take the people out of it, the movement, the talk, even the arguments, and it becomes a hollow shell.

Tobias has left a note on the hall table saying he's gone for an assessment at the hospital. He'd forgotten to tell me and has got a taxi.

In the sitting room his computer screen is on.

There are photos on the screen as usual, and I lean forward, recognizing a picture of our kitchen table, the cloth we used in the old days when the kids were little. The cloth that Irena pulled off that fateful day, over twenty years ago now.

It was one I'd bought at a *brocante* – a flea market, near my mother's house in the South of France. French white embroidered linen, too big, really, for our table, and a hopelessly impractical colour with small children around.

The grainy images show George as a baby in his bouncy chair on the floor, his face perfect.

And there is Irena, squatting, looking into a bucket where she has collected shells. The look of complete focus on her face as she gazes at her treasure trove of sea creatures reminds me of Xavier. I think how quickly these early years in a child's life pass, how they are there and gone in a flash.

Tobias has reached the time when our children were infants. Next he'll find the ones when Irena, and before that, Mia, were babies – a time that seems to have been sucked into the past so fast, disappearing like bathwater down a plughole. If Mia continues not letting me see him, I will miss a time with Xav that is more fleeting and precious than she realizes; Mia has no idea yet how quickly her son's childhood will go. You don't realize first time around. Or perhaps it's true when they say time speeds up as you get older, so that you have a more urgent need to hang on, fiercely, to what's vanishing even as you touch it.

In the kitchen I remember it's bin day tomorrow. I take out the bin bag and shake it into the wheelie bin outside, and something catches my eye. There's a bright yellow envelope, one of those old ones photos used to come in when they'd been developed. I absentmindedly pick it up out of the rubbish. There are only two prints, the images Tobias has scanned onto the screen. But in the little pocket along the edge are a batch of negatives. I hold them up to the light, trying to see the images, but I can only make out the table again, the inverse images of the children.

I remember suddenly a little gadget we had – a mini projector that magnified them. I scrabble about in Tobias's desk but can find nothing. Then I remember his box of printed photos, and sure enough, at the bottom is the slide viewer. Sitting down at his desk, I feed the negatives into the slot, and put my eye to the lens. Now I can see clearly; the slides are from the same batch as the one on the screen.

The first negative shows the big white tablecloth stretched out to the side of the table, held down on the old sideboard we had then with a pile of my recipe books, to make a kind of tent. I slide the strip along. Here are the children again with a little plastic tea set under the table. It occurs to me Tobias has thrown away the rest of the prints from this batch because it's the day George got his burns. No wonder he didn't want to keep them. Neither of us wanted to remember that day.

In the next one, Mia has her hand on the corner of the cloth. The cloth is sliding off the table, the teapot with it. Irena is beside Mia, and Mia has hold of Irena's hand with the one that isn't pulling the cloth. And George, in his bouncy chair, is right under the table, his face screwed up, crying.

Irena and Mia had looked alike as children, with their dark curly hair. So I look again. I look once, twice, three times. I look away. I look back again. My eyes are not deceiving me. Mia is about to let the teapot topple, and it's right above George. The teapot in the picture is teetering on the edge.

Irena is pulling away from Mia.

It comes to me, a muscle memory, my body leaping up at the piercing scream, my running down the stairs, the howling. Tobias drenching George with cold water to cool the burns, while screaming into Irena's face, 'See what you've done? See what you've done to your baby brother?'

Irena, just three, staring back at him blankly, her little face showing no emotion, while her bigger sister Mia looked on, her hands over her ears, sobbing.

I remember feeling a surge of fury at Irena, as Tobias told me what she had done to my beautiful little baby boy. And then all the commotion as I rang 999 and Tobias continued to tend to George's burns, and Mia continued to sob hysterically, asking if her little brother was going to die.

That night, as we waited in the hospital, the clenching in my stomach, the terror George wasn't going to survive his burns, were accompanied by a creeping resentment at Tobias for not watching the children properly while I was busy working upstairs. And guilt that I hadn't been there to supervise.

'How could you take your eyes off them, Tobias?' It wasn't the time to apportion blame, as we sat there in the visitors' room, awaiting news, but it burst out of me anyway.

'I'd just told them' – Tobias's voice was tight – 'I'd just told the girls to be careful, there was hot water in the pot. I'd just told them, and as usual, Irena was defiant.'

And my feelings for my daughter, Irena, our middle child who had done this to my beautiful little baby boy after being told to be careful, wavered.

*

Now, I stuff the negatives and the viewer into my bag, pick my keys up from the hall table, slam the front door, get into my car and drive too fast, along the coast road, over the causeway, around the mainland to the harbour. I'm aware of a vast hole in my life, the last six years, when I thought I had lost my middle child for ever. I'm aware how fragile our relationship still is, how easily it might be broken again.

Already I feel it disintegrating. Already I feel my grip on Irena loosening, as she floats inevitably away from me again.

The air around the houseboats is filled with the scent of woodsmoke; thin blue trails rise into the air. There's the smell of winter in the air, the wind has a sharp edge to it and I hug my coat tighter around me. I pass Jonah's boat. I wish I was free to stop, pop in for a long talk beside his wood burner. But I have to reach Irena.

'Mum.' Irena opens the door. 'This is a surprise. Jonah explained Mia gave you a choice between her or me.'

'Irena, it's impossible for me, I—'

'He didn't want to tell me, not without your permission; but I was upset you'd not been to visit, and I think he thought telling me was the lesser of two evils. And I guessed you'd go for her and Xavier. Because Xavier's too young to understand why you would disappear from his life when he's been so close to you. And because Mia's been here for you.'

She turns and walks down the two steps into her cabin.

'Irena,' I say to her back. 'Please, it isn't like that . . . It's . . .'

Everything I'd planned to say evaporates. This is more complex than I imagined.

Now I'm here, I have no idea how I reveal to Irena that she was never responsible for her brother's facial scars. What will it do to her sense of identity? The incident defined her. It had, whether we liked it or not, influenced how our family saw her, how her school friends saw her, how she had seen herself, all her life.

It must have been behind the reason she left us for all those years, although I still can't quite piece together what the final trigger was.

Other questions occur to me. What will it do to Mia's sense of *herself*, as a sister, and as a mother, when she knows it was her, not Irena, who pulled the teapot onto her screeching brother – to shut him up, I guess? But what does Mia remember of the incident? Oh my God, has she lived with the guilt of knowing the truth all her life? Or was she too young to remember what happened? Pushed it deep down into her own unconscious? Mia has such high standards for herself. The truth would never have sat well with her. How will I put it to her without causing her damage?

But Irena, as the wronged one, has a right to know. She

has a right to know now, even if it's years too late. Even if it means it's the end.

'Sit down, Mum.' Irena waves her hand towards the sofa. 'You're making me agitated pacing around in that way. I've just put some bread in to warm and I'm going to make an omelette. Do you want some?'

'I'm fine, thank you, Irena. I'm not hungry.'

I examine her, try to work out how she is. At least she's been eating, there is colour in her cheeks. She looks – somehow – more self-contained than when she first arrived home, so cowed and pale.

'I came to tell you something. I don't know how to say this.' I collapse back onto the piles of cushions on her sofa.

'Here, have some wine.' Irena fills a plastic beaker with red wine and hands it to me. I put it on the table beside me and take a deep breath.

'Irena, Dad's been sorting through family photos, and putting them into files on the computer. It's something he's got quite obsessed with since his stroke. It's one thing he can do, you know, that doesn't require too much fine motor control or co-ordination.'

'Well, that's good. I'm pleased he's found something to occupy himself.'

I glance at her but her face is still, giving nothing away.

'This is hard for me. Because I know how hard it's going to be for you to hear. When you were little we didn't have mobiles, as you know. We took photos on cameras and had to get the films developed. And you could put the camera on a tripod with a timer, so you didn't have to be looking into the lens all the time and . . .'

'OK, Mum. You don't have to give me a history lesson. I know how people used to take pictures.'

'As you know, Dad was taking photos the day George

got his burns. Photos of you and Mia and George playing "house" under the kitchen table. George was so little he was still in his bouncy chair. They show him before . . .'

'Before he was so badly scalded he nearly died?' Irena's tone is hard.

'Dad must have thrown the other photos in that film away. And I mean, it wasn't an afternoon Dad or I wanted to reminisce about. In fact, it's an afternoon we wanted to forget for ever. But he failed to throw out the negatives. Today, Irena, was the first time I've ever set eyes on those images.' I pause. This is so hard to tell her. 'Irena, what one of those pictures shows is . . .' I take another deep breath. 'It was never *you* who caused the teapot to fall off the table. The boiling water that nearly killed George.'

I wait for Irena's reaction, but she is silent.

'Irena?'

She doesn't speak, she just looks at me with an expression that's impossible to read. What's going through her mind? How long will it take her to process this new version of herself? She smiles, stands up, pours herself more wine, sits down cross-legged on the rug by the fire. 'You're telling me you didn't know?' She pokes the fire with a stick.

'Of course I didn't know. That's what I'm telling you. I had no idea . . .'

She swivels round.

'Mum. *I* knew! *I* knew it was Mia.' Her face is open, her eyes wide, her mouth still half smiling.

'How can you possibly have known? *I* didn't know! I don't think Mia knows either. You were both so little – far too little to remember the details of that day. George obviously has no idea. And Tobias . . .'

Tobias. Tobias, who had taken the photos, who had presumably sifted through the prints once they were developed,

212

he had decided to throw them away. The implication hits me. My husband must have known. *My husband had known he was blaming the wrong daughter.*

'Mum . . . last time you were here,' Irena begins slowly, 'I told you there was more, but your phone rang and you had to leave.'

My mind spirals back to how we were interrupted by the phone, my panic that Mia might hear I was with Irena and prevent me from seeing Xav. That she'd believe I'd chosen Irena over her and Xav. I'd left in a rush, too anxious to stay and hear the rest of Irena's story.

'So, what I was going to tell you is this . . .' Irena turns and looks at me. 'That day I came home, when Xav was tiny, and you all went out to the pub and I stayed behind? Because Mia wouldn't let me hold my baby nephew? *Because of what I did to George when he was a baby?* I found those photos. I told you that much last time. What I didn't get to tell you, because your phone rang, was that I found the negatives too. And I got the little projector thing out and *I saw the one showing Mia pulling the cloth.* The teapot was teetering on the edge of the table. She was obviously pulling the cloth off the table. She was holding my hand, pulling me, trying to make me join in.'

'Oh Irena.'

'I knew in that instant, seeing the photo, that what I always thought I'd done, I hadn't. It was Mia.'

The wood burner spits suddenly and the logs shift.

'I believed it was me all my life. I'd lived with, not just the guilt, but the trauma of it.'

Trauma.

The trauma of it.

'That evening I learned it was never true. I also realized Dad must have known it was never true because he had photos of what really happened. He took the photos.' She swallows. 'Knowing my own father had deliberately blamed me for something I never did was the end for me. The end of trying to belong. I'd been trying and failing for so long.'

I stare at Irena, lost for words. That was the day before Irena left for Paris and barely got in touch for six years.

A chasm opens behind me, a sense of what might have been. How could I have missed what my youngest daughter was going through that weekend? A mother is supposed to see, a mother is supposed to know. I hadn't seen, I hadn't known. I had failed Irena again. If I'd been more aware, I would have taken the time to talk to her. Irena might not have left us for all those years. The past would have been very different.

'Why didn't you say anything, Irena?' I manage at last. I reach out to hold her hand. 'Why didn't you say anything that evening? When you found the negatives? Instead of *leaving* us?' My voice cracks.

'What?' Irena stands up. 'How could I stay after that? How could I stay when I'd just learned I'd been blamed for injuring my brother who I loved, when I was so very little, and when it wasn't me at all? When Dad had this evidence that it wasn't me, and hadn't told me?'

Irena's right. What else could she do? Knowing her own father – and, for all she knew, *both* her parents – had let her believe she was responsible for a near-fatal accident she had never caused?

'I'd grown up thinking I was some kind of psychotic monster who destroyed everything she touched,' Irena continues. 'That I'd nearly killed my brother. I didn't belong anywhere. Not at home. Not at the local school. Not really at boarding school either, though I put on a mask there and tried. But the version of me I believed, that everyone believed, wasn't the real me at all. And when I saw those projected images, I knew *Dad* knew it wasn't the real me either. But he hadn't told me! Which was the biggest betrayal of all.' She stands up, reaches for the wine bottle, fills her cup and takes a long gulp. 'I thought you knew the truth too, Mum. I thought, *My parents both know, they've got the evidence right here in these photos. And yet they've chosen to let me believe I destroyed half of my little brother's face.*'

A wave of heat rushes through me and my head spins again.

'Can we sit outside? I'm feeling very hot. I need to get some air.'

'OK. Yup. I need a cigarette.'

I follow Irena up the little wooden steps. We sit on the deck and I breathe the night scent of the sea, and it begins to restore me a little so that I can think a bit more clearly.

Irena lights a cigarette.

'I want you to know I had no idea what actually happened that day, Irena. I wasn't there when the accident happened.'

I stop. I hear myself, trying to wriggle out of responsibility, the way I tried to wriggle out of failing to pick Xav up from school. My words sound pathetic to my own ears.

And yet on I go. 'I only knew what Dad told me. And of course, I had no reason not to believe him. I tried to convince you it wasn't your fault, you were so little. In fact, I was furious with your dad for not watching you. We both agreed you were too young to know what you were doing.'

She gives a little sound, a half-laugh.

I gabble on.

'We had no idea the story would take on such a monstrous life of its own. That it would haunt you throughout your childhood – your whole life!'

Even as I say these words, I know something is wrong, something nags at me.

'So. You *didn't* know it was actually Mia?' Irena says at last. 'It was that that hurt me more than anything. I thought you, my own mother, let me believe I'd done something I hadn't. I couldn't understand why you or Dad would do that. It felt almost vindictive.'

'It must have done.'

'*Such* a betrayal.' She takes a long drag on her cigarette, as if to stem the turmoil of feelings. She begins to speak again, softly this time.

'I always wondered. It didn't sit right with me that I would have done something to hurt George, even by accident. I loved George so much. I was very protective of him. But then, of course, later, when I was a bit older, I wondered whether I'd learned to feel that sense of protection towards him *after* causing his scars. Because of doing that to him?'

And now I do realize what has been nagging at me.

As a mother, how *didn't* I know? I should have known my own children. Known how much Irena wanted to protect her little brother. Known that he drove Mia mad. I had let Tobias's conviction that it was Irena persuade me. I hadn't questioned it.

A picture comes back to me: Mia covering her ears while George screamed, her face screwed up in fury. Oh God, I should have realized. I should have at least questioned Tobias more about what happened that day. Why hadn't I?

'It never felt right,' Irena says again. 'That I would have done something so awful, even accidentally, to my baby brother . . . I was in thrall to Mia and didn't want to admit to her how I felt about him.' She lowers her voice. 'When we were at primary school, she used to find George really annoying. So I didn't tell her how much I loved him and wanted to protect him. In the same way I became in thrall to Hermione and didn't want to tell her how much I missed you all. My family.'

We sit in silence for a while then.

There's the sound of someone playing a guitar on one of the other boats. A laugh, the clatter of some pots.

Irena.

One incident had defined her for her whole life. I hadn't been able to see the child who wanted to please her sister, and protect her brother. The child who wanted to belong. But couldn't.

'I understand why Mia might have blamed me for something she felt bad about,' Irena says now, and when she turns to me there are tears in her eyes. 'She was a kid herself and probably frightened out of her wits by what she'd done. But Dad blaming me feels so unfair. Why would he do that?'

'I don't know, Irena. I'll talk to him about it. I haven't had a chance yet. I came here the minute I found the photo.'

Had Tobias felt too ashamed that he'd blamed the wrong child to tell any of us once he realized? Is that why he'd thrown those print photos away? Along with all the other unpalatable things he felt didn't belong in the albums?

'Well, so now you know why I left, Mum.' Irena blows more smoke into the night air. 'I saw the whole of my life flash past my eyes when I found that photo. George teasing me, telling me I was possessed. The children at school telling each other I tried to kill my brother. Trying to get away to boarding school, so I might become someone different, to try and work out who I really was. Dad telling me I destroyed everything I touched. And Mia refusing to let me hold Xavier when he was a baby, saying she couldn't trust me after what I did to George.'

I listen with a growing sense of unease.

I had thought of Irena as a puzzle, impossible to solve. And I'd said so, I remember with another shot of guilt, that day she came home from boarding school. I had been riddled with doubt about my middle child each time she did something that seemed to confirm her destructive side.

'And so now you know, too, why I didn't come home when Dad had his stroke. Seeing that picture told me he didn't love me. Because if he loved me, how could he lie to me like that? And Hermione convinced me I shouldn't come, that he should suffer for what he'd done to me.'

I grapple to find words that will contradict what she believes, but I can't.

'And I suppose that's why I took Xavier and didn't tell anyone,' she finishes. 'Yes, I wanted to care for him, keep him safe. But I was also making up for the time I'd been denied him because Mia didn't trust me with him. In a way, by doing it in such a thoughtless way, I suppose I was also living up to expectations.'

'Will you ever be able to forgive us? For making this mistake?'

I look at Irena and she looks back at me through her big brown eyes.

And I have the horrible feeling the damage might have gone too deep.

23

RENEE

When I get in from Irena's, the familiar sight of Tobias at the computer, scanning and deleting photos, infuriates me. I march over to him, prop the strip of negatives containing the ones of Mia pulling the cloth in front of him.

'Look at these, Tobias.'

He turns slowly, frowns.

'What is this, Renee?' He picks up his reading glasses, puts them on, painfully slowly.

He stares at the negatives for what seems like ages, then he looks back up at me like a frightened child.

'You may need this.'

I put the little hand projector in front of him, slide the strip through, pick it up and hold it to his eyes.

He gazes into the viewfinder for a few minutes.

'Where did you find these? I thought I'd got rid of them. You weren't ever supposed to see those.'

'But I have seen them. I need an explanation.'

He turns away from me.

'Have you always known it was Mia, not Irena?' I say to his back.

He shakes his head.

'No. Renee, please. Please don't let's revisit that day again. We'd agreed to put it behind us.'

'Tobias, please look at me. I need you to look at me. I

219

need to understand what this means. Did you know from the start? Did you blame Irena deliberately?'

He sighs, puts his head in his hands.

'I need the whole story, Tobias. What did you know? When did you know?'

'OK.' He pushes himself up, moves over to the sofa, stumbles, then puts a hand out so he can steer himself down onto the seat.

'OK. OK.' He speaks as if I've been haranguing him about this for years. 'I admit I was mistaken in assuming it was Irena. But it's over and done with. We put it behind us. We agreed to.'

'Did you actually see what happened at the time? Have you always known?'

'How can you think that? Of course not. I wouldn't have deliberately blamed the wrong daughter – why would I do that? I told you, I had the camera on the tripod, on the timer, so I didn't see what happened. But Irena was, as you know, our more, let's say . . . more impetuous daughter. When I heard the commotion, before I realized quite how serious it all was, it was quite understandable that I would assume it was her. And Mia, who, as you agree, Renee, was always so sensible, mature beyond her years, said it was her. She said, *It was Irena, she pulled the cloth and the tea spilled on George.*'

'Oh God. I hope you're not blaming Mia.' I walk across the room to the window. 'Because Mia must have said that out of fright. She was only tiny herself. She should never have been left with a pot of hot tea. She must've been terrified of what she'd done.'

I'm trying to make sense of all this. I turn, look at my diminished husband, slumped now into the corner of the big Chesterfield sofa.

'I think perhaps Mia had an inkling of how serious it was,' he sighs. 'That George's life was in danger. But I didn't question her because I was frantic, and furious and feeling guilty.'

'Guilty, Tobias?'

'Of course I felt guilty, Renee!'

'Stop shouting, Tobias. It's not fair of you to get angry. You've never told me the truth before, and I need to know.'

'Of course I felt fucking guilty. I was to blame! I was afraid of what I'd allowed to happen. I thought my son was going to die! Maybe I did take it out on the girls. Anyone would have floundered in that situation.'

'You thought it was better to blame tiny children than admit you'd allowed it to happen?'

'I wasn't thinking rationally, Renee. I was upset and confused. I shouted into Irena's face and she didn't deny it. I know now that was because she'd done nothing. But at the time I interpreted her blank look as defiance. It enraged me. Even more, I believed she had deliberately hurt her brother, because he'd usurped her position as the youngest. You would have assumed the same. In fact, I think we discussed it at some point, the psychology of what she did.'

I stare at my husband. I'm about to object to this assertion, but I'm aware suddenly that he's right. We had explained it away as natural sibling rivalry. And we'd decided to move on. To reassure the children it wasn't their fault. Everything he says is true.

I'm astonished to see there are tears in Tobias's eyes. I feel myself softening, the beginnings of forgiveness, of sympathy for him for how awful those moments, after George was scalded, must have been.

'It wasn't until many years later I found the canister containing the undeveloped film from that day.' Tobias's voice is quieter now, and hoarse from his shouting. 'I had no idea what it contained. I took it to be developed. It was only then I saw the evidence of what actually happened. It was only then, Renee. Only then that I knew I'd blamed the wrong daughter. But it was too late to change anything, so I didn't tell you. Or Irena.'

'And you threw the prints away.'

'Yes.'

'When was this, Tobias?' I ask quietly.

He shrugs. 'Does it matter?'

'I think it does.'

'It was around the time Irena was begging to go to boarding school. Yes, it was then. Once I realized what I'd done, I decided I'd give her what she wanted. It was a kind of way of making it up to her. I suppose it made me feel better about it all. Much good that school did her.'

This is getting worse. My husband thought it was better to pay for our daughter to go away than to tell her what he'd just discovered about her?

'It was too late to change the story,' he repeats, looking at me with a cowed expression as if he is afraid of what I'm going to say next.

And he should be.

'Too late?' I walk over and look down at him. 'Was it too late to gather us together, say to your daughters, to me, to George, *I made a mistake; I've only just realized. It wasn't you, Irena, who spilled hot water on your brother after all. So, Irena, you are not, and never were, "the child who tried to kill her brother". You can stop feeling like a misfit who has to go away to a boarding school rather than confront people who bully you and call you names and . . .'* I'm ranting. I take a breath. 'You could have said, *These photos show it was Mia. But you, Mia, are not to blame either. I*

222

am to blame for putting that teapot within reach of a tiny child with a new baby brother sitting under the table.' I stop, suddenly exhausted.

I pull up a chair. Sit opposite him, lean forward.

'Go on,' I say. 'Finish what you were saying.'

'OK. If you're prepared to listen.'

'I am. I am listening.' And I am – now.

'So – Irena went off to boarding school. As she'd begged us to allow her to. What good would it have done Mia to know that it was she who had scarred George, not Irena? As far as I was concerned, in fact, as far as we were both concerned, if you remember, it was over and done with. I decided it was best to let sleeping dogs lie.'

'But it wasn't over and done with. God, Tobias, I couldn't be a therapist if I believed traumas that happened in people's pasts were over and done with, just because they happened long ago.'

I move over, sit down next to him, hoping that if I'm physically closer to him, we'll somehow be able to bridge the emotional distance between us. 'I've just spoken to Irena. She'd seen those pictures. She believes you – and I – *deliberately* blamed her for what happened to George. Imagine what that has done to her sense of worth, to her trust in you, in us?'

'Irena saw the negatives?'

'She found them. The day before she disappeared from our lives. She believed you – no, *we* – blamed her for George's injuries when we knew it was really Mia. She felt she had to leave her family, not because she'd scalded her brother, but because we'd chosen to blame her for something she never did.'

'Oh God,' he groans. Puts his good hand to his face. 'I was going to bring it up that weekend. The last weekend we were all together. I thought perhaps the effects were in the distant past and it would do no harm to right the story. I even imagined us being able to laugh about it. But Mia and Eddie were so happy to be new parents. I couldn't spoil that for them, could I? Then Irena went off to do her protesting and didn't say goodbye.'

He pauses again, takes a deep breath as if this is exhausting for him.

'She put all that environmental stuff before us. Then before me when I had my stroke. How do you think that made me feel, as her father, Renee?'

'You were hurt. I know. But I hope you see now *why* she did that. I hope you see that you have an apology to make. To Irena. But actually to Mia too. Because the choice you made to conceal the truth from them both underlies, I think, why they've been estranged from one another for so long. I need to straighten this out so I can have access to all my children again. To Xavier too. Because it's been breaking my heart.' I don't add that it's been breaking my heart to have lost my husband – or at least, the man he used to be – as well, because I think it might be too late for that.

I go into the kitchen and pour myself a glass of wine, and sit at the counter to turn over the facts in my mind.

Tobias had always needed Mia to be perfect. To achieve high grades the way he had always done. To walk in his footsteps. To be there for us when he was ill. He would certainly find it hard to believe Mia had it in her – as we all do – to do anything mean or destructive. And what a burden, if so, for Mia to carry. Never being able to get anything wrong. Or to accept anyone else for getting things wrong.

And perhaps that's why Tobias had projected everything less palatable onto his other daughter? Who had, eventually, lived up to this expectation, failed to come home when he had a stroke, let him down, as he expected, almost forced her to do?

But Tobias has a chance to correct the situation now. He has a chance to repair the rift in our family. There is time, I think, and, as Jonah told me, hope. I pull on my coat and go out for a walk. I need to breathe the sea air.

When I arrive back at the house, it takes a while for me to make sense of the scene before me, as if I'm adjusting one of the photos on Tobias's computer, slowly bringing it into focus. A hand in a pool of liquid, a smashed mug, its contents seeping into the floorboards. Tobias's head turned to one side, his face away from me. His body loose on the floor, like a puppet with its strings cut. Glossy photos strewn across the floor around him. Moving across to him, I lift his hand, feel it limp in mine. I sit next to him and feel for a pulse. It's there, I can feel it, a tiny, barely perceptible throb beneath his thin skin.

I pull out my mobile, press 999, speak to the voice on the line. 'My husband. I think he's had another stroke.'

The night goes past in a blur. The ambulance comes, and the paramedics fill the house with their equipment and their monitors. Then a doctor arrives and at last someone asks if there's somewhere we can sit quietly while she explains to me her assessment of the situation. I try to take in what she tells me, that the stroke is catastrophic, that it's best we make Tobias comfortable, that it won't be long. She's going to send the palliative care team to help him through the night. Is there anyone I need to contact? Anyone who should come before my husband dies?

Two nurses arrive at dawn. When one of them has

examined Tobias, she turns and packs away her paraphernalia. I watch her, wondering how it must feel to do a job that involves administering to the dying every day, day in day out.

'It will be today, almost certainly,' she says softly. 'If you have any family members who would like to see him, they should come today.'

'Thank you.' The words float out of my mouth, as if from someone else.

When she's gone I text Mia and explain what's happening. She will want to see her father. **If you want, I'll go out, so you can see him alone,** I write, because I don't know if she will agree to be in the same room as me. While I wait for her reply I phone George, explain as gently as I can the situation, suggest he comes today.

Irena's phone is on voicemail so I text Jonah, ask him to tell Irena that her father is dying, that it's definite this time, he isn't going to pull through. That in spite of everything, if she wants to see him, she must come today. I add that I will understand if she cannot come, can't let it go. **She'll know what I mean,** I add.

When I've contacted my children I go up to the bedroom.

Tobias seems peaceful now, on the bed, the one in the front room where I usually sleep alone these days. It felt right to put him in our marital bedroom for his last hours. The sun comes in through the window, falling on his face, filling the room with a golden light. It's funny, I'd always thought death was dark. But this is a bright winter morning; I hear the drone of the van that delivers the milk that still does the rounds here, as it moves along the street, the cry of children playing in one of the neighbouring gardens. Life seems fuller than ever out there, amid the shadows of clouds, the clanking of boats and, down in the garden, the holly berries that shine bright red in the bushes. I take up Tobias's hand. His fingertips are cold.

'It's a beautiful day out there,' I tell him. 'Would you like some music?'

He opens his eyes briefly, makes a noise that I interpret as affirmative.

I reach for my phone, find the playlist we used to put on in the evenings sometimes, that we would listen to over a glass of wine. Van Morrison, Leonard Cohen, Joni Mitchell. I sit beside my husband, letting the music ripple up and down and over, the sunlight and cloud patterns dappling the room.

I think back over our marriage, its ups and downs, the times he's driven me mad with his fixed ideas about everything, including the children, never seeing nuances. I pity him, that he needed to believe only one thing about each of his daughters, and was unable to alter this even when he had the evidence in his hands. It has meant an estrangement from Irena that has lasted to the end of his life. For his sake, I wish he had agreed to see Irena, knowing she was back, to tell her he loved her, apologize for any mistakes he had made over the years. Why hadn't he done that when he could? Now Tobias will die with no closure. And perhaps Irena will be denied closure too.

As I sit beside my husband, I think of the last years since his stroke, how he had become more rigid in his thinking, more short-tempered. We hadn't slept in the same bed since his first stroke three years ago. I had missed the warmth from his body sometimes, but there was something else that had come between us, and now I know what it was.

His deception.

I don't want to give this thought room, but it creeps in

227

anyway, filling me with unwelcome feelings, with hurt. He knew for several years that it wasn't Irena who had injured George, and he hadn't told me! How could he withhold that from me, when if he'd admitted it, and been prepared to apologize, it might have brought Irena home?

At eleven there's a sound behind me and I look up. It's George, coming quietly into the room. My heart lifts as he comes in, my handsome film star son. He drags the stool over from the dressing table and sits on it, next to me, leaning over to look at Tobias.

'Dad,' he says. 'It's George here. Came straight from London when I heard. Wanted to tell you what a great dad you've been.'

He glances at me, questioning whether I think Tobias can hear.

I nod.

'Speak to him,' I whisper. 'Tell him anything you need to. I'm going to make us some coffee.'

Downstairs in the kitchen, the clock ticks, and the fridge hums. The back garden is in shade. There are the holly berries, blood-red drops in the bushes. A robin hops about on the bird table, pecks at crumbs. Everything is heightened. The aroma of the coffee when I open the canister. The lingering scent of toast from earlier that hangs in the air.

There are things that punctuate a marriage, routines, habits, little arrangements of mugs or plates or bottles or flowers or cups on a tray. Tobias's wine glass on the shelf waits for his evening snifter that won't come tonight. How many times have I boiled the kettle for Tobias over the years, spooning coffee into the cafetière, not thinking with each coffee I make, there will be one less in the future, not paying any attention to this incremental seeping away of time? Not suspecting that the man I've been attending to, caring for, was keeping a secret from me that had injected the last six years of my life with a constant, aching sadness. Everything familiar seems suddenly to be a different shade, a different texture, as if I am viewing it through a filter. Nothing is as I thought it was.

I wait while the kettle hisses and finally boils and clicks off. I wonder what George will make of all this. How will knowing the truth about his scars impact on his relationship with either of his sisters?

I hear a gentle knock on the front door and go to open it.

Mia stands there, groomed as ever, dark hair straight and glossy, wool coat over a sleek skirt, pale pink jumper, ankle boots. My body instinctively relaxes as my eyes rest on her, my eldest child, who has been so much part of my life for the last three years but who then stopped me seeing her so abruptly.

I've missed her, our daily chats, hearing about her work, helping her out with Xav. I've even missed her arch comments about my beliefs and attitudes. And yet she, too, seems subtly altered, as if the filter has enveloped her as well. She is somehow different to the person I'd always thought she was.

'You aren't at work today?'

'I was. When I got your text I asked if they'd let me take compassionate leave. Is Dad OK? What's happening?'

I give her a look, and tears spring to her eyes.

'Has Xav gone to school?'

'Eddie took him. He'll pick up to give me time if I need it.'

Maureen is right, then. Eddie is living at Mia's. A little sinking of my heart. She won't need me to help with Xavier any more.

'George is in with Dad at the moment. They're in our bedroom. I'm making some coffee, will you have some?'

'OK. Please. Can I go up?'

'Of course.'

I take my time putting the mugs and a seed cake I've got in a tin in the cupboard on a tray. On a whim I go out and cut some holly sprigs to put in a jug and put that on the tray as well. I want to give Mia and George time together with their dad, time to talk, to reminisce.

After another ten minutes or so I take the tray up the stairs.

George and Mia chat quietly, flicking through one of the photograph albums Tobias had printed for them. The images chosen carefully so as not to mar the depiction of a happy, wholesome family. These are pictures of Mia, Irena and George as teenagers.

Mia and George are laughing gently. 'Do you remember this day? We had that Easter egg hunt and Dad hid those mini bottles of fizz, because you'd almost reached drinking age . . .'

George laughs. 'He could be quite a good sport at times.'

I look over at Tobias. Something has changed even while I was downstairs making the coffee. It's hard to define, but something in his colour, or the depth of his breath has altered. I know, instinctively, he is moving away from us. If Irena doesn't come soon, she'll miss him. My heart starts to race. This will be it. This will be the end. The end of the story that began with a misjudgement and led to a lifelong estrangement.

I glance at my phone. There's a message from Jonah, saying he's been to see Irena, told her what I asked him to.

It's all I could do, and I know, in those few words, he's telling me that she won't acquiesce. She won't come.

'Mum?' Mia catches me looking at my phone. 'Mum, put that away. It will only make you feel worse. We're here. George and I are here.'

'I know. And I appreciate you coming, Mia.'

'Of course I'd come. And I ought to tell you. Eddie's decided to move back in with us and to live here. He likes it here now he's got over the gossip.'

I glance at her.

'So stop it, Mum.' She takes my hand. I realize we have barely touched recently. Today I imagined her hand would be cold but it is warm and soft. 'Stop trying to make Irena be the person she isn't capable of being. She's not coming. She chose this. There's nothing you can do. It's time you let her go. She's gone.'

Her words hang in the air.

She's gone.

'I think his breathing's changed. Dad,' Mia whispers. 'Dad, I do love you. You've been such a good dad. More than that, a friend to me. And the best granddad to Xav. I will miss you so much.' A tear rolls down her cheek and lands on his chest. 'Goodbye, Dad.'

24

IRENA

Jonah put his head through the cabin door as I was pulling on my trainers. I needed to get some air before heading for the boatyard.

'Irena.' Something in Jonah's expression told me this was serious. 'Message from your mum. She's tried to ring but says your phone's on voicemail.'

'It was on silent.'

'I'm so sorry. Your dad's had another stroke. Your mother says if you want to see him, you need to go today. Now.'

A sweat broke out, creeping up my body, yet I felt freezing cold. I'd been here before.

'I can't go.' My dad, the big, blond man who I was a little afraid of in my childhood – dying? I continued to pull on my shoes, and reached for a jacket. It looked as if it was going to be cold out there, so I'd need the thick padded one I got from an Emmaus in France.

'He disowned me, Jonah.'

'It must have hurt very badly, Irena.' Jonah's face is kind. 'But *he* was feeling hurt that you wouldn't see him last time he was ill. It sounds very paradoxical, I know, but in a sense, your dad's rejection was a proof of his love. He decided to cut you off so you couldn't cause him any more pain. We don't feel hurt by people we don't care about, you know.'

I could be there in ten minutes.

'All I can say is, sometimes people regret it when they don't take these opportunities.' Jonah was insistent. 'It's none of my business, I agree, before you tell me to shove my words where the sun don't shine. Just saying.'

Normally Jonah's funny turn of phrase would have made me laugh. But I didn't laugh. The vision kept looming into my mind, my dad unable to move, turning grey. My once tall, domineering dad, who ruled the family, made the decisions, let me live a lie about myself, who I had felt justified in hating, was now pale and weak and fading away.

'I'm going for a walk, Jonah. I need air.'

'Suit yourself. But remember, there's only one chance for this.'

The tide was far, far out this morning, the grassy shore stretching for miles to a thin line of silver horizon. The air was sharp and clear and the sun was shining and the seagulls were wheeling, calling. It was too bright for a morning in which my father was dying. It made no sense. But it made no difference either. He wasn't my father any more. He'd made that very clear when he recovered from the stroke last time.

I didn't see how telling me I was dead to him was proof of his love; Jonah's capacity for believing in the good in people was astonishing.

As I walked, I thought about the day I met newborn Xavier, how Mia told me I couldn't be trusted with him. Hermione had told me I was always going to fail in my family's eyes. And unless I shook off my whole family, I would never become the person I had the potential to be. But then, meeting Hermione in London, finding she had stopped loving me too – it had occurred to me that she had said those things about my family when she wanted me to stay with her, until she didn't need me any more either.

Who was I then?
Was I Hermione's version of me?
Or was I my father's version of me?
Or was I someone else entirely?

The man coming towards me across the mudflats was tall and black. I blinked. I hadn't met Eddie for a long time, but I remembered his gentle manner, the interest he took in me. Now I could see straight away that he'd lost weight; his once smooth, even skin tone had a marbled appearance to it as if he'd been deprived of sunlight.

'Irena?' he said.

I turned away from him. Mum had mentioned he was back with Mia. Perhaps my sister's resentment at Eddie for gambling all their money away had lessened? She must have realized how valuable her support network was, now she'd given Mum that ultimatum, her or me. I don't think Mia probably ever appreciated how lucky she was to have Eddie. Or how lucky she was to have Mum nearby, to pick up Xavier, to provide childcare when she kicked Eddie out after he erred.

We all err at times.

All of us except Mia.

I thought of my sister, always the smart, capable one, the one who got the handsome men. The perfect exam results. Cambridge. She was the one who had ended up with it all, too, the marriage, the beautiful child, my mother, our father, our brother. Mia's one flaw, if she had any, was her inability to forgive. Eddie for gambling away their money – although it seemed she might have absolved him, finally. Mum for forgetting to pick up Xavier one afternoon. Me for spending time with my nephew without asking her permission. Because I knew she'd refuse.

If I were to tell her *she* was the one to have scarred our little brother in a moment of rage, all those years ago, would she ever be able to forgive herself? I doubted it.

Eddie began to walk alongside me, silently, out towards that shimmering horizon.

'You know your dad is dying,' he said quietly. 'Don't you think you should go and see him?'

My breath came in sharply, a gasp.

'What is it with you and Jonah?' I said. 'You both seem to think it's your responsibility to persuade me to visit my father who disowned me quite some time ago.'

'He thinks you disowned him.'

I turned to look Eddie in the eye.

'Eddie, my dad allowed me to believe I caused those terrible scars on George's handsome face. Even when he had evidence I didn't. That betrayal meant I went away and couldn't come home. Wouldn't be here now if I hadn't been homeless. I can't go and see my dad. I'm not one of them any more.'

'Your dad lied? About how George's accident happened?'

'Forget I said that. I didn't mean to.'

'No. Tell me. You have to. I want to understand too.'

'Really?'

'Really! Because Mia doesn't understand either. She's hurt, yes, because she said you two used to be close. She often tells me how badly she missed you when you went away to boarding school. And then to Paris. And how she didn't understand why you wouldn't come back when your dad was ill the first time. She needed you. So please, Irena, if there's something she doesn't know, tell me.'

The story came out slowly. I told my brother-in-law everything. The negatives I'd found. Learning I wasn't, after all, the one to have injured George. The bewilderment that my dad had let me believe I was.

By the time I'd finished we were approaching the bit of the mudflats where they would disappear under the shallow lapping waves of the sea. Although it was a feature of this landscape that the nearer you got, the further away this point seemed.

'Do you know what?' Eddie turned to me. 'That all makes a curious kind of sense.'

'What do you mean?'

'Mia told me that when she was pregnant, she was worried she might not be able to be a good mother to our baby, because babies crying really grated on her nerves. She said she couldn't stand it when George cried when he was a baby.'

I stood still. A light breeze had got up, and the longer grass was all leaning one way in the wind. My mind raced. Eddie was speaking again.

'Mia said she'd sometimes felt such a rage when George cried. She said George annoyed her because he was so perfect as a baby, and your parents doted on him, and she wanted to play with you but he would cry and spoil your games. Then, when he was scalded and ended up with those facial scars she was expected to watch out for him, keep you away from him, play the "good girl".'

'Eddie, did she remember scalding him? And blaming me for it?'

'No. At least she never said she did. But you were both very young then, weren't you? Four and five?'

'I was just three.'

'You were probably both too little to remember. But she said she'd felt a terrible kind of pressure from your parents. Always having to be the successful, helpful, "good" one and never, ever allowing herself to slip up for a moment.'

'I don't want you to tell Mia what I've just told you. Believing I had it in me to almost kill – to *want* to kill my brother – made it very hard to like myself. I wouldn't want to put that onto anyone else, ever. It's best Mia continues to believe the family story, even if it means she puts herself under pressure to be perfect all the time. Better that than the guilt.'

'But don't you see, Irena?' Eddie taps me on the shoulder again, emphatically. 'No one killed your brother. Or even wanted to. It was an *accident*. Well, perhaps not an accident, if Mia pulled the cloth deliberately . . . we don't know . . . but if anyone was responsible, it was your dad!'

'No, Eddie, it was—'

'Shhh. Listen. I mean, if I left a teapot of boiling water anywhere near Xavier and it spilled on him, for whatever reason, even if another child deliberately pushed it off the table onto him, because they found his wailing intolerable, I'd blame myself. You girls, you were so tiny, neither of you should ever have had to carry *any* blame. Or have felt *any* association with it whatsoever. Most children want to hurt their little siblings sometimes. The adults are supposed to stop them from actually doing it.'

We walked on towards the ever-vanishing line where the land would meet the sea.

'You know you broke your mother's heart when you went away and didn't get in touch,' Eddie said quietly. 'And Mia's.'

'*Mia's?*'

'Irena, Mia was heartbroken when you left for Paris. Then didn't get in touch for years.'

'That's quite hard to believe.'

'But it's true.'

'When I asked to hold Xavier, your tiny newborn son, Mia wouldn't let me. Because of what she believed I did to

237

George. Can you imagine how that felt? When you know you are seen a certain way, it's impossible to change that. I had to get away to shake off that label. To try, somehow, to reinvent myself. My only choice was to leave, and find myself elsewhere. I had to – I *had* to shake off every last drop of influence my family had on me. Hermione – she's the woman I lived with in Paris – helped me see the truth.'

'Is she here with you now?'

'It's over.'

'I'm sorry.'

'It's OK. It had run its course.' As I say the words, I realize they're true. 'I think she did love me, but she used me, too. I didn't mind. I wanted to be used at first. I was so confused. She convinced me I was capable and independent and didn't need my family. But I think she liked the fact I was so lost and she could control me. And I was so in thrall to her. And we did have some very good times in Paris, protesting, being activists. But in the end she tired of me, of our environmentalist life. It's OK. I probably needed her to tire of me, in order to confront my family. To find a way back.'

I turned to Eddie again. 'So, she's out of my life now. And now I don't know who I'm supposed to be. Hermione's version of me, or my dad's, or Mia's – the child abductor.'

Eddie laughs and I frown.

'I'm serious, Eddie.'

'I know. I know what Mia accused you of. But you're Xavier's aunt, Irena. It wasn't abduction, not as I understand it. Whatever you did, it was cool as far as Xav's concerned. He keeps asking for you.'

'Really?'

'He loves you, and he loved that time in London with you. As for Mia, I'm working on her. Don't you worry. I think she'll forgive you for taking Xav eventually. After all, she's forgiven me at last. And I've had to forgive myself too. It isn't easy, but it is necessary. I had to forgive myself for the temptation that made me gamble and lose all the money Mia and I had saved between us.'

I watched my feet sink into the mud as we squelched on. Eddie wasn't used to mud, he was a city boy. I glanced at him to see how he was coping with being out in the wilds. The light breeze had become a brisk wind by now, and he tied his cashmere scarf tighter round his face. He'd clearly never stopped dressing well, even after nearly losing everything.

My sister had good taste, I had to hand her that. Eddie's face had a kindness to it, a depth that was attractive, and which Xavier had inherited. He had the same slightly uptilted chin, the same high cheekbones. I felt something rise inside me, I couldn't put my finger on what it was. A yearning for the kind of closeness Mia had with Eddie maybe. A sense of relief, a sense of love, of grief.

Relief that Eddie, at least, seemed to have forgiven me for taking Xav from school without telling them. Love for him, and for Xav and for Mum. Grief over losing touch with Mia, and for the fact my dad was dying. Sorrow that he'd never had the courage to apologize for betraying me. Sorrow for him for his surfeit of pride, for never allowing himself to be wrong.

All jumbled up, all bubbling up inside me.

We *had* reached the edge of the land now, and we stood in this hazy place where the grass turned to mud and the mud turned to water. The word liminal came to me, and I thought of my dad, hanging there, between life and death in his own liminal space. If I looked over to my left, I could actually see the roof of my parents' house behind the tall trees, beyond the fishing huts and the road. He was in there, right now, dying. How sad it all was.

How unnecessary our estrangement seemed, suddenly.

'I want you and Mia to be sisters again,' Eddie said into the silence. 'She might not show it, she might not even know it. But she needs you.'

'We should get back before the tide comes in.'

He put an arm out and placed it around me. It felt comfortable leaning against Eddie's shoulder in its wool coat.

The tide had indeed turned, I could hear it, rippling beneath us, filling the creeks. We'd have to walk quickly to reach the shore or the sea would get there before us. It had already begun to move in through the deeper channels.

'It's been a weight for both of you. Mia always having to be the high achiever, the "good" one who does the right thing all the time. You the one who was unpredictable and free-spirited. But it seems to me, getting the truth out in the open might enable Mia to recognize she doesn't have to be so perfect after all. That she needs to more easily accept the flaws in herself and in other people, such as myself.' He grinned. 'And you, Irena.'

We reached the harbour, and Eddie indicated that Suzy's was open and suggested we went for a coffee.

'What will you have?' he asked.

I hesitated.

'I'm not sure, Eddie,' I said. 'I'm not sure I have time.'

25

RENEE

We've been sitting in silence for a while now. The playlist has reached its end and I haven't the strength, or perhaps the belief, that Tobias can hear it, to put it on again. George continues to flick through the photos, and Mia bustles about, collecting our cups.

'I'll take these down to wash.' She scoops up the plates. 'Goodness, it's almost three. Time's gone all awry . . . it feels impossible that the world can be moving on out there. It feels . . . it feels as if it should have stood still while . . .'

She gives George and me a helpless, grief-stricken look.

'Lucky I asked Eddie to get Xavier from school. Does anyone want some lunch? We forgot to have any. I don't think I can eat . . .'

'We're fine. Go down, Mia, take a breather.'

The light in the room has changed. The golden veil that lent everything a soft feeling earlier has passed, and now the room is in shade, the light outside fading. The shadows sharp and gloomy. I glance again at Tobias. He's still breathing.

It takes longer than I thought for a person to die. Like birth, it seems it rarely happens instantly. There is nearly always a struggle to enter, or to leave, the world. But Tobias seems comfortable, his body still, his chest moving gently. I go to the window and look out across the estuary. The tide

241

is coming in, boats beginning to stir, little white horses edging the waves where the estuary opens up to the sea.

Mia's right, it seems impossible that the world is continuing out there.

The idea that my marriage might have been a sham comes to me in a shock. The fact Tobias could do something so fundamentally damaging to our children. A flash of something unsettling bolts through me again at the thought of what his withholding of the truth did to us all. It isn't quite anger, it's more a kind of disappointment. And still an underlying sense that I, too, am implicated.

We, the feted Gulliver family, are imperceptibly shifting shape all over again. Perhaps a family is never the thing you thought it was. Like the tides, it comes in and out and it re-forms in a different way each time. We are no longer Renee and Tobias and their three children, the family of the feature in the magazine. We are something different, smaller, sadder. We, the parents, are certainly more deeply flawed than I ever realized.

I feel a movement beside me. George has come to stand next to me, and is gazing out of the window too. I look back at my husband. I wonder what he's going through, whether there's the tiniest bit of consciousness left that tells him he's dying. George puts an arm around me.

'I'm sorry, Mum,' he says. 'I'm sorry Irena never came. I know what it's done to you.'

My head rests on his shoulder.

'I don't blame her. Later, George, I'll explain. Now's not the time.'

'Let's sit down again.'

There are footsteps on the stairs, Mia coming back up with some late lunch. Though I know I won't be able to eat

242

either. George and I take up our positions on our chairs alongside Tobias.

'I don't think it's going to be long,' George says. 'I think we should open the window. It's said it lets the spirit out.'

'It'll let some air in, anyway.'

Mia has reached the door, is struggling to turn the handle while holding the lunch.

George stands up and goes to open it.

But it isn't Mia in the doorway at all. The person standing there has aubergine-coloured hair in a huge halo around her head, the sinking sun from the landing window backlighting her.

'Hello, Mum,' she says. 'Hello, George.'

Irena crosses the room. She stands for a while, breathing deeply, her eyes closed as if unable to move.

'Mia told me you were up here.' She still has her eyes closed, still hasn't moved.

'Where is Mia?'

Irena lowers her voice.

'She's gone. Didn't want to be in the house with me, I guess.'

Her words sting, and tears spring to my eyes. Even now? How can this rift slice through everything? How can Mia persist when her father is dying?

Irena has opened her eyes and is gazing at Tobias. She's trying to pluck up the courage to confront a deep-seated fear. I know this now. She takes another deep breath, walks forward, picks up her dad's hand.

'Dad,' she says. 'It's Irena.'

I'm about to tell her it's too late. He's beyond responding. I don't think he can even hear the music we're playing – George put the playlist back on – although the nurse assured me hearing was the last sense to go.

But then Tobias opens his eyes. He looks at his youngest daughter.

His lips flicker upwards, into a small smile of recognition.

She bends down and kisses him on the cheek.

'I wanted to see you,' she says. 'I wanted to say that I do love you.'

Tobias suddenly tries to sit up, his breath rasping, and grasps his daughter's hand. He tries to say something, but he's too weak.

Then his breath changes.

He takes one, two, three more breaths.

And then it all stops.

26

RENEE

'You can go biodegradable.' The woman at the Co-op funeral parlour flicks through a glossy brochure. 'If you think that feels right for your loved one. A lot of people do these days. Or this is the more expensive, high-end range.'

She turns to a page of mahogany coffins with brass or gold handles.

My head swims.

I look at George.

'Have you any idea what Dad would have preferred? He didn't specify in the will. I know he liked churches, though he wasn't actually religious. And he didn't believe in God, or an afterlife.'

'Mum.' George puts his hand on mine. 'Dad's dead, I think we should do what we want. And I suggest we go bamboo or cardboard. The most biodegradable. It will please Irena. And be good for the environment. I think we should go with the woodland burial ground as well.'

'OK.' I'm numb, my mind completely unable to process thoughts.

'Now, the next thing I need to ask is, are you choosing a religious service or a celebrant?'

The woman on the other side of the desk has a badge on her lapel saying 'Susan'.

I stare dumbstruck at Susan, at her round face, short silvery grey hair, fashionable bright-yellow-framed glasses,

245

wondering what it must be like dealing with the people who come into her office stunned by loss, unable to make sense of the simplest questions. She seems unfazed by my silence. Susan's face is kind, but not overly emotional.

I wonder if she's had training? Been told not to let herself show too much empathy, not to encourage a surfeit of grief during this time of practical arrangements.

'When you've decided, let us know.' She puts her pen down on her desk. 'But can I suggest you consult the rest of the family? Any siblings, children, anyone at all really. You wouldn't believe the number of disagreements we see over funerals, how they should be carried out.'

I gaze at her.

She strokes the brochures on her desk. 'It's an emotionally charged subject.'

George nods at her. 'We'll bear that in mind. I think we'll go for the bamboo coffin and probably the celebrant option. Our dad wasn't religious. But I'll consult the rest of the family first to prevent any disputes.'

He steers me out of the office into the fresh air.

It feels like a weird non-time, the period between Tobias's death and the funeral. I have things to do, the death certificate to organize, people to inform, decisions to be made about the service, whether to go civil, as George suggested, or to have a church ceremony. But decisions feel slippery, impossible to grasp.

The evening after Tobias's death, after the undertakers had carried his body away, Irena, George and I had sat together around the kitchen table. Mia had not come back. She still hadn't spoken properly to Irena.

George opened a bottle of red wine and refilled our glasses as we sat and tried to make sense of what had just happened.

We found ourselves remembering things about Tobias we'd forgotten. We talked about the way he could be so dogmatic about things, and laughed about his sometimes ridiculous pomposity. Then we remembered other things, like the time he built himself a wine shed, determined to make the best wine ever but only ever succeeding in making disgusting wine that no one could swallow.

Our feelings were all churned up as we grappled to understand he had gone for good. We shared memories that made us laugh, and cry, and realize that however difficult Tobias could be at times, the gap he had left was too vast to contemplate yet. It would take many months to work through what had gone, what he'd left behind, what he'd taken away with him. And to come to terms with what he'd chosen to let us believe about the past.

I looked at Irena and wondered what was going on in her mind. She had never had a chance to speak to her father properly about his deception. And yet she'd said she loved him. Eventually George said he needed to get some sleep and when he'd gone upstairs it was just me and Irena left at the table.

She sat silently for a while.

'What enabled you to come? Was it because you wanted to absolve Dad before he died? If so, I have huge admiration for you. I'm not sure I've been able to forgive him yet.'

'I had a conversation with Jonah. He said Dad's rejection was to do with hurt, and that it was a sign he loved me. Then with Eddie. I think it helped. We talked about how Mia found it so hard to forgive Eddie for his gambling. When Eddie had been convinced he was going to make them all more money – so his motives were pure. I realized Dad must've had his reasons for not changing the story. Like I had my reasons for taking Xavier to London. If we try and

see beyond the action to the person, if we try and understand the motivation, there is always a reason, isn't there?'

'There is always a reason,' I agreed. 'I spoke to Dad when
I left you yesterday evening. He tried to explain why he
didn't correct the story when he saw the photos. You're
right that he had his own reasons, to do with not upsetting
the apple cart. Thinking there was nothing to be gained. But
I'm not sure I'm quite able to let that go.' I put a hand on
hers. 'I wouldn't blame you if you couldn't forgive him, you
know, Irena. He kept the truth from you all your life. No
wonder you felt betrayed. No wonder you felt at odds with
yourself.'

She smiled.

'Dad felt trapped by his own mistakes,' Irena said, suddenly. She paused and then said something that reminded
me of how our children can sometimes put their finger on
what we can't. 'Dad was always afraid of being seen to get
anything wrong.'

Yes. Tobias, my husband of thirty years, had been more
afraid of being seen to be wrong than of losing touch with
one of his children – until the end.

'Irena, I think now we have this information, Mia needs
to know the truth, too.'

'Won't it devastate her, though, Mum? Perhaps, as Dad
thought, there's nothing to be gained by her knowing. Eddie
knows, but I said he shouldn't tell her.' She ran her hands
through her hair. 'I don't know if you fully realize how terrible it was believing I had it in me to harm my little
brother – even if I was only three at the time. It will be terrible for Mia to know she had it in her. Couldn't we just
keep things as they've always been?'

I thought of Mia and Xavier and Eddie in their home

settling down for the night. Mia's voice, telling me I had to choose between her and Irena.

The shocking realization that I was going to have to lose touch with one of my daughters, if I was to keep contact with the other.

The sense of Mia's intractability.

The sense that her ultimatum was insoluble.

If Mia was never given the opportunity to understand what was behind Irena's disappearance, and why she took Xavier from school, she would almost certainly continue to force me to choose between them.

But it was late, and we were reeling from Tobias's death, and I was beginning to feel a little drunk. And I couldn't make any further decisions tonight.

'Perhaps you're right,' I told Irena. 'Perhaps it's better Mia never knows.'

27

IRENA

'Irena, will you pop to the hardware store? We need some screws and a tin of resin.'

Terry's voice came from under the hull of a small wooden yacht, hoisted up onto a rack in the boat shed. Only her legs in their paint-stained dungarees and her battered trainers were visible. 'Use the business card.'

It was a few days after Dad had died and I was still feeling shattered. The world had changed. Although Dad and I had never properly reconciled, he had always been there as a concept, as a possibility. Even when I'd lived in France all those years. Even when he'd told me I was no longer one of his family. I'd always felt him, a kind of spectre, who one day might, somehow, become solid again. Now he was gone for good, I kept having the sensation I was reaching out for a foothold that was no longer there. I felt the slightest thing might tip me over the edge. Only work at the boatyard helped, a welcome distraction.

'Sure, I'm on it,' I told Terry now and I left the boatyard and cycled into the village centre, got the bits she needed, came out of the hardware store and walked straight into Mia.

We stood looking at each other for a few silent, stunned moments. Then she said, as if there hadn't been years since we last properly met, 'I'm waiting for Eddie. He's just popped to get a paper. We've been to the florist's, organizing the flowers for Dad's funeral.'

My sister had changed in the years I hadn't seen her. Hadn't seen her properly, I mean, face-to-face, up close. I'd seen her from afar, those days I waited outside Xav's school, hoping to catch a glimpse of him. And briefly, in passing, when I'd gone to see my dying father, but she'd left rather than be in the same house as me.

She was still my big sister, though, with the Mediterranean beauty that had come straight down the line from my maternal grandmother Estelle. Those deep-set dark brown eyes, high pointy cheekbones, straight nose. Long, thick, dark hair that was naturally as curly as mine but that she managed to straighten so now it looked long and silken. The olive skin that was a shade darker than mine. But she looked older, more tired. Like a woman, not the young girl-mother I last knew.

'Mia . . . I . . . we need to talk. Before the funeral. Or it's going to be terrible for Mum. I can't bear to see the pain on her face. She's lost the man she had been married to for thirty years. Surely we, her daughters, don't want to make things any more difficult by refusing to speak to one another?'

'I'm not sure I'm ready for this.' Mia turned aside as Eddie came out of the flower shop and put his arm around her.

'Irena!' Eddie smiled in a warm way that accentuated how chilly Mia had been. 'Why don't you come and have a coffee at our house?'

Eddie looked at me, trying to communicate something. I wasn't sure what.

'Eddie, thank you, that's kind, but I'm not sure if Mia wants me to.'

I looked to Mia for a sign.

'I always thought you were close once upon a time,' Eddie went on. 'That's what you told me when I first knew you, Mia. I think it's time for you two to sit down together. Accept your dad blamed the wrong daughter for injuring your brother. And kept it from you. You need to work out what that's meant to you both.'

I looked from Eddie to Mia as the realization sank in slowly.

Eddie had told Mia what I had told him, during our walk on the marshes together.

I had a momentary sense of dread, that this was only going to put the last nail in the coffin of our relationship. Mia would feel hurt that I'd told Eddie. And betrayed. And changed by it. And even, possibly, guilty for something she did long, long ago. So long ago it should have been forgotten, the way our dad – and mum too, of course – had wanted it to be. But truths didn't vanish, as I knew only too well. They rose to the surface at vulnerable points in our lives, nudging at us, confusing us, making us question everything about ourselves.

'Perhaps we could sit at Suzy's on the deck?' I suggested. 'Neutral territory?'

And Mia gave a reluctant nod.

Suzy's was quiet at this time on a weekday morning.

Mia and I sat at a table overlooking the estuary and Eddie went in to get our coffees. We gazed out over the marshes, green and brown now, the sky grey and still above us, and I felt the chill air was freighted with our unspoken words. The silence blossomed between us. At last Mia shifted, looked at me and spoke.

'Eddie told me what really happened to George,' Mia says quietly. 'I didn't remember doing it, before you ask. I have no recollection whatsoever of that day. Once you knew, why didn't you say? Instead of vanishing and disowning us for years, and then coming back without telling us and snatching Xav from me? Did you *want* to put me through hell?'

'Oh Mia, I didn't—'

'Was it some kind of punishment?' I could see tears standing in the corner of her eyes, waiting to fall. 'If so, it wasn't fair, Irena. Because I was too young to remember how George got his scars. I'd been given the wrong narrative as well.'

'My only intention in taking Xav from school was to look after him,' I told her. 'I wanted to keep him safe.'

'By taking him to London, without telling Mum or me?'

I begin to babble, my voice high, shaky.

'I knew you'd never let me get close to Xavier, and this seemed like my opportunity. I was there at the school gates at home time and you weren't. I didn't plan to take him. But one thing led to another. I thought if I tell you I've got him, you'll take him away. I wanted to show him the blue whale at the Natural History Museum, and then once we'd got to London I realized I'd already gone too far and I couldn't turn back.'

I realized how hard it was to explain my behaviour to Mia. How far down one route we'd gone and how relearning our narratives was like manipulating a great juggernaut into a tiny space.

Eddie came back with our coffees and he went and stood at the fence of the deck, looking out over the marshes.

Mia didn't speak, her lips tightly drawn into a thin line. I went to join Eddie; I was afraid of Mia's silence. It was hopeless. She might have forgiven her husband. But she needed Eddie. She didn't need me.

The tide was out. I gazed across the saltings, at the silver and emerald tussocks, at the bronze muddy banks of the creeks that snaked between them, and thought about how

Eddie and I had walked there just the week before, while my father lay dying. And I'd thought about liminality, being on the cusp of two important but opposing sides of life. I was there again. I could feel it.

'It's going to be OK,' Eddie said to me quietly. 'Look, I'm going off home, I'll leave you two to talk alone.'

'Please, Eddie. Don't go. I can't do this.'

'I'm afraid I have to go.' He looked over at Mia, communicating something I was unable to interpret. 'I've got stuff to do.'

A few minutes after Eddie had gone, I felt a movement beside me.

Mia had come to stand at the fence with me.

'Mia,' I said quietly, 'I now realize that what Dad did, when he saw the photo and realized his mistake, but couldn't bring himself to take it back, was very like what I did, taking Xavier and finding I couldn't bring him back.'

'A mistake that runs away with you.'

'Exactly. We were perhaps more alike, Dad and me, than I realized. Wanting to do the right thing, but finding ourselves on a path into a place we could no longer return from. And frightened of the repercussions of our actions.'

'I thought *I* was the most like Dad,' she said. 'Dad always had to be right. He could never admit to getting anything wrong. Including blaming the wrong fucking daughter for almost murdering our little brother.'

I wondered if she was thawing. At least we were talking.

'How do you feel about that, Mia?'

'I feel shit, of course.'

'Oh Mia.'

'And shit that you took the blame and felt you had to leave. But why *did* you leave? Losing touch with you was awful for me. I wondered if you'd been brainwashed by Hermione or by the environmental campaign. You hurt me very badly. I needed you. Especially when Eddie and I split up. And when Dad was so ill, and I needed some moral support, because the thought of looking after Mum if Dad died, on my own, was terrifying to me.'

'Terrifying to you? You always seemed so capable, so brave about everything. You always knew what to do.'

'I was terrified of the responsibility. Of caring for Dad if he became disabled. I didn't have the strength, emotionally. But I said I'd do it. And when Eddie and I split up I came home to live near Mum because it was the right thing to do. Because that's the person I was expected to be. The one who always did the right thing. The one who got the best grades, the perfect results, was there for our parents.

'A little bit – maybe a large bit of me – envied you, Irena. When you'd been gone for a year, then two years. I often used to think, *oh, to go away, to reinvent myself*. It seemed so desirable at times. On nights when Xav wouldn't sleep and Eddie was out somewhere I'd think, *how have I become tied down and so staid so soon?* I would think of you and wish I could be you.'

'*Be* me?'

'Yes! Free. Independent. Rebellious. Instead, I was stuck with this responsible version of myself that I realize now . . . Mum and Dad had kind of carved out for me.'

'It wasn't easy, you know. To go away, to feel I didn't belong in my own family and could never come home.'

A gust of wind rushed over the salt flats. It clouded over, so for a moment we were in shade, before they parted and light filled the estuary again. The tide had begun to come in. I could hear and smell it before I could see it.

'Irena, I need to walk. I need to move.'

'OK.'

We gathered up our things and began to walk along past the creeks that were filling now with tidal water. We didn't speak for some time. We found a grassy tussock and sat down and watched the creeks fill beneath us. I had tried to reclaim my French and North African roots in Paris, but the call of this east coast in England never left me. Being torn from my homeland, my hometown, my family, had left me feeling afloat, like one of the mudbanks that had come loose from the sea. This landscape was part of me. I had grown up here and the mud and the salt and the sea made us who we were. The Gulliver children. I realized how much I'd wanted to come home over the last six years. How painful it had been constantly resisting it.

'I missed you when you went away to school too,' Mia says suddenly. 'I remember how quiet the house seemed. I used to talk to the empty bed next to me in our room.'

'You didn't!'

'I did. I used to pretend you were still there, under the covers, and I told you all about the problems I was having with friends and the issues I had with Mum and Dad, and my anxiety about needing to get the best grades at school in the exams. But you weren't there. Because you'd got away. And I envied you so much for that. I thought you were the lucky one.'

'I thought I was the misfit. That you were the blessed one.'

I fiddled with the packet of screws in my pocket and then I remembered Terry.

'Oh fuck,' I said, 'I only popped out for some screws from the hardware store. Terry's going to wonder where the hell I've got to.'

'I'll come with you,' Mia said. 'I'd like to meet her.'

256

28

RENEE

In the end we compromise. We arrange a small church service in honour of my mother, who is Catholic, and because somewhere inside I feel Tobias would have wanted the tradition of it.

In fact, it makes no difference to me in the end where we hold the ceremony because the day of Tobias's funeral goes past without me, as if I'm only partly there, only able to grasp snatches. I'm astonished at how many people are here as we follow the coffin in, up the aisle and take our place in the front pews. Faces from Tobias's past, his old work colleagues, and his brothers, people I don't even recognize. Distant relatives maybe? Old friends. There are Maureen and Dave, and Sunanda and Nat. Charlie and her husband. They have all come.

George reads a eulogy he's written himself. He stands at the front, unfazed by these people – although, of course, he's used to this, he's used to being on stage – and his voice is resonant, mesmerizing. I don't hear everything; I just watch my son, my boy, simply feel the vibration of his voice as it reaches me, letting occasional words or phrases register: 'ambitious . . . successful . . . a man of high expectations . . . us children . . . yet always deeply sensitive . . . fun . . . loving grandfather to Xavier, seriously affected by the stroke that forced him to give up the work and the family life he loved . . .'

It's this that gives me pause. Had I taken on board how very frustrating Tobias had found the limits placed upon him by his first stroke?

Had I realized how desperate he was after that for his old life, and how deeply hurt he was to be rejected at that time by Irena? Had he felt somehow that after he was diminished, he wasn't lovable any more? As George reads, I realize my own idea of Tobias had become rigid, set; I hadn't seen him the way others saw him. The way George saw him. Mia. *The best father, the best grandfather.*

George is finishing. 'And as we all know, he loved the good things in life. Sailing, good wine, music, the best food. He would want us to continue to enjoy the good things in life in his memory, and that's what we're going to do today, after this, when we ask you to join us for drinks and food back at the house. Even after his stroke, and in defiance of the doctors, Dad continued to enjoy a glass of good wine every night, and it had to be in a beautiful glass, one of a set Irena gave him on his fortieth birthday.'

George looks up from his reading then and I see he's searching for Irena in the congregation and his eyes find her and she looks back at him frowning, and then suddenly she gives him a cautious, tear-strewn smile.

Then Mia steps up and reads a Dylan Thomas poem, and there's another reading from one of his work colleagues, and then the priest finishes the service and we pray and sing and then it's time to leave.

We walk out behind the coffin to Van Morrison singing 'Into the Mystic'.

'This, George?'

'Mia suggested it. She remembers you and Dad listening to it when she was little, in the evenings.'

'We did. We did in the old days.'

Nights when the children were tucked up in bed and we would unwind with a bottle of wine and music. Good nights. Before the cracks began to appear.

After the church service, we walk behind the hearse, to the woodland.

It's the bamboo coffin George suggested, arguing Irena would approve, and that in these times it was important it was biodegradable. It was more like a basket than a coffin, woven with leaves and berries Mia and Xav had spent the early morning gathering from the garden. And with the bouquet she had organized from the florist's displayed on top.

It's a pale, winter's day, the sun filtering through, hardly giving any warmth. I'm aware of the bare branches of the trees making a fine pattern of intricate shadows, like a veil over us as we move, this quiet procession towards the burial ground.

I wonder, as we walk, if this is what Tobias would have chosen. A woodland burial in a bamboo coffin? And something about this thought, this question, releases a giggle that rises from inside me that I can't stifle.

'Mum?' George puts out a hand, clutches my upper arm. 'Are you all right?'

I turn to him. I can't stop, the giggle is just tumbling out of me, I have no control. Tobias, my CEO husband, in a bamboo coffin, on his way to a woodland burial? The giggles are rising, I can't stop them, they're a torrent, they're turning into a wail. There are tears streaming down my cheeks.

'It's OK.' George's hand is still on my arm, still squeezing it through the sleeve of my charity-shop trench coat that isn't warm enough. I should have worn wool. George hands me tissues and says, over and over again, 'It's OK, Mum, it's OK.'

It's unstoppable. It's everything. I'm letting everything tumble out.

It's the image of Tobias in a biodegradable coffin.

It's the weight of my anger at him.

It's my sorrow for him for losing the things that were important to him, his work, his status, his sailing days, Irena, after his stroke.

But it's also sorrow for *myself* for losing the man he was when I married him, the man who listened with me to 'Into the Mystic' and drank wine with me, rather than staring alone at a screen.

It's the grief that my daughters aren't speaking to one another, the grief of being a mother who failed her children.

It's little Xav, walking in front of me now, holding his dad's hand, with his life ahead of him, unaware of how complicated it all is. How many relationships he's going to have to navigate, how much love there is to lose, how many conflicts to endure, to attempt to solve.

It is so easy to get it wrong.

It is all so much hard work.

We've moved to a place where the trees are closer together, a little thicket, to Tobias's place, the hole that's been dug, that is waiting for him.

It's watching the body I used to cleave to, that was once young, tall, muscular, vibrant with optimism and ambition, disappear in its bamboo casing into a hole in the ground.

It's watching George, half his face ruined by Tobias's momentary distraction, step forward to put the first shovel of earth onto his father.

The crowd begins to dissipate, but I stand for a while longer by the grave, letting the tears dry on my face. Two birds, fluttering their wings loudly, take off from the tree overhead into the pale sky. I look round. The woodland is almost empty.

Just George and Irena, over by the gate, with my mother. I suddenly realize – why hadn't I registered this before? – that Irena has been pushing my mother in her wheelchair all day. Irena is talking to George now, and at one point she puts up her hand and strokes the scarred side of his face, and I remember how she told me she was never able to look at it. Never touched it, was afraid of what she thought she'd done to him. And then I spot Eddie; he's holding Mia's hand and Xav's, and they are approaching George and Irena, and Irena turns, and Mia and she are talking together. As I watch, Mia drops Eddie's hand, lifts her arm, and puts it around Irena, and she pulls her to her. For a few moments the two sisters stand still, their arms around each other. They are hugging.

I'm astonished by this. I know from my work that death, funerals, have a habit of widening the cracks in a family, turning those cracks into irreparable breakages. I think of Susan at the funeral parlour, her warning about how family disputes often happen over funerals. I know from my work these kind of fallouts tend to be a displacement of grief; that anger at losing one person – the one who has died – anger for their leaving, spills over into resentment of those who are left.

So what I see happening between my daughters defies all my expectations, all my worst fears. It's the opposite. It's as if Tobias's final disappearance into the hole in the ground has somehow released something that enables the girls to be sisters again.

I move towards them. But Xav is tugging at Mia's arm by now, saying he wants to go, he's hungry, he wants the sandwiches. And they are moving away again, Eddie and Mia and Xav.

Irena turns to me.

'I'll bring Grandma, Mum. You go in a car with George.'

'How? How will you bring Grandma?'

'In Jonah's car. Go now, go, Mum.'

She waves towards the road and I see that Jonah is there. Has he been here all day? He's standing a little way away, beside his car, dressed smartly for him in a tweed jacket and black trousers and a scarf. And now he's helping my mother out of her wheelchair and into the passenger seat of his car. Irena gets into the back seat and they set off.

At the house, it's noisy, people chatting, laughing, leaning over Tobias's computer looking at the photos Mia has turned into a slideshow. Friends and relatives watch Tobias change from a tall, handsome, confident young man in a dinner jacket at our wedding, into a young father, playing with the girls on the beach, carrying George on his back, then older, with a bit more weight, barbecuing in the garden, summer evenings, sailing sessions, big birthdays – his fortieth, my fortieth, his fiftieth, then mine, his sixtieth, my mother's eightieth, Xav's first visit home, then the more recent, more distinguished, aged version of Tobias. They watch our life – our curated life – as the Gulliver family grow and blossom and then begin to diminish again.

They don't know, none of them can see what lies beneath.

Tobias's heartache, his guilt. What they can see, however, is his enduring love.

29

IRENA

A few months later

After picking him up from school I took Xavier down to the nature reserve on the marshes. His limbs had elongated, and his face had narrowed a little; it was losing the chubbiness of boyhood.

He had brought his fishing net and he lay down on his tummy so he could look into the pools and examine what he found. He scooped some things up into his net carefully, like a naturalist.

'You can wait for ever to see beavers or kingfishers,' he explained. 'But minibeasts are here all the time and easy to find and look at. They are going to be my speciality when I'm a naturalist.'

'And we need them more than anything,' I said, quoting some of the environmentalists I'd met in my Paris days. 'If we don't care for our smallest creatures, we fail the biggest ones, including ourselves.'

I could spend hours out here in Xavier's company, roaming out towards the area where the grass turns to mud and the mud to sea and the sea to sky, before turning back, the wind behind us, and heading to the cafe for tea and cakes.

But Xavier was growing up. He'd become interested in football, like his classmates. I wondered if he was humouring me sometimes when we went on our walks after school together on the days I collected him.

He still had a fascination for the sea creatures he's always loved, as Mum told me. He would collect discarded shells and dried seaweed and bring them back to the boat with him to identify and look at through a magnifying glass. He still often referred to our day at the Natural History Museum, and how we lay on our backs and looked at the blue whale skeleton from underneath and pretended we were smaller fishes in the sea and how it was the best day of his life.

After a little while I told him the tide was coming in, it was time to go.

We took the boardwalks and mini bridges over the creeks and channels, treading carefully all the way back to the boats. We went inside to offload his haul of seashells and dried-up crabs and fish eggs. Later, there was a knock at the door and I saw Eddie's tall silhouette and he came in. The sight of Eddie restored my sense that the world was solid, that it wasn't all about to fall apart at any moment.

He had also restored in Mia a kind of calm. I thought this was partly due to the weight of resentment lifting. Mia had learned to forgive Eddie for the error in his ways that had made him gamble their hard-earned cash away in the early days of their marriage. She had also forgiven me for abandoning the family for so long.

Best of all, she had begun to trust me with her son.

She had learned to forgive herself, too, for the accident she now knew *she* had caused in a moment of childish fury and frustration at George's crying.

She understood the injuries were not intentional. That they were caused by our father's oversight in leaving a teapot of boiling water on the table. But she said she was learning to accept that we all have destructive impulses and by recognizing them, we can more easily accept those in others.

And I think we'd both begun to understand our dad, now we knew he'd believed it would do no good to change a narrative we'd grown up with – not realizing how this decision would backfire when I stumbled upon the truth. I wasn't sure I'd entirely forgiven him, but I was getting there.

'Hey, Xavier, my boy!' Eddie cried, squatting, opening up his arms. 'Am I glad to see you!' Xavier ran to him and leaped into his arms.

Sometimes I went round to the house to be with them. There was a kind of poignancy for me in going back to my family home. Something I didn't expect to feel. I'd spent my childhood here. Stepping through the door now Dad had gone, and Mum had moved out, threw into sharp relief all the years I hadn't come home.

I looked at the chart etched on the wall at the top of the stairs that recorded Mia and my and George's heights every year until I'd left for boarding school.

Xavier's had now been added to this, but I'd missed the measurements he'd reached at the age of just one, then two and three, four and five.

I thought of every birthday I'd missed, the tradition we'd had of leaving a pile of croissants out in the morning in the kitchen on birthday mornings. I thought of every Christmas, every Mother's Day, Easter, summer, the others' birthdays, everything I'd missed, not just when I was in Paris, but at boarding school too.

But it's too late to go back.

Those lost years are gone.

Dad's gone.

It made sense for Mia and Eddie and Xav to move into

the family home once Mum said she didn't want to stay there. For now, they needed the space and she and I didn't. So Mia and Eddie moved into the family home and I stayed on my boat where I was happier than I had been anywhere. To everyone's surprise, Mum rented one of the other boats in the mud berths.

I waved Eddie and Xav goodbye from my boat. Dad's little glass, the antique one, the only one left from the set I'd bought him before I left for boarding school, the set I'd smashed that awful night six years ago, sat on the side. Now I poured myself a small glass of Entre-Deux-Mers, and went up on the deck to drink it, listening to the sound of the curlews calling as the sun began to go down.

30

RENEE

It's spring, and the grass is new and bright green, a swathe of jade reaching as far as the thin blue line of the sea. George has come home for a couple of days and we go together to pick up my mother and then to drive her to spend some time at home with me. She sits beside me in the passenger seat of the car, a diminutive figure, but still beautifully dressed. Still smelling divinely of the Guerlain perfume she's worn all her life. George is in the back, and I feel that warmth I get when my son is home, when any of my children are home, especially when they are here together, even now they are grown up.

'Is this where you live, Renee?' my mother says as I take her arm and lead her along the path and across the gang-plank to the houseboat. 'But it can't be. It's not big enough, surely?'

'Mum, you live in one room. I can surely manage to live on a houseboat.'

'One room? What are you talking about, Renee? I live at the *manoir*. It has eleven rooms, at least, and a terrace and a veranda.'

I hear George stifle a giggle. I should sympathize. Like my mother, I once thought I was a person who needed a big house, sofas, a kitchen island, a beautiful garden.

Or perhaps the Renee that went before, the one that married Tobias, did need those things. In the same way she

267

needed a nuclear family, regarding it as something that would provide security, solidity in a world that often felt unpredictable. But there is no such thing as security, solidity; everything in life is mutable; change can come from left field, and nothing stays the same for ever.

Now, the new me, the post-Tobias me, is discovering I can live with very little, very frugally and accept that things move on. I have learned, I suppose, to let go. Of stuff, yes, but also of needing to make everything all right for everyone all the time.

When you pare back everything to the bare essentials, Jonah says, it is, in some ways, easier to navigate life. Especially as you get older. You want less stuff, less practical baggage, so that you can deal with and begin to shed the weight of the emotional baggage that you have gathered over the years.

Every morning after my shower I fling on the cleanest of my clothes, gather one or two necessities to take to work. I wonder how I ever filled a whole great big handbag with paraphernalia, when all I need is my notebook, a pen, my phone and a lipstick. They all fit into a tiny pouch I wear on a belt around my waist.

I've recruited some new clients, and seem to have re-established my reputation, at least in part, since the previous year, after I failed to pick up Xavier from school.

Charlie was right that I needed some time off, and I took it, and it restored me.

There was a lot to work through after Tobias died and it took some time to deal with the bereavement, what it meant, and what I felt Tobias had done to our family, however inadvertently. It was difficult to work through the resentment I felt towards him but harder still to admit my own part in the mistake, my willingness to believe the wrong thing about Irena, and to perpetuate the labels we'd attached to our two daughters, unquestioningly. I was not without guilt.

I think I have begun to forgive both Tobias and myself now, to accept the flaws in myself as well as in him.

I've aged in the last year, and am acutely aware of this. I still check my hair in the mirror before going to work, a habit drummed into me, of course, from years of trying to gain my mother's approval. I've grown to like the aubergine lowlights Ella recommended and have continued to go back to her to have them refreshed. I have also begun to accept the lines, the shifting body weight, have even come to quite like these changes that mark me very firmly now as Xavier's grandmother, not his mum, as Harriet first thought I was.

Mia and Eddie have moved into our big family house now, and Irena stays with them sometimes, helping out with Xav. The rest of the time she lives on the boat next door, and it lifts my heart each morning to see her go off to work with Terry at the boathouse on her bicycle. My other joy is that Eddie and Mia are expecting another baby.

The sun's still out, so I help my mother onto the deck and sit her in a fold-up chair. George and I sit on the step and Jonah comes round to join us. Jonah's brought the blanket he has been knitting with him. It's finished now, and he spreads it over my mother's lap.

'To keep you warm.'

'It's a beauty, Jonah,' I tell him, and he laughs and points out the dropped stitches and the crooked edges.

'They're what give it character. Its imperfections,' George says. 'Like my scars.'

I kick off my pumps and move my bare feet about on the deck. I breathe deeply in through my nose. Salt, and mud, and seaweed. The wind is brisk, cooling as it ruffles my hair.

This reminds me of the day I first came to see Irena living on the boat next to Jonah's. How the euphoria at seeing my middle daughter after so long meant I clean forgot to pick up Xavier from school. The horror of it, and then the slow realization that it was Irena who had him, the relief and yet the anxiety about what it might mean for Mia.

'It's funny, Jonah.' I turn to him when George is busy on his phone. 'Mia thought I was having an affair with you. You know? The day I forgot to pick up Xavier? She was so upset, thought I'd cheated on her dad, and let that come before the safety of her child.'

He turns his head slowly to look at me.

'I can see how that would be upsetting.'

'I know. But when I told her the truth, that I was visiting Irena, she said she preferred her first theory. Seeing Irena behind her back felt like a betrayal of *her*. Back then, she'd have felt happier if I *had* been seeing you.'

Jonah laughs, glances sideways at me. I give him a quick smile, wondering what my mother has noticed about how he and I are together. But my mother is too busy watching the cloud patterns that are forming and shifting overhead to be interested in us.

'Mum, Jonah.' I look up. Irena's coming along the boardwalk with Xav, and she stops as she often does these days on her way back to her own boat.

'Irena! Xav! Come and join us.'

Irena comes up onto the deck and Xav empties his collection of dried seaweed and fish eggs onto the floor.

'Hey! Is there room for me?'

It's Terry, the boat builder, approaching us from the boat huts.

'I was on my way to yours, Irena,' she says. 'But then I spotted you all and I thought, that looks like a jolly little gathering. And I saw that you, Irena, and Xavier were here too.'

'Come and join us,' I say.

Standing up to let Terry onto the boat, I move onto the towpath, and stay there for a minute looking at the little gathering on the deck of my houseboat.

Here we all are then, I think.

We might be a different configuration to the one I once thought was my perfect family, the one my clients imagined, the one displayed in photos in the interiors magazine all those years ago.

We might be cobbled together; a bundle of oddballs.

My eighty-six-year-old mother in her chic French skirt suit, the blue and green blanket spread across her knees and her hair in its perfect chignon with its silver streaks framing her pretty face; my blond son with one side of his face severely scarred, the other side heart-droppingly handsome; my wild-looking daughter Irena with her dungarees and crocs and her halo of purple hair; my grandson Xavier, looking more than ever like his dad, Eddie; Jonah with his white hair and dark eyebrows in his faded shorts and old grey sweatshirt; Terry with her cropped hair and dungarees and leather work apron. But we are here. We are here together.

My mother looks up at me suddenly, spotting me looking at them all.

'Renee,' she calls out loudly. 'What *have* you done to your hair?'

I don't care, I think. *I am not going to let anything she says bother me today.*

Then she speaks again. 'It looks really quite pretty in this light.'

I glance at Irena, who *knows*, and we both laugh.

271

'Oh my days,' Irena says. 'That *is* a first!'

Then we sit and chat and wait for Mia, or perhaps today it will be Eddie, to come and pick up their son from his grandma and her best friend, and his aunt and her lover and his uncle and his great-grandma, before they take him home to the house on the front for his tea.

Later, when they've all gone, I go below deck. My boat is another one of what Jonah jokingly calls his 'property portfolio' that I am renting from its owner. I strip off in the cabin, pull on my costume. It's still warm outside, so I don't bother with the socks or gloves. The tide is in. I go to the prow of my boat, and climb down into the water, which is icy in spite of the weather. I count to five, taking slow strokes as my body adjusts to the cold, and then it comes, sweeping over me, the moment I love. No one needs me in this moment, and I need no one. Jonah's words come back to me: *It's important for all of us to keep a little bit of our inner selves alive, even when we have people who seem to need us and make demands of us. Because in the end, we're all on our own.*

In this moment, with the birds calling across the estuary, in the water, the wind sending ripples across its surface, I am just me, Renee; no thoughts, no worries, only the sensation of liquid holding me in its cool embrace.

With the wind on my face, I swim out towards the horizon and a curlew calls, and I remember I told Jonah I found its song mournful, and Jonah told me he found it full of hope.

Now its rising notes as I swim out into the still evening air seem more than ever like a question, whose answers lie in the unknowable future.

ACKNOWLEDGEMENTS

Heartfelt thanks go to several people:

To my inimitable agent Jane Gregory and Stephanie Glencross at David Higham for their continued loyalty.

To Sam Humphreys at Mantle – the best editor a person could wish for.

To the rest of the team at Mantle, especially Samantha Fletcher and Lorraine Green for their copy-editing, cover designer Ami Smithson and proofreader Pippa Wickenden.

To my writer friend Anna D'Andrea, who always so patiently reads and feeds back on early drafts.

To those whose brains I picked for theories on family psychology, relationship therapy and counselling terminology. Any mistakes are my own.

I would also like to thank Molly Guest at Young Lives vs Cancer, whose auction for character names always raises huge amounts for this life-changing charity. I hope the winning bidders are happy with the depictions of the teacher Christina Walker, Renee's friend Maureen, the school caretaker Paul Kicks and the manager at the counselling centre, Charlie (although any character similarities are purely accidental).

Most of this book was written during lockdown in 2020 and 2021. Untold thanks go to the NHS and key workers who did such an amazing job in keeping us safe and enabled those of us who do less risky jobs to get on with them.

Penny Hancock

And I couldn't have written at that time without the support, conversation and excellent catering skills of Andy Taylor and Jem Hancock-Taylor, or Zoom calls with Polly, Tom, Emma, Will and the rest of my family.

Thank you for everything.

274

If you enjoyed *The Choice*, discover Penny Hancock's previous novel *I Thought I Knew You*

Who do you know better? Your oldest friend? Or your child? And who should you believe when one accuses the other of an abhorrent crime?

Jules and Holly have been best friends since university. They tell each other everything, trading revelations and confessions, and sharing both the big moments and the small details of their lives: Holly is the only person who knows about Jules's affair; Jules was there for Holly when her husband died. And their two children – just four years apart – have grown up together.

So when Jules's daughter Saffie makes a rape allegation against Holly's son Saul, neither woman is prepared for the devastating impact this will have on their friendship or their families. Especially as Holly, in spite of her principles, refuses to believe her son is guilty.

Read on for an extract . . .

1

HOLLY

He's alone again. Head bowed. Cumbersome bag hanging from bony shoulders. Trousers flapping around clownish shoes at the end of lanky legs. He's at that age where nothing's in proportion. Elongated but not filled out. A curtain of straight dark hair swings across his face, hiding the angry smattering of acne on his cheeks.

Saul finds himself a space on the green and stares at a patch of ground where the grass has been trodden bald by decades of school shoes. A girl approaches from the far side. One of Saffie's friends, but more bookish-looking. Less confident. *Go to him. Talk to him*, I urge her. *Please. He's nice. He's gentle and sweet.* She gives my son a wide berth and makes a direct line to the popular crowd.

I wish he didn't have to go to school. I wish he didn't have to mix in the world. Nothing about him fits.

More gaggles of girls appear, laughing, skirts short, shiny hair bouncing, hands clutching their mobiles. Then a group of handsome almost-men. Glowing skin, sharp haircuts, perky quiffs. They gleam with good health. These groups of children have been passing my front window for the last half-hour, gathering for the bus that will carry them off to secondary school before the village falls silent again.

'You're too attached,' Pete says, coming up behind me, surprising me. 'You have separation anxiety.' Pete's a psychotherapist. Attaching labels to feelings is what he does.

'I have not got separation anxiety,' I say, my breath misting the window. 'I'm simply a mother worrying for her son. Who still doesn't have friends.'

'Come here.'

Pete's arms slip round my waist. He lifts my hair, kisses me on the neck. I lean back into him.

'Saul's fine, Holly. He's sixteen. Searching for an identity. You need to let him be. Believe me, I see enough kids with problems. Saul's quiet, and sensitive, and he lost his father six years ago. But he's not displaying behaviour I'd consider a reason for concern. It's you who needs to back off a little, if I may say so.'

I rub a circle of condensation from the glass. Saul remains alone on the green.

'It's hard. After everything he's been through.' I turn and kiss Pete on the cheek. 'I need to go.'

Money, mobile, make-up. The mantra Jules and I use to check we don't forget anything in the morning. All ready in my bag. The pizza dough's in the fridge, waiting to bake when I get home.

'Wish I was in tonight,' Pete says. 'I'll get back as soon as I can tomorrow. D'you want a lift to the station?'

'I'll walk,' I say. 'Thanks, Pete. It's the wrong direction for you.'

'See you tomorrow, then,' he says, and his lips on mine send a fizz through my whole body. An unexpected bonus of my two-year-old relationship: Pete and I married soon after we met. A brisk ceremony at Cambridge Registry Office. That's how certain we were about each other.

Once I'm at work, I won't think about Saul. Not until tonight when we begin the argument about homework. The nagging that masks my worry about how unhappy he seems since I moved him from his London school for a fresh start in the Fens.

My mobile vibrates as I set off along the side of the green, head bowed against fine rain. The school bus draws up and swallows the teenagers.

'Where are you?' Jules asks.

'On my way to the station. I haven't got any tutorials until eleven, so I'm getting the eight thirty-five. It's horrible out here. Peeing down. Pete's taken the car.'

'You should have said.'

'It's fine. Good exercise.'

'You haven't forgotten about tonight? Tess's birthday drinks at that new gastropub in Fen Ditton. Girls' night out.'

'Oh, of course. Yes. That's something to look forward to.'

'Come round to mine first? Rowan's away. We can have pre-drinks, then get a cab together.'

'Sounds good. You OK?'

'Apart from dealing with the mood swings of a thirteen-year-old,' she says, 'fine. You?'

'Better for hearing you. We'll talk later.'

When she's gone, I tuck my mobile into the pocket of my parka and pull up the hood. It will be good to get out after a day dealing with students and their stresses and their heartbreaks. I haven't had a chance to get to know the local women, never made those school-gate friendships you form when you have primary-age kids. Saul was already fourteen when we moved here two years ago. I envisage sharing my concerns about him tonight; there's always another mother worrying about her own child who'll help put things in perspective.

The fields either side of me as I leave the village are striated with puddles of water shimmering to a black fuzz of trees on the horizon. Brown, muddy fens and high, colourless clouds. It's hard to say which seems longer, this narrow road leading beyond the level crossing to a vanishing point where the land meets the sky or the ribbons of ditch water fading to nothing where they merge with clouds. Squeeze your eyes half shut and everything blots into a watery murk.

Soon after we moved here, I thought I'd made a terrible mistake. The land seemed a place with the life – along with the floodwaters – drained out of it. Not a tree or a flower or an animal to draw the eye. Industrial storage units built from concrete breezeblocks and corrugated iron the only features on the vast flat fields. The sky so huge you could turn in a circle and only see one continuous line of horizon. I didn't belong here. It wasn't my home. I knew no one but Jules, and found it hard to make inroads into the tight-knit community. I'd had to do something, though, despite the fact it meant leaving the place where Saul was born and where Archie had died. Saul was miserable at his London secondary school. And the mortgage repayments on our Hackney house were crippling us.

'Move up here,' Jules had suggested. She'd moved out of London herself four years earlier, when Saffie was going into Key Stage Two. It was Rowan's home village. 'There's a really supportive community. And all this space. You'll love it.'

She swiped through property sites on her iPad. 'Look at this. Two-bed terraced house with garden. In this village. For half of what you'll get for your Hackney house. You could probably buy it outright.'

'I'd feel I was betraying Archie,' I said. 'If we moved.'

'Holly, it's been four years. You have to let him go. And so does Saul.'

Jules was right. In the four years since Archie died, Saul had grown from a ten-year-old primary-school child to a

towering teenager. We both needed a fresh start. I was cling-
ing on to an old plan, an old dream.

'What about work?' I'd asked Jules. 'I'll never find another creative writing lectureship. They're in high demand.'

'Commute, like everyone else.'

'You think?'

'It's only an hour to King's Cross. It could take you as
long on a bus from Hackney. Look, no one can afford to
live in London any more. This village is deserted by day, but
in the evenings, barbecue smoke fills the air and everyone's
popping corks and levering tops off beer bottles.'

'Very poetic!'

'Every night's a party night. And there's loads for kids to
do. Rowing, tennis, riding. Much more wholesome than
London. Saul will love it.'

In the end, I put an offer on the little house Jules had
spotted, got it for just under the asking price. Unheard of in
the South-East. Perhaps it said something about the village.
Perhaps I should have taken it as a warning.

Saul wasn't keen on the idea. But what teenager wants to
be shifted sixty miles from his birth home to a village where
he knows virtually no one? I persuaded him he'd grow to
like it. The school would be an easy bus ride, unlike the
two long tube journeys he took to his London one, where,
anyway, he wasn't happy. And so two years ago, when he
was fourteen, we moved into our small terraced house, just
off the green. Two years. And even though I have Pete, I still
feel an outsider here.

*

The train this morning is full of kids travelling to the private
schools and colleges in Cambridge. They fill the space by the
doors, laughing, showing each other their phones, talking

about their latest Instagram posts and WhatsApp groups. I try to spot whether there are other loners, like Saul, but fail. The high-spirited youngsters get off at Cambridge Station and I manage to find a seat. The train passes between flat ploughed fields, flooded in places, glassy water throwing back reflections of trees turning red at the tips. Then the land begins to roll, green slopes dotted with redbrick villages, station signs – Hitchin, Stevenage, Welwyn Garden City. Within an hour we're among the first trailing suburbs of North London. My mobile pings as we pass the Emirates Stadium. I hesitate, then check it anyway. As I feared, it's a tweet from 'the Stag'.

@Hollyseymore says yes, but who'd fuck her anyway? #sex #consent #feminazi

A troll, responding to the freshers' workshops at my university on sexual consent. The students' union set them up to tackle the increasing problem of 'lad culture' in the university. As one of the longer-standing members of staff, I'd been asked to help advise on the issues they wanted to address. The students had also discovered (thanks to Google) that I had volunteered for Rape Crisis many years ago as an ardent young student myself. In those days, I'd been unable to resist a cause or a protest, an opportunity to 'reclaim the night', or to argue for a 'woman's right to choose'.

The workshops, however, had raised heated debate. Some students questioned whether a half-hour discussion was the best way to teach young men that the absence of a 'no' does not equal consent. The students who most needed to think about it, the 'lads', probably wouldn't attend the discussions anyway. Others were furious we considered workshops like this necessary. They found it patronizing. I wrote a piece for one of the broadsheets suggesting better sex education at school, particularly for boys, might be more effective than non-statutory meetings for students, but that given the status quo, consent workshops were the only way of tackling sexual harassment and the escalating problem of campus rape. I had been trolled on and off ever since.

The tweet leaves me shaken. The hatred in it. *It's just words*, I tell myself. *Ignore it.* Which is ironic when words are my stock-in-trade.

*

When I emerge at King's Cross, the rain's stopped and London's shining, wet pavements, glistening windows. I'm in good time, so I walk to the university, taking the streets of early-Victorian terraces leading south from Euston Road, then right through an alley and past a block of 1950s council flats. This area of the city is quiet, just an old Bangladeshi man sweeping the pavement in front of his general store and a few people drinking coffee behind the steamed-up windows of one of those small independent Italian cafes that still exist away from the busier thoroughfares.

On the other side of Woburn Place, in Gordon Square, trees cast shifting shadows on the gravel paths that wind between the now ragged flowerbeds. The shrubs are laden with bright berries, the tall grasses are turning gold.

The surrounding townhouses have a proliferation of literary blue plaques. Christina Rossetti, Virginia Woolf, Vanessa Bell all lived here. Emmeline Pankhurst lived on the site of the Principal Hotel. I feel as if the square contains the spirits of those writers and feminist trailblazers. Archie used to tease, 'You believe you'll imbibe their talent by osmosis!' He didn't understand – how could he? – that it wasn't as simple as that. I felt, still do, a connection with those women who loved the city the way I do.

Our plan back then was that he and I would take it in turns – Archie would earn the money as a lawyer so I could write in the gaps when Saul was at school. ('One day, there'll be a blue plaque outside your office,' he joked. 'Holly Seymore got the idea for *A Stitch in Time* as she drank her latte in this very building!') Then, when I'd finished my PhD, which consisted partly of the novel I was working on, I would return to work as a course leader, on a better salary, so he could write *his* book.

Instead, abruptly widowed, I'd had to take a basic lecturer's job, teaching undergraduates creative writing. It wasn't quite the literary career I'd had in mind. But I still love working here, within sight of the British Museum and among the Georgian terraces, with their white stucco facades and black railings. And Archie was right: part of me did – still does – feel only good can come of working in the geographical slipstream of so much feminist thought and literary talent.

I cross Montague Street to the forecourt of the university, unlock my office. On my laptop, I click on the file marked, 'Novel – A Stitch in Time.' I had some idea, and it seemed so bright and alive at the time, of writing about two women, one in this area of London – Bloomsbury – in the interwar period, one now, linked by a single object – an inkwell – the contemporary one finds in her attic. After Archie died, however, the idea deflated like a balloon. I could no longer believe in it. I've barely looked at it since. Fifty thousand words gone to waste. Once I was bereaved, I lost the plot. Literally. I ought to bin it.

*

'How do I get it published?'

Jerome, my first student of the morning, has written an

experimental novel that omits the letter 'e'. He is a blue-eyed hipster with a red beard and a flesh hole in his ear. His face is full of naive optimism. I hand the work I've marked back to him, and we talk about whether these kinds of constraints – lipograms, made popular by the Oulipo group – paradoxically give writers more freedom to be creative. I suppress the urge to tell him to write something a little more mainstream if he wants to sell his work. He has impressive self-confidence, arguing his case when I suggest that constraints like these shouldn't be at the expense of story. He leaves full of the self-belief that will propel him through life even if his writing doesn't.

Mei Lui's a quiet, wan-looking second year whose skin I've always thought belies a poor diet or too many late nights. She's written 60,000 words of a novel in which she describes a Vietnamese girl's experiences working as an escort to pay for her degree in England. We discuss point of view and agree that the confessional tone lends itself to rewriting in the first person. As she leaves, she turns.

'It is . . . semi-autobiographical,' she says.

'Ah. D'you want to talk about it?'

She shakes her head, embarrassed, and hurries away down the corridor. I'm about to call her back when Luma, our head of department, appears.

'Holly. Hanya says she'll chair the consent workshop scheduled for next Friday but she'd like you to check what she's prepared.'

'That's fine. She could pop in at lunchtime.'

'You been getting any more tweets?'

'One or two,' I say. 'I'm ignoring them. It's just some guy with a chip on his shoulder.'

'Nasty, though. And I'm sorry they've targeted you.'

'Better me than one of the students.'

'You think so?'

'There's something particularly unpleasant about the anonymity of a Twitter troll. I'd hate to see students become victims. But I've a duty to help publicize their workshops. I'm not letting the Stag have his way!'

Luma steps into my office and closes the door behind her.

'I've just had Giovanna in. She's that first year – the talented one. Italian? Long dark hair? She spent the tutorial in tears. Turns out her boyfriend's threatened to dump her if she won't sleep with him. I suggested she attend one of Hanya's sessions. She's afraid he's going to leave her. Which would be a blessing IMHO. She says she loves him. That he's a genius. He's writing something based on an idea of the Oulipo group, but he's made her feel her writing's rubbish.'

'Not called Jerome, is he?'

'How did you know?'

'One of mine. Rather too confident if you ask me.' We exchange a smile. 'It's he who should attend the session, not just Giovanna, but I can guarantee that won't happen.'

'I still wonder what makes these kids take writing degrees,' she sighs. 'What comment by some English teacher set them down a track that probably won't go anywhere. So many of them are too young to take the knocks on the way.'

'Dreams?' I suggest. 'The desire to make sense of a world that makes very little sense otherwise?'

The trouble with having lectured for so long in the same institution is we've seen it all before. The ones who are too young to cope, the mature men who believe they're imbued with comedic genius, the experimental ones like Jerome who might or might not have the commitment to see it through. More often, sadly, not. Our students come with their writing but also a litany of other concerns. Almost all suffer from anxiety. Several have money worries. A few are struggling with gender identity. At times I feel treacherous that I'm earning a salary on the back of the belief that our students can and will make a living from writing, when I know how much they're up against. And when I've failed to do so myself.

*

After a chat with Hanya about her screening for the next consent workshop, and delivering an afternoon lecture on Pillman's 'Lean and Mean' theory, ('Pare your writing back until you can pare no further,' I tell my earnest sea of young faces, wondering if I'm helping or hindering their creative flow), I walk back to King's Cross. There's the smell of crisp leaves, a sweeter tinge of smoking chestnuts, and the shops are filling with pumpkins. Autumn's arrived. I pass the Friend at Hand, a pub Archie and I frequented, opposite the Horse Hospital. (Once used to stable sick horses, it's now an arts venue.) The pub's filling with post-work crowds; a glimpse through the doorway reveals pints on tables, candles guttering. I have a fleeting nostalgia for the days when I would have stepped inside, sat at one of those scrubbed wooden tables, drinking and chatting until late. As it is, however, I pick up balls of fresh mozzarella for Saul's pizza and a jar of artichoke hearts from Carlo's Italian deli, tucked away in a corner behind Marchmont Street, and walk on towards King's Cross.

*

I'm back in the village just after seven.

'D'you wanna cup of tea?' Saul asks, leaping down the stairs as I get in the door.

'You're a sweetheart. That's exactly what I want. How did you know?'

He shrugs and I want to hug him, tell him how he lifts my heart. How I love him more than words can say.

'How was your day?' I ask instead, pulling off my boots.

'Shit.'

My mood dips.

He switches the kettle on, puts a teabag in a mug for me.

'Not getting better?'

'It was school. So what d'you expect? I don't really want to talk about it now, Mum. What's for supper?'

'You OK with pizza? I'm off out tonight. With Jules.'

'Sure. Pizza's cool.'

'The dough should be ready. Oh, and I got you some of that nice mozzarella from Carlo's.'

'You could've just got a bought one,' Saul says, and I grin at him. He knows how I frown on shortcuts when it comes to food. When I've assembled Saul's pizza and put it in the oven, I take my cup of tea upstairs. I've had a shower, changed into clean clothes, sprayed a bit of Coco Mademoiselle behind my ears and am putting my earrings in when Saul appears in my bedroom doorway.

'I can't get on the internet,' he says. 'Broadband's down. That's going to screw up my evening.'

'Shouldn't you spend it doing homework?' I say to his reflection in the mirror.

'It's done.'

'Saul, you can't have done it in an hour.'

'I'll show you the essay I've written on *An Inspector Calls* if you like, but it'll bore you to tears.'

I have to restrain myself from launching into a lecture about the nuances of the play, its subtle shift of blame for a woman's suicide from one character to another to another until we realize everyone's implicated.

'It's dumb we can't get broadband,' Saul growls.

'Saul, we do have broadband. It's just—'

'It's just it doesn't work. What's the point in living here? What's the point in a fucking house with no broadband?'

It's true our connection is erratic, and that neither Pete nor I have had time to sort it out.

'You want me to do my homework, but half of it they put on the fucking website, and if I can't go on it, how am I supposed to do it?'

Saul raises his iPad, knocking my bottle of perfume flying as he does so, narrowly missing my ear, and for a second looks as if he's going to hurl it at the mirror.

'Saul, watch it.' He stops at the last minute, but not before my bedside lamp has tumbled sideways, smashing onto the floor. He's only got to lift an arm these days and things go flying. He doesn't realize how long his limbs have become.

'I'm so bored! There's nothing to do in this arsehole of a village.'

I take a deep breath. Saul's mood swings are new. I know rationally they're due to the massive hormonal changes he's undergoing. Changes that mean he can't cope the minute he's overtired, bored or hungry. But when he's in this state, my sweet boy seems possessed by someone else entirely.

'Your pizza will be ready. Go and get it out of the oven.'

*

He's playing some game on his phone, thumbing the screen, eating pizza with the other hand when I go down to him fifteen minutes later.

'I was starving,' he says without looking up.

'Can't you use your phone,' I say, nodding at it, 'if you must go online?'

'Used up my data allowance.'

'How about I ask Jules if you can use her internet round there? Then you could come over with me.'

He doesn't reply.

'Saul?'

'I guess.'

*

'Of course,' Jules says. 'Saul's welcome. He can keep an eye on Saff at the same time. Rowan's away and she's objecting that she has to do her homework. Saul can be my security guard.'

I laugh, go back to Saul. 'All sorted. Rowan's away and Jules was worried about leaving Saffie so she's thrilled to have you there.'

He glances up. 'Why's Jules worried about leaving Saffie?'

'She's been acting out lately. Finding her teenage feet. You can keep an eye on her. Make sure she doesn't spend the whole evening on *her* computer.'

'So Jules wants me to be, like, her minder?'

'All you have to do is be there. She says Saff's got homework to do. You can watch their home cinema. And they have everything – Netflix, Sky, the lot.'